RESCUE AFTER DARK

GANSETT ISLAND SERIES, BOOK 22

MARIE FORCE

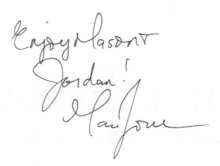

Rescue After Dark
Gansett Island Series, Book 22

By: Marie Force
Published by HTJB, Inc.
Copyright 2020. HTJB, Inc.
Cover Design: Diane Luger
Print Layout: Holly Sullivan
E-book Formatting Fairies
ISBN: 978-1950654840

View the McCarthy Family Tree *marieforce.com/gansett/familytree/*

View the list of Who's Who on Gansett Island here *marieforce.com/whoswhogansett/*

View a map of Gansett Island *marieforce.com/mapofgansett/*

The Gansett Island Series

Book 1: Maid for Love (*Mac & Maddie*)
Book 2: Fool for Love (*Joe & Janey*)
Book 3: Ready for Love (*Luke & Sydney*)
Book 4: Falling for Love (*Grant & Stephanie*)
Book 5: Hoping for Love (*Evan & Grace*)
Book 6: Season for Love (*Owen & Laura*)
Book 7: Longing for Love (*Blaine & Tiffany*)
Book 8: Waiting for Love (*Adam & Abby*)
Book 9: Time for Love (*David & Daisy*)
Book 10: Meant for Love (*Jenny & Alex*)
Book 10.5: Chance for Love, *A Gansett Island Novella* (*Jared & Lizzie*)
Book 11: Gansett After Dark (*Owen & Laura*)
Book 12: Kisses After Dark (*Shane & Katie*)
Book 13: Love After Dark (*Paul & Hope*)
Book 14: Celebration After Dark (*Big Mac & Linda*)
Book 15: Desire After Dark (*Slim & Erin*)
Book 16: Light After Dark (*Mallory & Quinn*)
Book 17: Victoria & Shannon (Episode 1)
Book 18: Kevin & Chelsea (Episode 2)
A Gansett Island Christmas Novella
Book 19: Mine After Dark (*Riley & Nikki*)
Book 20: Yours After Dark (*Finn McCarthy*)
Book 21: Trouble After Dark (*Deacon & Julia*)
Book 22: Rescue After Dark (*Mason & Jordan*)
Book 23: Blackout After Dark

More new books are alway in the works. For the most up-to-date list of what's available from the Gansett Island Series as well as series extras, go to *marieforce.com/gansett*.

CHAPTER 1

*S*ummertime, and the living was *not* easy for Gansett Island Fire Chief Mason Johns. During the seemingly endless winter, year-round residents on the remote island counted down to the summer season. For Mason, Memorial Day weekend signified the end of peace and quiet and the start of insanity.

His department went from three to five calls a week to five to ten calls per day, and it continued like that for months. Summer on Gansett was an endless cycle of moped crashes, alcohol-related incidents, sun poisoning, falls from the bluffs, near drownings, bicycle pileups, surfing accidents, unauthorized bonfires and the occasional house fire. At least once a week, they evacuated someone for trauma treatment on the mainland via helicopter. On the island, the saying went, if you saw the chopper coming, someone was in big trouble.

The drama didn't end until after Labor Day weekend, and while Mason enjoyed helping people and being part of the Gansett Island community, he found himself craving time away from the madness.

He rarely took a day off during the season, which meant he had to make the most of the free time he did have to get in a workout. Exercise was critical to keeping seasonal stress under control and maintaining his sobriety. Now that another wild Race Week was in the books, he'd been determined to get out for a bike ride after work. As he rode his mountain bike over rugged trails on the island's north end while fighting the brisk northerly wind that had been howling all day, he tried not to think about the piles of work he'd left behind at the station, the quarterly reports that were due to the mayor's office or the long night he still had ahead of him as he tried to stay caught up.

Two weeks into another season, and it was living up to its reputation thus far. In fact, this year was looking to be even busier than usual. He'd stolen a rare hour to ride his bike and get away from it all before he returned to the office with a takeout dinner to finish the endless paperwork that came with the uptick in calls.

The sun inched closer toward the western horizon, giving him another hour of daylight before it became unsafe to ride on the trails, even with the headlight he'd installed on his bike. After dark, he stayed on paved roads, but he preferred the trails that wound through some of the most scenic real estate on the planet.

Or at least he thought so. Despite the madness that descended this time of year, he loved this island and all its wild beauty. He wouldn't want to live anywhere else. When he first moved to Gansett, he'd feared that island life would be too confining, but he'd discovered the opposite was true. Island residents were masterful at keeping themselves entertained, even in the dead of winter, and he'd come to love everything about living there.

He'd reached his favorite part of the trail, the top of a hill that always sent him airborne down an embankment that veered off to the right. More than once, he'd nearly ended up in the seagrass that grew along the trail, but he always managed to right the bike at the last second. He laughed out loud at the thrill of flying through the air on the bike and landed hard, still on the bike and on the trail. But just barely.

Thirteen years after giving up alcohol, he got his thrills from exercise these days. A binge-drinking habit from his college days hadn't aged well, and he'd had the choice of quitting drinking or finding another line of work. Since he couldn't imagine doing anything other than working in the fire service, giving up his new job as a probationary firefighter in Worcester, Massachusetts, hadn't been an option. The department had sent him to thirty days of rehab with the edict to quit drinking or find another job. So he'd kicked it, but it had been the hardest thing he'd ever done, hands down.

Staying sober had been his primary goal ever since, and fitness played a huge role in making that happen by giving him a more productive way to spend his time away from work. He pushed himself until he was so exhausted, he fell into dreamless sleep when he finally went to bed at the end of every long day.

Sobriety was a daily challenge. He'd never lost the desire to drink, but he'd learned to control it, to channel it into more productive pursuits. Daily AA meetings helped, and he tried to never miss a day, although that became more difficult this time of year.

Mason completed one lap around the land conservancy Mrs. Chesterfield had deeded to the island upon her death and, after gauging the sun-to-horizon ratio, decided to take a second loop around the four-mile path. Approaching the jump, he sped up, looking for even more height this time. As he cleared the incline, he noticed flames and smoke in the distance, which took his attention off the landing—only for a second. But that was all it took. He came down wrong and flipped over the handlebars, landing hard on his left side several feet from the path.

The impact knocked the wind out of him for a full minute. He lay on the ground, staring up at the sky, watching as daylight faded to twilight and wondering if he was badly injured or only momentarily stunned.

And then he remembered the flames and forced himself to move, to breathe, to shake off the crash. Standing, he glanced in the direction of the flames and found the smoke plume had doubled in size in the time he'd been flat on his back. Wincing at a sharp pain from his left elbow, he found his phone in the pocket of his jacket and called dispatch.

"It's Mason. There's a fire on the west side. Might be Eastward Look. Dispatch all units. I'm on my bike but heading there now."

"Right away, Chief."

He ended the call, stashed the phone in his pocket and fished his bike out of the tall grass, groaning when his left elbow refused to bend. "Crap." The last freaking thing he needed right now was an injury, so he gritted his teeth and pretended his elbow wasn't messed up as he pedaled hard toward the flames and smoke.

SOMETHING WAS WRONG. Jordan didn't know what or where or how she knew something was wrong, just that it was. The sleeping pill she'd taken hours ago had made it so she couldn't move to do anything about the feeling of danger. Her chest hurt, like it had during the first major asthma attack she'd suffered as a child.

That'd been the first time she'd thought she was going to die, but it hadn't been the last.

Don't think about him.

She was so tired—mentally, physically, emotionally. She'd taken the pill out of sheer desperation for some much-needed rest. While the pill had made it so she couldn't move a muscle, her mind was wide awake and spinning, as usual. With her identical twin sister, Nikki, and Nikki's fiancé, Riley, off-island for a few days, Jordan was home alone in the house that Nikki and Riley had restored over the winter. Technically, the house belonged to their grandmother, but Evelyn had all but given it to the happy couple, which was fine with Jordan.

She wanted nothing more than Nikki's happiness.

Jordan had come to Gansett for the grand opening of the Wayfarer, where her sister was the general manager. After all the years of support Nikki had given to Jordan and her career, such as it was, the least Jordan could do was fly across the country to be there for Nik during her big weekend. Two weeks after the grand opening, Jordan hadn't worked up the energy to return to her so-called life in Los Angeles.

Things were a mess, and the last place in the world she wanted to be was alone in that massive, empty house in Bel Air. So she'd stayed on Gansett, even if she suddenly felt out of place in the house that'd always been home to her and Nik.

Nikki and Riley were so ridiculously happy that being around them was almost painful for Jordan to watch after the disastrous end to her horrible marriage to Brendan. Known as Zane, the eponymous —and yes, he'd referred to himself as such—rapper had beaten the crap out of her in a hotel room last winter, putting her in the hospital.

Even after she'd blocked his number, he'd popped up again and again, using other people's phones to plead with her to talk to him, to beg for another chance. She'd read online that he was taking "time away" from the tour to deal with "personal issues" and had checked himself into a facility to contend with substance abuse and mental health concerns. But that hadn't stopped him from finding numerous ways to call her.

Jordan was glad he was getting the help he needed, but wished he'd leave her alone. Each message she received from him only further lacerated her already shredded heart. She'd put everything she had into their marriage, even long after he hadn't deserved anything from her. After she'd lived through a custody battle as a child, stuck between warring parents, the failure of her marriage weighed heavily on her heart. She'd tried so hard to make it work, because she didn't want to be divorced.

Distressing thoughts spiraled through her mind, reminding her of the mess her life had become. The sleeping pill had made her anxiety worse, which was the last thing she needed.

Her chest hurt all the time, but worse than usual now.

She wanted to rub her aching breastbone, but couldn't seem to make her arms cooperate with the directive from her brain.

Something is wrong.

Alarm flooded her system, reminding her of the panic that came with asthma attacks.

A piercing noise sounded, adding to her anxiety. Was that the smoke alarm?

Jordan struggled to find the surface, to open her eyes, but her eyelids felt like concrete weights.

Pounding footsteps came toward her, a shout that sounded like concern. Then she was flying through the air, more loud noises, a rush of cool air over her face, the press of warm lips to hers, a flood of air to starving lungs. The lips were soft against hers. She tried to get closer, to keep them there, to open her eyes so she could see the face that belonged to the lips, but her eyelids wouldn't cooperate.

Her chest hurt so badly, it was almost all she could feel, except for those lips against hers.

A panicked shout, more loud noises, the lips were gone, something covered her face, a sharp pain in her arm and then, blissfully, nothing.

"Is she breathing?" Mason asked Mallory Vaughn, a nurse practitioner who filled in periodically on the rig, and Libby, one of his best volunteer paramedics.

Mallory held a stethoscope to the stunning young woman's chest and nodded in response to his question. Their patient had long, silky dark hair, lovely olive-toned skin, eyelashes that other women would kill for and sexy lips. "Her breathing is shallow with wheezing, and her heart rate is through the roof. Let's get her to the clinic. I'll call David on the way."

Dr. David Lawrence, the island's only doctor, was always on call.

"Do we know her?" Mason asked.

"She's Nikki Stokes's sister, Jordan," Libby said. "They're identical twins."

That was why she seemed familiar. She looked like Nikki, but he noted subtle differences between the sisters. He'd read about Jordan and her troubles online, curious about Nikki's famous sister after he got to know her while inspecting the Wayfarer—and after catching Jordan's show, *Live with Jordan and Gigi*, a few times.

"Where are Nikki and Riley?" Mason asked Mallory, who was Riley's cousin.

"Off-island."

"Good," he said, relieved to know that all occupants were out of the house.

Mallory and Libby moved with precision to stabilize Jordan while

Mason's team extinguished the blaze that appeared to have started on the roof and then somehow engaged the chimney—or vice versa.

If he had to guess, the flames on the roof had jumped to the chimney. A creosote build-up had probably caused the chimney to ignite, which had sent smoke into the house. They would have to fully investigate, but that was his hunch.

"Good thing you saw the flames," Libby said. "She's in the midst of an asthma attack."

Adrenaline coursed through Mason's system, making him feel amped up the way he always did after a rescue. "She's breathing, though, right?" He always cared about the people they saved, but for reasons that made no sense to him, he was extra concerned about this woman.

"She is, and we're giving her a breathing treatment." Mallory glanced up at him and did a double take. "What'd you do to your face?"

"Huh?"

She pointed to his left temple.

He reached up, felt wetness and winced at the flash of pain. "Fell off my bike."

"You need to get that looked at."

"I'll come by the clinic after we finish here." He didn't mention that his elbow was either broken or dislocated. He'd see to his injuries as soon as he got the chance.

They loaded Jordan onto a gurney and rolled her into the back of the ambulance.

"Let's go," Mallory called to the firefighter driving the rescue.

The rig took off with lights flashing and siren screaming.

Jordan was in good hands with Mallory, Libby and Dr. David at the clinic, so Mason turned his attention to the smoking hulk of stone that was Mrs. Hopper's chimney and the singed roof on the north side of the chimney, wondering what could've sparked a fire on the roof. Nikki and Riley had done a ton of work to the house over the winter. Hopefully, there wouldn't be too much damage inside from the fire that'd been contained mostly to the roof and chimney. They'd need some repairs to both.

He tried to shake off the jitters that followed the rush of running into a burning building and bringing someone out alive. The amped feeling stayed with him as he supervised his firefighters, inspected the damage and tried to pinpoint the source of the fire.

The whole time, though, his mind raced while he tried to process a strange occurrence.

When he'd put his mouth on Jordan's to blow air into her lungs, something he'd done hundreds of times in the past, the craziest thing had happened. She'd moaned and moved her lips as if to kiss him. That'd certainly never happened before, and it was for damned sure he'd never felt a current of electricity zip through his body while administering mouth-to-mouth resuscitation to anyone else.

What the hell was that about?

CHAPTER 2

*E*verything hurt. That was the only thought in Jordan's mind as she opened her eyes to a flood of bright light and frantic activity happening around her. Where was she? What'd happened? Then she remembered her fear that something was wrong and felt panicked as she struggled against the mask on her face, wanting it off.

"Easy. You're fine."

Jordan recognized the female voice, but couldn't place it. Her eyelids were still too heavy to stay open for more than a second or two.

The next time she came to, she was in a dark room, the mask still on her face and something beeping next to her. In her hand, she found a device with a button on it that she pushed, recalling the look and feel of the nurse's call button from too many hospital stays to count while battling asthma as well as the recent one after Brendan.

No. Don't. Just don't go there.

Jordan didn't want to think about him now or ever.

A young woman wearing light blue scrubs came into the room. Her blonde hair was in a ponytail as she quickly checked the monitors and adjusted the IV taped to Jordan's right hand. "You're doing great.

EMS gave you a nebulizer treatment, and your breathing is much better."

The words *nebulizer treatment* took Jordan back to a childhood filled with asthma attacks and other associated respiratory illnesses.

Jordan recognized the woman as Katie McCarthy, who was married to Riley's cousin Shane. She'd met them at the Wayfarer opening. She reached for the mask covering her nose and mouth.

Katie held it aside for her.

"Do I have to stay?" Jordan's tongue felt too big for her mouth, and her throat hurt.

"Just for the night so we can monitor you."

Jordan closed her eyes against a rush of tears. It'd been years since she'd had an attack, and she couldn't figure out what would've caused one out of the blue like this. She tried to put the pieces together, to think about how this could've happened, but she was so out of it that the pieces refused to add up. "Someone was there..."

"Yes, thankfully the Gansett fire chief, Mason Johns, saw the flames and got you out of there. You were barely breathing when he found you."

The lips. She remembered the lips. Had they been Mason's lips?

"My chest hurts."

"I know." Katie's eyes and demeanor were kind and caring.

Jordan wanted to beg her not to leave. "The house..." Nikki would kill her after the time and effort she and Riley had devoted to remodeling it.

"From what I heard, the fire was contained to the roof and chimney, and the fire department got there quickly. The house should be fine."

The flood of relief made it easier to breathe.

Katie set the mask back in place, over Jordan's nose and mouth. "Shane called Riley to let them know what happened."

Jordan absorbed that info with a sinking feeling. Nik and Riley had been so excited to spend her rare night off on the mainland to shop for their upcoming wedding.

"Slim is flying them back to the island. They should be here soon."

She felt sick knowing she'd caused their getaway to be ruined, not to mention that Nik would be panicked to hear Jordan was in the hospital—again.

No matter how hard Jordan tried, she couldn't stay awake, but the noises of the machines kept causing her to jolt awake, as if she'd been dreaming of being chased and came to at the critical moment of being caught.

One of the times, she awakened to see a large man sitting in the chair next to her bed. In the murky light, she could make out only the shape of him, and at first, she thought she was still dreaming. His arm was in a sling, and a white bandage on his forehead stood out in stark relief against tanned skin.

"Hey." He leaned in toward the bed. "I'm Mason Johns from the fire department. Katie asked me to sit with you while she tends to another patient. How're you doing?"

She fumbled with the mask over her mouth and managed to remove it. "I'm okay. You were the one who rescued me." Her chest hurt a little less than it had earlier, which she took as a good sign.

"That was me." His deep voice projected warmth, empathy and competence.

They'd been his lips, then. "Thank you."

"No problem."

"Your arm and your head. Did that happen when you rescued me?"

He smiled, the flash of straight white teeth visible from the glow of the monitors. "Nah, that happened before, when I crashed my bike."

Jordan was a sucker for a good smile, and his was excellent. "How did you do that?"

"I like to ride on the paths out by the bluffs, and there's this one little hill that's like a ramp. I was on the ramp when I noticed the flames and smoke coming from your place, got distracted, and next thing I knew, I was flat on my back. My elbow took the brunt of the fall and was dislocated."

"Ouch."

"Hurt like a mother-you-know-what when they put it back where it belongs."

"You rescued me with a dislocated elbow."

"I did."

"That's very heroic."

He laughed. "Not really. It's kind of my job."

She liked the sound of his laugh almost as much as his voice and wanted to hear more of both. "Have you been a firefighter a long time?"

"About fifteen years now, but you shouldn't be talking. You need to put the oxygen mask back in place."

Jordan made a face that she hoped conveyed her displeasure. "I don't like it."

"No one does, but you need it."

"I feel better."

He affected a stern expression. "Doctor's orders."

She scowled at him. "And here I thought you were nice."

He laughed again. "I *am* nice, and I want you to get better."

Katie came into the room. "How's the patient?"

"She doesn't like the mask."

"No one does." She checked the monitors and said, "Your oxygen saturation is better than it was. I think we can switch to the nasal cannula."

"Oh yay," Jordan said.

Katie smiled at Jordan's lack of enthusiasm. "I'll be right back."

"Congrats on the upgrade," Mason said.

"I guess it's better than the mask, but what I really want is to get out of here."

"That's not happening tonight."

She stuck her bottom lip out. "I know. I heard."

"It's better to let them monitor you before you leave. You wouldn't want to have problems when you're home alone."

"I won't be home alone. They called my sister and her fiancé. They're on their way back to the island now."

"You won't be happy to see them?"

"I feel bad that their night away got cut short because of me. They were looking forward to it."

"I'm sure they're concerned about you."

"And how their house nearly burned down on my watch."

"They won't blame you."

"What happened, anyway?"

"Not sure yet, but if I had to guess, something sparked the roof, which sparked the chimney and forced smoke into the house. My guys are investigating. We should know more in the morning."

"You're the boss, huh?"

"Yep. I'm the fire chief."

"I heard I got saved by the big boss."

"That's right," he said, smiling. "Some of the guys were jealous because I got to rescue you."

"Because they know who I am." That left her feeling deflated. Of course they'd seen the video. Mason probably had, too.

"I guess so."

She turned her head toward him. "You don't know who I am?"

He shrugged. "Maybe, but only because I saw your show a few times."

"You did?" Jordan found that shocking. "Seriously?"

"Yes," he said, laughing. "It was good. But for the most part, I don't follow social media or pop culture. I'm told I'm a dinosaur."

"I find that rather refreshing."

"I don't get why people have to live their whole lives online. I'd rather be riding my bike or out on a boat or anywhere other than chained to a computer or phone. Although I can't go far without my phone, especially this time of year."

She chose not to mention her ten million Twitter and five million Instagram followers to someone who disdained social media. "The summer is busy for you." In all the years she'd been coming to Gansett for the summer, she'd never once considered what the season would be like for public safety workers.

"It's insane."

"Do you hate it?"

"Nah. Fortunately, it's only a couple of months. The rest of the year is a cake walk in comparison. What about you? Is there a busy season in your job?"

Jordan thought about that for a minute. "I'm not really working right now." Her attorney and best friend, Gabrielle "Gigi" Gibson, was working to try to get Jordan out of the contract for the last season of their show. Jordan and Zane were her biggest clients. She'd also starred as Jordan's sidekick on the show, which had made Gigi a celebrity in her own right.

Jordan also had a divorce to contend with, but nothing could happen there until Brendan got out of rehab. "I'm trying to figure out what's next."

"Gansett is a good place to do some thinking. A lot of people come here to regroup."

"I guess."

Katie returned with the nose prongs, which were a big improvement over the mask, but Jordan had always hated them, too. She'd had far too much experience with medical breathing equipment to like any of it.

"Better?" Katie asked as she removed the mask and the tubes attached to it.

"Much. Thank you."

"Do you need anything?"

"I'm actually kind of hungry."

"I am, too," Mason said. "How about I make a run to Mario's for us?"

"You don't have to do that. You must be wanting to go home after working all day, not to mention your elbow has to be killing you."

"It's fine. I don't have anything else to do tonight, and we're both hungry."

"If you're sure it's not a problem."

"I'm sure. What do you like?"

"A house salad with vinaigrette would be great."

His brows furrowed comically. "That's an appetizer. What do you want for a meal?"

"That is a meal for me."

"That's not enough. I'll get a pizza. You can have some of that."

"I'll only eat cheese or veggie. I'm a vegetarian."

"I can do that. Be right back." He stood to his considerable height and was gone before Jordan could object to his desire to feed her.

She couldn't recall the last time she'd had pizza, but the thought of it had her mouth watering in anticipation. "That is one tall dude," she said to Katie.

"I know. I asked him once how tall he is, and he said six-six."

"Damn." That made him more than a foot taller than her five-two.

"Nicest guy you'll ever meet. Everyone loves him."

Jordan wondered why Katie was telling her that. Was she playing matchmaker? Because the last thing in the universe Jordan was interested in was anything having to do with the male species. She was done with men and all the nonsense that came with them. The last one had nearly killed her, and had ruined her interest in other men.

She agreed that Mason seemed like a nice guy. He would make some lucky girl very happy someday. That lucky girl was not going to be her.

While Mason was gone, Jordan dozed and dreamed and woke to the scent of pizza. "You're back."

"I told you I would be."

Jordan was conditioned to expect nothing so she wouldn't be disappointed, which forced her to admit she hadn't actually expected him to come back. Brendan would've gotten sidetracked by a fan or a post or a video or something and forgotten all about her being hungry. That's what she was used to. She started to push herself up in the bed.

"Hang on." Mason found a button on the side of the bed that did the work for her.

"That's handy." Until she'd tried to sit up, she'd had no idea how exhausted she was. Between the asthma attack and the lingering effects of the sleeping pill, she had the coordination of a weak kitten.

Mason set the food on a tray, dropped the rail on the side of her bed and rolled it in close enough for her to reach.

"Thank you. It was nice of you to bring me food."

"I'm hungry, too, so no problem."

While she picked at her salad, he dove into a meat-lover's pizza, devouring three slices in the time it took her to take five bites of lettuce and cucumber. Mario's always included shaved parmesan cheese on their house salad, which she loved.

Mason put a piece of cheese pizza on a paper plate and pushed it in her direction.

Jordan eyed it with lust in her heart. The days of having to watch everything she ate had ended with her reality TV career, but the habit of denying herself was so ingrained as to be almost impossible to overcome.

He pushed it another inch closer. "I told them to keep two slices meat-free for you. You're not going to let me down, are you?"

"You're the devil."

A smile lit up his warm eyes. "You had a close call tonight, super-star. At this point, I'd be asking myself—if this had been it for me, would I be glad I'd given up pizza for years so I could look a certain way? My answer would've been *hell no*." He gave the plate another nudge in her direction. "Eat the pizza. Dance in the rain. Live your life. You never know how long you've got. Don't have regrets."

He would never know how much she'd needed that reminder or how far she'd strayed from living her best life in the last few years. Jordan picked up the slice of pizza and took a huge bite.

Mason grinned at her, letting her know he wholeheartedly approved of her decision.

Jordan had never tasted anything better than that sinful bite of cheese pizza. She took a second and third bite in rapid succession.

"Don't choke. I've already had to save your ass once tonight."

She sputtered with laugher and nearly lost the mouthful of pizza. In addition to being bad for her diet, he was also funny and seriously cute, if a six-and-a-half-foot-tall man could be called "cute."

His brown hair was streaked with blond highlights, and even though it was only June, his handsome face was already as tanned as most people would be by the end of the summer. He must've spent a lot of time outside.

"Thanks for getting the food. It's really good. I owe you for my half."

"Don't worry about it."

"I will worry about it."

"Suit yourself. *I* am not worried about it."

"I'll pay you back."

"Have some more pizza and stop fretting about things that don't matter."

"Are you always so blunt and bossy?"

He paused before attacking his fourth piece of pizza. After chasing the bite with a mouthful of water, he blotted the grease from his lips with a napkin.

Jordan zeroed in on the lips that had breathed air into her lungs and electrified the rest of her, which was so silly. He'd been saving her life, not trying to kiss her.

"I guess I'm pretty bossy sometimes, because I have to be. Got a lot of younger people working for me, and they require a certain amount of *direction*."

"How so?"

"Well, for one thing, they all think they deserve an award for showing up. Blaine, the police chief, says it's because they were raised in the everyone-gets-a-prize generation in which they got certificates and trophies for ninth place. We got them, too, but they didn't make us feel like we're special."

Jordan laughed. "I've got a few of those on my shelf at home."

"What did you play?"

"I was a cheerleader and dance team member, and I played soccer and lacrosse. Lotta trophies and certificates."

"I'll bet."

"What else do your people do that annoys you?"

"They're cell phone addicted."

"Guilty as charged. I was just wondering if you'd thought to grab my phone when you were rescuing me."

He gave her a salty look. "Sorry that I was more concerned with the fact that you didn't appear to be breathing than I was about your phone." His tone positively dripped with sarcasm.

Jordan loved sarcasm. "I'll let it pass this time, but the next time you rescue me, if you could make it a package deal with my phone, I'd really appreciate that."

He rolled his brown eyes dramatically. "I'll make a note of that."

"You won't make a note, because you don't get it."

"You're right. I don't get the obsession. I'm tied to a phone around the clock due to my job. If I didn't have to be, I wouldn't. Trust me on that."

She gave him her best horrified look. "But how would you keep in touch with everyone you've ever met if you didn't have your phone with you?"

"I can think of much better ways to 'keep in touch' than through a cell phone."

Jordan also appreciated a good double entendre. Her rescuer was not only handsome and sweet, he was also witty and charming, which was far more dangerous than smoke for a girl recovering from a badly broken heart.

CHAPTER 3

*D*amn, she was gorgeous and funny and sarcastic. Normally, sarcasm drove him mad because he was overrun with youthful firefighters and paramedics, many of whom had never been taught not to talk back to their boss. He put up with it because they were a small, tight-knit department, and for all their faults, his firefighters and paramedics did an excellent job serving the Gansett Island community.

But coming from Jordan, sarcasm took on new meaning. He liked that she gave it right back to him and more than held her own when it came to bantering with him.

He liked her. While he'd waited for the pizza to be done at Mario's, he'd taken a quick look at Google to get the latest lowdown on her. What he'd read about her husband had infuriated him. Other than seeing her show a few times and having been entertained by it, Mason didn't know much about Jordan Stokes. However, he'd certainly heard about Zane and had even liked his music before reading about what he'd done to his wife in a hotel room in Charlotte, North Carolina.

There'd been tons of speculation over what'd become of Jordan since the meltdown with Zane. Apparently, she hadn't been seen in public or posted to her social media accounts since the night of their fight in the hotel. People were speculating as to whether they'd seen the last of her or if she'd be back for another season of her reality TV show.

With the pizza finished and Jordan settled back against her pillows, with her face pale and her dark eyes big from the ordeal, he knew he ought to leave her to get some rest. The paperwork waiting for him back at the station wasn't going to do itself, but he wasn't in any rush to leave her.

So he stayed until Jordan's sister and future brother-in-law came rushing into the room a short time later.

Nikki hurled herself at her sister, sobbing as she clung to Jordan. "Oh my God! You scared me to death!"

"I'm so sorry about the fire and the house. I don't know what happened."

"Who cares about that? All that matters is you're all right. I've been shaking for two hours since we got the call."

"I didn't want them to call you. It was your night away."

"Don't be silly, Jordan," Riley said. "All that matters is that you're all right."

Nikki hugged her sister for so long that Mason worried Jordan might be having trouble breathing and was about to say so when Nikki finally pulled back to study the face that was just like hers, only with subtle differences.

For one thing, Jordan had a tiny mole on the left side of her upper lip, and her right eyebrow had an arch to it that Nikki's didn't.

And honestly, why in the world did he care about the differences between the twins, and why was he even still there?

"I, um, I'm gonna get going. I'll, ah, check in with you tomorrow, and we'll be by for a look at the roof and chimney in the daylight."

Jordan nudged Nikki to the side so she could see him. "Thank you so much, Mason, for rescuing me, keeping me company, feeding me, entertaining me. I really appreciate it."

Nikki surprised him when she got up from Jordan's bed and hurled herself at Mason, narrowly missing a full hit to his injured arm.

"Whoa," he said as he absorbed the impact.

"Nikki!" Jordan said. "Watch out. He's hurt!"

"Thank you so, so, *so much* for saving my sister, Mason." Nikki broke down into tears again. "You saved us both, because there's no me without her."

Mason patted her awkwardly on the back and was relieved when Riley rescued him.

"Come here, love. You're freaking the poor guy out with your hysterics."

"Sorry, Mason," Nikki said, sobbing into Riley's chest.

"No worries. Glad I was in the right place at the right time." He thought it wise not to mention that Jordan hadn't had much time left when he'd arrived on the scene.

"We're eternally grateful, Mason," Riley said, shaking his hand.

"Just doing my job." He gave a small wave to Jordan, who looked so small and adorable in the big hospital bed. "Feel better."

She gave him a smile that did funny things to his insides, making him wish they'd had more time to talk before her family showed up. "Thanks again, Mason."

"Sure thing. We'll see you all tomorrow when we come back to take a look at the house in the daylight."

"See you then," Jordan said.

As he walked out of the hospital into the warm late-spring evening, he couldn't wait for tomorrow.

NIKKI SAT on the edge of Jordan's bed, holding her hand. "What happened? Do you remember?"

"I'd taken a sleeping pill, so I was kind of out of it. I remember my chest hurting and feeling like something was wrong, but I couldn't do anything about it. Then Mason was there, and he was running me through the house. I couldn't figure out what was happening. Apparently, there was smoke from the chimney, and I had an asthma attack."

"Shit," Riley said, "I bet I left the flue open the last time we had a fire. I'm so sorry, Jordan."

"It's not your fault. You couldn't have known what would happen."

"I'd really like to know how the roof caught fire in the first place," Riley said.

Nikki brushed Jordan's hair back from her face. "Shane said you were barely breathing when Mason found you. I almost had a heart attack when he said that! Then we heard it was an asthma attack. You haven't had one in years."

"I know. I actually thought I'd outgrown it."

"The smoke probably triggered it," Riley said.

"I guess," Jordan said. "It's kind of scary to know it's still lurking in there after all these years." Asthma had been the story of her life as a child and teenager, but the condition had improved as she moved into her twenties.

"Let's hope it was a onetime thing and not the start of a new phase," Nikki said.

"God, I hope so." Asthma was terrifying, with the attacks often coming with little or no warning. One minute, she could breathe fine, and the next, she'd be straining to get air into her lungs. It was the worst feeling she'd ever experienced, and she used to live in fear of each attack. Of course, freaking out over the attacks had only made them worse.

"What did Dr. David say?" Nikki asked.

"I haven't had a chance to talk to him yet. Katie was in earlier and said my lung sounds were much better."

"We'll make an appointment with him for as soon as possible," Nikki said. "If necessary, we'll find a pulmonologist on the mainland to give you a complete workup. Try not to worry."

"I should just go back to LA and see my doctors there."

"No! You promised to hang out for the summer. You can't leave yet."

After her marriage ended in spectacular fashion, she'd put her career in LA on indefinite hold. Since she had nothing pressing she needed to get right back to, Jordan had agreed to spend the summer with Nikki and Riley. However, she still felt weird about being at the house when they were crazy in love and not afraid to show it. She felt like the awkward third wheel in her sister's love affair. "You guys don't need me underfoot. I'll come back a couple of weeks before the wedding."

"Please don't go. I love having you here. It's made me so happy to know we were going to do the wedding stuff together." Nikki paused, tipped her head and added, "Unless it's too painful for you after what's happened with *him*." Nikki had refused to say his name after Charlotte. "God, I'm such an ass. Of course you don't want to help plan a wedding when your own marriage just ended."

"That's not it, Nik. I'm super excited for your wedding. I swear. I just feel like you guys need your privacy and—"

"We're *fine*," Nikki said. "We get plenty of privacy, right, Ri?"

"That's right," Riley said. "We're happy to have you spending the summer."

Jordan eyed him skeptically. "As if you'd ever tell me otherwise."

"He would," Nikki said. "He'd come right out and say, 'I want to be alone with Nikki.' You've heard him say it!"

Riley laughed, because he couldn't deny that he was rather blunt when he wanted Nikki to himself. "The house is huge, Jordan. There's plenty of room for all of us. It's no sweat, and we like having you there. You make Nik so happy, and I like happy Nik."

Jordan drew in a breath and exhaled, relieved that her breathing had returned to normal, even if the attack had left a lingering ache in her chest. "You guys are too nice."

"You're *family*, Jordan," Riley said. "I have my own version of a Jordan, too, don't forget. Finn and I aren't identical twins, but we might as well be."

"That's right," Nikki said. "He practically lived with us all last winter while we were renovating. Riley owes me big for putting up with Finn."

Riley scowled at her, but his eyes conveyed amusement. "Finn is a bit of a handful. You're nothing compared to him."

Jordan had spent time with Finn and his girlfriend, Chloe, and liked them both a lot. "Fine. If you guys are sure you don't mind a third wheel underfoot, I'll stay. But I've got to go home eventually and figure out my life." In addition to the show, she had numerous endorsement contracts she'd put on hold after the trouble with Brendan, and Gigi had been after her to think about getting back to work before someone decided to sue her for breach of contract.

Despite the fact that Brendan had assaulted her, she'd been the one receiving death threats from his loyal fans after he'd been arrested and charged. Her grandmother had insisted on hiring security for her that she'd recently dismissed after the initial furor had died down. Gran and Nikki had been upset with her for ditching the security, but she couldn't bear to be watched all the time. Besides, no one knew she was on Gansett, so she certainly didn't need them on the remote island.

It'd been a relief to be on Gansett, where she and Nikki had spent summers with their mother and grandmother. Those had been the happiest times of her life, and Jordan loved any chance she got to return to the island and to spend time at the house that had been more of a home to her and Nikki than anywhere else they'd ever lived.

She wasn't ready to return to the madness that was her real life. A few more weeks on Gansett would help her mentally prepare to reenter the maelstrom. Prior to the fire and the asthma attack, she'd been thinking it was time to go back and face the proverbial music. Now, she had a good excuse to take more time off.

Jordan glanced at Nikki, who'd once been her full-time manager as well as her twin and closest friend. She'd never admit to anyone, especially Nik, who was so happy in her new life, how lost she'd been without Nik at home and at work. "Can you ask them about a note?" A doctor's note about the severe asthma attack would buy her a few more weeks.

Nik would know what she needed. She always knew. "Of course. Don't worry about a thing. I'll take care of it."

Jordan's eyes filled with tears as she looked up at her sister. "I thought this shit was behind us."

"I know. Me, too, but it was probably the smoke."

"I hope so. If it's back…"

Nikki laid her hand over Jordan's. "It's not. It was triggered by the smoke. I know it."

Dr. David Lawrence came into the room, looking rushed and flustered. "I'm sorry it took me so long to get back to you, Jordan. A car accident resulted in several patients being brought in, so I got waylaid."

"Anyone we know?" Riley asked hesitantly. He was related to half the island, or so it seemed.

David shook his head. "Tourists who took one of our famous curves too fast and found out how unforgiving Gansett Island trees can be."

The doctor was tall, dark haired and good-looking. Jordan had met him and his fiancée, Daisy, at the opening of the Wayfarer.

"Are they going to be all right?" Nikki asked.

"They will be." David sat in the chair at Jordan's bedside. "Anyway, about you, Ms. Jordan. How're you feeling?"

"Better. My chest hurts, but it always does after an attack."

"Talk to me about your history with asthma."

Jordan glanced at Nikki.

"If I may?" Nikki said.

Jordan nodded. She was too tired and wrung out to tell that story.

"Jordan had her first asthma attack when we were six. It came out of nowhere, and at first, our mom thought she was choking. She called for rescue, and the paramedics immediately realized what was happening. That was the start of a cycle of attacks that went on for years, well into high school when the situation seemed to stabilize. She'd go years without an attack, and when she had them, they were less severe than they'd been when she was younger."

David nodded as he took notes. "That can happen. People grow out of it in many cases. Others continue to struggle with it into adulthood."

"She hasn't had an attack in more than seven years."

"I kind of thought my asthma issues were behind me," Jordan added.

"They probably were until you were stuck in a smoky room, which will trigger the old demons."

"So you don't think it's back like it was before?"

"I can't really say for certain, but it's probably safe to assume this particular attack was situational due to the smoke. We can only hope it won't lead to others. Do you still carry an inhaler?"

"No. I haven't needed it in years."

"I'm going to prescribe one, and I'd like you to keep it with you for the next three months or so. I'd recommend a check-in with your pulmonologist to update them on this latest incident."

"Can we take her home?" Nikki asked.

"I'd like you to spend the night so we can monitor your breathing. Just as a precaution. There were no signs of burns in your throat or upper airway," David said, "and your chest X-ray was clear. We just want to be sure you're okay before we release you.

Jordan groaned. She'd spent so many nights in the hospital as a kid that the thought of even one more was unbearable.

"I'll stay with you," Nik said.

"Absolutely not. Go home. I'm fine."

"I don't want to leave you."

"Riley, take your fiancée and get her out of my hair, will you, please?"

"Come on, Nik. Let's give Jordan the chance to get some rest. We'll come back in the morning to bring her home."

"Can we, Doc?" Nikki asked David. "Can she come home in the morning?"

"Provided her vitals are where they need to be, she can go home in the morning."

Seeming to realize that was his best offer, Nikki leaned across the bed rail to hug Jordan. "Will you call if you need me?"

"I don't have my phone, but I'll make sure they have your number in case you're needed."

"You can give it to me," David said. "I'll be here all night." He wrote down the number Nikki recited. "Try not to worry. Everything is looking good, and we'll keep a close eye on her overnight."

Jordan had given Nikki plenty of reasons to worry about her, especially lately. Her sister was now preconditioned to worry. Jordan hated being the cause of the line that had begun to form between Nikki's brows from all the time she'd spent jammed up over Jordan's shit.

It was time to make some changes. She just wished she knew what changes she wanted to make or how to actually reset her life.

She would use this time on Gansett to do some deep thinking and contemplation. Hopefully, by the time she left, she'd have a plan that would give her sister far less to worry about.

Because neither she nor Nikki could go on this way for much longer.

CHAPTER 4

*R*iley half-dragged Nikki out of the clinic and held the door for her while she got into his pickup truck.

She went through the motions of putting the seat belt on.

"Hey," Riley said.

Nikki glanced at him.

"She's okay," he said. "David's only keeping her as a precaution. Everything is fine. We'll come back in the morning to pick her up."

"I know."

While Nikki stared straight ahead into the darkness, Riley walked around to the driver's side and got in. His phone rang, and he took the call from his dad, Kevin, who'd apparently heard about the fire at Eastward Look.

"Yes, we're fine, and Jordan is spending the night at the clinic, but she's okay. No, the house is fine. From what we heard, there's a little damage, but nothing we can't handle. Sorry to freak you out. How's Summer doing?"

At times like this, Nikki thought while Riley talked to his dad about his new baby sister, it was handy to have a contractor for a fiancé. Riley, his brother and cousins would have the place back to rights in no time.

Riley promised to check in with Kevin in the morning and ended the call.

As they drove home in silence, Nikki relived the last few hours, from the time Riley received the call from his cousin Shane about a fire at Eastward Look, how Jordan had been rescued by Mason and found to be in the midst of a severe asthma attack.

She shuddered remembering the frightening attacks from their childhood that would turn their lives upside down, sometimes for weeks at a time. The utter terror of realizing Jordan couldn't breathe was something Nikki had never forgotten, and tonight's incident had brought back the horror.

Nikki's thoughts were so mired in the past that she'd almost forgotten about the incident that had led to Jordan's more recent attack. She was quickly reminded of it when Riley took the turn into the driveway at Eastward Look where fire trucks were still at the scene, serving as a grim reminder of what'd taken place earlier and how close she'd come to losing her sister.

"Wait for me," Riley said when he parked out of the way of the fire department vehicles. He came around to help Nikki from the car, which, under normal circumstances, wouldn't have been necessary. But since she could barely bring herself to move, she accepted his assistance and welcomed the warm hand he wrapped around hers. She felt cold all over as they went to talk to one of the firefighters.

"Hey, folks," the man said. "Is this your house?"

"Yes," Riley said. "Were you able to determine the source of the fire?"

"It started on the roof and spread to the chimney, but we can't seem to figure out what sparked it. We're wrapping up here for tonight. We'll be back in the morning for a closer look in the daylight."

"Is it okay for us to stay here tonight?"

"Absolutely. The damage was contained to the roof, chimney and living room, where you've got some water and smoke damage. Luckily, the chief spotted the flames and smoke before the fire moved past the chimney area. Otherwise, you might be looking at a total loss. Doesn't take much for these old houses to burn to the ground."

Nikki began to actively tremble as images of the house fully engulfed in flames with her sister inside took up residence in her imagination.

Riley dropped her hand and wrapped his arm around her.

Having him with her made everything far more bearable than it would have been before she'd had his unconditional support.

They waited until the firefighters packed up and left before venturing inside.

"Not sure I can bear to look," Nikki said as Riley led the way to the front door. They'd spent months working on every square inch of the downstairs and had brought it back to gleaming life.

"Whatever it is, we'll fix it and make it good as new. We just have to keep reminding ourselves that it could've been so much worse."

"I know. When I think about Jordan stuck in there, knocked out by a sleeping pill." She clutched her stomach as a wave of nausea overcame her.

At the top step, Riley stopped her from going in. "It's going to take a while to get those images out of your mind, but just keep thinking about how she looked just now at the clinic. She's totally fine."

Nikki nodded. "Thanks for being my rock. Always, but especially the last few hours."

He laid a gentle kiss on her lips. "Being your rock is my favorite thing ever."

When Riley opened the door and the pungent stench of smoke greeted them, Nikki's heart sank. He flipped on lights and walked ahead of her into the living room. The rug and sofa were soaked and sooty, the hearth singed and the ceiling black. "Could be way worse," Riley said. "This will be nothing to fix. Probably have to get new furniture, but whatever. That's no biggie."

Seeing the discarded blanket that had covered her sister on the sofa and Jordan's phone on the coffee table brought home just how close Jordan had been to the fire.

Riley noticed she was fixated on the sofa and came to gently redirect her toward the stairs to their room. "You feel like a bath?" He knew how much she loved the claw-foot tub he'd restored the previous winter.

"I don't think so. Not tonight. But thanks." Nikki changed into pajama pants and a long-sleeved T-shirt because she still couldn't seem to get warm.

"Is there anything I can do for you, love?"

"Warm me up in bed?"

Riley sent her the special smile he saved only for her. "Always happy to help with that." He stripped down to boxers, and after they'd both taken a turn in the bathroom, he crawled into bed next to her and wrapped his big body around hers, making her feel safe, loved and warm. "Better?"

"So much better."

"I'm sorry this happened to Jordan and to you."

"I feel so bad for her. She's had more than enough lately."

"So have you. It's okay to feel a little badly for yourself, too."

"It's always been this way."

"What way?" he asked, running his hand over her hair and back.

"Everything is harder for her for some reason. We're identical twins, so we're supposed to be similar, but it just seems that every-thing is hard for her in ways it wasn't for me. She had awful asthma when we were kids. She was in and out of the hospital for years. She had trouble keeping friends, and I could never understand why. She's the nicest girl, but for whatever reason, people would turn on her. And then her husband did the same thing. I just keep wondering when she's going to get her break. When will it be her turn to be happy?"

"It'll happen, honey. When the time is right. Jordan is a great girl. She's going to meet someone who'll make what's-his-name seem like a distant bad memory."

"Any time now. I want her to be happy. I'm not saying she needs to fall in love to be happy, but she's always wanted to find someone special. I think it goes back to the way we were raised and how betrayed we both felt by our dad. We just wanted to find stability anywhere we could. She's done a lot of dumb things trying to achieve that goal, such as marry *him*."

"Did you always hate him?"

"Always. My dislike for him was immediate and visceral. And vice versa."

"He only disliked you because his oversized ego couldn't handle the fact that you had him nailed for what he really was from the get-go."

Nikki raised her head off his chest to look him in the eye. "How do you know that?"

"I know his type. He's a malignant narcissist. It's all about him, and everyone around him needs to get on board. You refused to do that, so you were of no use to him, especially since you had significant influence over Jordan."

"That about sums up the dynamic. Have you known people like him?"

"There was this one guy I knew in college who was like that. His way or the highway, and anyone who questioned him was automatically excommunicated from his life."

"Did you get excommunicated?"

"Yep. I intervened when he was hassling a girl at a party, and he didn't like that. Tough shit. I wasn't going to walk away and pretend I hadn't seen what he was doing. I knew her from a math class I took freshman year, but I would've done the same thing even if I hadn't known her."

"My hero."

"Oh, please. I was just doing what any decent person would do when they see someone in a bad situation."

"Not everyone would do that, Ri. In fact, I bet most guys would've kept on going."

"Not if they were raised by Kevin, Frank and Big Mac McCarthy, they wouldn't have."

"They raised good men."

"I'm glad you think so."

"It's not just me who thinks so. Everyone does."

"I only care what you think."

Nikki turned Riley's face toward her so she could kiss him. "I think you're the best man I've ever known. I just wish my sister could find someone like you."

MASON SLEPT FITFULLY, the pain from his elbow waking him several times during the night, forcing him to take painkillers at two a.m. He decided to forgo his usual morning workout in deference to the injury, but that would make him doubly cranky. He relied on exercise to keep him grounded and had made it a habit for years to start each day with a vigorous workout. Once upon a time, he'd been a competitive weightlifter, and since he quit drinking, exercise had helped him stay sober. He'd learned not to ask questions about the things that helped. Whatever it took to keep from going back to who he'd been before he got sober.

Mason went through the motions of showering and shaving with an electric razor, since his left arm was in a sling and he didn't trust himself to use an actual razor with his right hand. Of course he'd injured the elbow on his dominant side. He hoped it healed quickly, because doing things one-handed seriously sucked. When he was ready, he left the small house he rented on the island's east side and arrived at the meeting he attended seven days a week at the nondenominational church in town.

Mallory and her fiancé, Dr. Quinn James, were already there. Mason fixed himself a coffee and went to sit with them. They'd become good friends over the last year, and he looked forward to seeing them every morning.

"How's the arm?" Mallory asked.

"Hurts like hell."

"It will for a few weeks," Quinn said.

"I was afraid you'd say that."

"Are you taking time out of work?" Mallory asked.

"Hell no. That's not an option this time of year. And besides, my arm hurts. Otherwise, I'm fine."

Mallory smiled at his testy response. "You can't go out on calls with your arm in a sling."

"I can still supervise and deal with the never-ending paperwork and all the other crap that goes on every day."

"True, and Lord knows the world might end if you're not there to supervise," she said, laughing.

He gave her a pointed look. "You know full well what I deal with." The two of them had had many conversations about working with younger officers and the generational differences in their work ethics.

"I do, and I understand. But if you were to take a few days off, I think they'd survive."

"I don't want to risk it and then have to spend the rest of the summer cleaning up whatever mess they make of things."

Before Mallory could reply, Nina, the facilitator, came rushing in, a few minutes late as always this time of year. She ran the Summer House Hotel, so this was her busy season, too. She began the meeting with the Serenity Prayer before asking everyone to introduce themselves. As usual in-season, they had a few visitors among them today. They didn't bother with introductions during the off-season when it was just the regulars.

When Nina asked if anyone wanted to share, Tori, one of the visitors, raised her hand.

Upon closer inspection, Mason noticed Tori had been crying. He put her in her midthirties maybe. She had dark hair and eyes.

"I'm here with my family on vacation," Tori said haltingly. "I'd been sober about four months, and last night." She shook her head and wiped away tears. "I threw away all that hard work for six margaritas that led to yet another fight with my husband. He says he's had enough this time. This is really it. He's taking my kids and leaving me."

Mason felt for her. Giving up alcohol was the most difficult thing he'd ever done, with more stops and starts than he could count before he finally found a path to lasting sobriety. Not that he could say exactly what had done the trick, but something had, and he kept up a rigid routine that revolved around maintenance. He rarely spoke up in the meetings, preferring to listen and absorb the wisdom of others, but he felt like he had something to add to Tori's situation that might help.

"I think it's really important to forgive yourself for the slipup," Mason said. "You're here, which means you own what happened, and you're taking the steps necessary to get back on track. If you didn't care about staying sober, you wouldn't be here."

Tori broke down into sobs that had Mallory shifting over one seat to put her arm around the woman.

"I can't lose my kids."

Over the next hour, the group pulled together to support Tori. Nina offered to go with her to speak to her husband, to help arrange for rehab or anything else the woman might need.

As the meeting broke up, Mason felt drained and yet also uplifted by the way the group had supported Tori during her crisis. AA had saved his life and that of so many others, and to see its powerful impact at work never failed to overwhelm him.

"I don't know about you guys," Mallory said, "but I need food and coffee after that."

"I'm with you, love," Quinn said.

"Me, too, if you don't mind a third wheel," Mason said.

"Oh, stop," Mallory said. "You're never a third wheel with us."

They walked to Rebecca's diner in downtown, which was busy as always in the summer, and took the last remaining booth.

Rebecca delivered three mugs to the table that she filled with coffee. "Be right back to take your order."

"You gotta love the summer around here," Quinn said, taking in the chaos in the island's number-one breakfast spot.

"Do I?" Mason asked, inflicting his tone with sarcasm.

"Yes, you do," Mallory said. "It's the price you pay for having it easy the rest of the year."

"If you say so." Mason stirred cream into his coffee with his right hand and then gave his phone a quick look to make sure nothing was going on—yet. He had no doubt there'd be plenty going on once the revelers woke up, shook off the night before and got started on another big day of partying.

So went the cycle, seven days a week for three months. Mason took advantage of the quiet mornings to attend a meeting, spend some time with friends and ease into a workday that would get progressively more insane as the day went on.

"Pretty intense meeting today," Mallory said, sipping from her mug.

Quinn nodded and stretched his arm out on the back of the booth. "Been a while since we had someone in full-blown crisis."

"Thank goodness for Nina," Mason said. "She always knows what to do."

"You were good in there," Mallory said to Mason. "Hearing that other people had multiple false starts on the way to sobriety is helpful. It's good for her to know it rarely sticks the first time."

"True. It didn't for me." When Mason thought about the last few years before he finally got sober, he was always filled with shame over the way he'd behaved. The three years prior to finally giving up drinking hadn't been pretty. "I nearly lost my job and my firefighting career before I got a clue."

"Took a few times for me, too," Quinn said.

He rarely spoke at the meetings, so Mason didn't know a lot about his story, only that he'd lost a leg in Afghanistan and had spiraled after he left the military. But he and Mallory were happy together. Mason saw that every time he was with them.

Rebecca came by to take their orders. Mallory asked for an egg-white veggie omelet, Quinn ordered eggs sunny side up, and Mason requested scrambled eggs with ham and a grilled English muffin.

"Coming right up," Rebecca said before taking off to tend to other customers.

"We're having a dinner party this Saturday and wanted to invite you to come if you're able to get away from work," Mallory said.

"I'd love to. Thanks for the invite. What can I bring?"

"No need to bring a thing, unless you have a friend you want to invite."

Mason immediately thought of Jordan, which was insane, but he had the thought anyway and immediately felt uncomfortable about it.

"What do you suppose he's thinking about over there?" Mallory asked Quinn.

Mason looked up to find them both fixated on him. "What?"

"You just got all silent and broody," Mallory said. "Something on your mind? Or maybe *someone*?"

Mason shook his head. He absolutely couldn't talk about this with her—or anyone. They'd think he needed his head examined if he told them he'd had a strange reaction to blowing air into Jordan Stokes's lungs or how much he'd enjoyed keeping her company in the clinic until her sister arrived.

He'd mulled over their conversation several times since he left the clinic the night before and found himself smiling every time he recalled her sarcasm, not to mention her reaction to the first bites of pizza she'd allowed herself in far too long. The blissful expression on her striking face as she'd taken the first bite of pizza was unforgettable.

"Mase, your face is red."

He glanced at Mallory. "No, it isn't."

"Yes, it is! Who is she? We see him every day, and he's been holding out on us, Quinn!"

"Leave him alone, babe. You're embarrassing him."

"Oh, please. It's Mason! He doesn't get embarrassed."

"Yes, he does." Mason glared at her playfully. "And I'm not holding out on you. It's nothing." But he'd like it to be, and how funny was that? What interest would a woman like her have in a small-town firefighter? She was used to the glitz and glam of Hollywood and a fast-paced celebrity lifestyle. His lifestyle would bore her to tears. Hell, it bored *him* to tears in the off-season.

"Come on. Spill it. You know you want to."

Mason was trying to figure out when Mallory had become like a sister to him, needling him the way only a sibling could. He huffed out a deep breath, full of annoyance. "I had pizza with Jordan Stokes at the clinic last night, and it was fun. There's your big scoop."

Mallory's eyes went wide with excitement. "*Ohhh*, I like this. Jordan and Nikki are so *gorgeous*."

"Are they? I hadn't noticed."

"I only know Nikki, because she's engaged to my cousin Riley," Mallory continued as if Mason hadn't said anything. "She's as nice as she is pretty, and so great at running the Wayfarer. My dad sings her praises on a regular basis." Mallory had been nearly forty when she found out that Big Mac McCarthy was her father, and the two of them had forged a close relationship since they found each other. "If Jordan is anything like her, and hello, she must be—identical twins, after all—you should ask her out."

Mason held up a hand to stop her. *Whoa.* To Quinn, he said, "Can you please do something about her?"

"Yeah, I've tried." Quinn smiled and shrugged. "She is what she is."

"That's right." Mallory smiled at her beloved. "And I'm too old to change now. I like her for you."

Rebecca brought their food—along with a reprieve for Mason that he knew was temporary. Mallory wasn't going to let this go.

They dug into breakfast while Mason waited for her to make her next move.

She didn't disappoint. "What harm would come from inviting her to dinner with some friends? Everyone needs to eat, right?"

"You're like a dog with a bone," Quinn said, smiling at her.

"Woof," Mallory said, returning his grin.

"I think it's possible she's been spending too much time with her siblings and cousins," Quinn said. "She used to be such a nice girl until they ruined her."

Mason laughed at the face Mallory made at him.

"They've taught me well about how to be a total pain in the ass."

Quinn snorted. "They sure have, but I still love you, even when you're being a total PITA."

"Aww." Mallory leaned in to kiss him. "Thanks, babe."

Mason flashed them a teasing grin. "Barf."

"Don't change the subject," Mallory said. "Ask Jordan to come to dinner."

"It might be easier to ask Jordan than to put up with Mallory badgering you about it," Quinn said, earning an elbow to the ribs.

"You might be right about that," Mason said.

Mallory beamed with pleasure. "So you'll ask her, then?"

"I'll think about it. Now talk about something else."

"I'd much rather talk about you and Jordan. I really like the idea of you two together."

Mason signaled to Rebecca. "Check, please."

CHAPTER 5

"You really ought to leave the poor guy alone," Quinn said to Mallory when they were in his car on the way to work at the Marion Martinez Elder Care facility they ran together in an old school that had been converted into a nursing home.

Funded by Quinn's obscenely wealthy brother and sister-in-law, Jared and Lizzie, the facility helped island residents remain close to their elderly loved ones who needed more care than could be provided at home. The facility was named for the mother of local businessmen Alex and Paul Martinez. Marion's plight with dementia and her sons' struggle to care for her had given Lizzie the idea.

"What fun would that be? He's a nice guy. I want to see him as happy as we are."

"Our kind of happiness isn't for everyone. You know that by now."

"I do know that, but Mason has been looking for someone for a long time."

"And how do you know that?"

Mallory tried not to squirm. "I might've collected a bit of intel on him."

"Mallory!"

"Don't 'Mallory' me. He's had some hard knocks on the dating front, and it seems he's sort of given up lately. We can't have that."

"Has it occurred to you that maybe he's happy by himself and prefers that to the hard knocks of dating?"

"No, that hasn't occurred to me. Mason is one of the nicest guys I know. He'd do anything for anyone. He deserves to have someone who'd do anything for him."

"You're off the deep end on this, babe. He's a grown man who can take care of himself. You don't want to make him not want to hang out with us."

"That is *not* going to happen. We're *friends*. Friends look out for each other. That's all I'm doing. And you mark my words—he wants to ask Jordan out. I just gave him a little push."

"A little push," he said, grunting out a laugh. "More like a shove off a cliff."

"Would you consider a friendly wager on the outcome of my campaign to get him with Jordan?"

"So now it's a campaign? I feel like I should call and inform him there's been an escalation."

Mallory laughed. "You're very funny today, Dr. James."

"And you're seriously unhinged, Nurse Vaughn."

"About that wager…"

He glanced at her before returning his attention to the road. "Hundred bucks and the sex act of the winner's choice. Anything goes."

"Way to make losing a win."

Quinn laughed. "There's no losing when it's you and me."

"That's very true. I'll take your wager."

"Not that I want to bet against Mason, but I'm not sure I see him with Jordan."

"I'll bet you that within a month, they're a couple."

He reached out his hand, and she shook it. "No cheating to score a win. Let him figure it out on his own. Seriously, Mal. If you push him too hard, he's apt to not even try."

"True. I hear you, and I'll try to behave. It's just that I have a feeling about these two. I can't explain it."

"You don't even know her."

"Not personally, but I know *about* her."

"You know what the media shares about her, which is probably mostly bullshit. She might turn out to be the worst woman he could possibly hook up with, for all you know."

"We know Nikki. She's good people."

"Yes, she is, but that doesn't mean her sister is."

"I know. You're right—"

"Wait. Stop. I need to enjoy this moment. Could you say that again?"

She sighed with pretend exasperation. "You. Are. *Right*. But can you blame me for wanting all our friends to be as happy as we are?"

"No, I can't blame you for that, and Mason won't either as long as you don't go too far in this matchmaking scheme of yours."

"I hear you."

He took hold of her hand and gave it a squeeze. "I love you for wanting him to be happy, and he does, too."

"When Ryan died, I honestly thought I'd never be happy like that again." Mallory had never completely gotten over the sudden death of her first husband and had long ago accepted she never would. "But when I met you, I realized it was possible to be truly happy again, even after the worst possible thing had happened. I can be happy and honor the love I lost at the same time."

"You have no idea what you do to me when you say things like that."

"I mean it."

"I know you do. And I feel the same way. I'd given up on ever finding this kind of happy."

She smiled at him, mesmerized as always by his beautiful face and the way he looked at her with such love and affection, even when they were locking horns at work, which they did often. "It's your fault for making me into a total sap who wants to spread my happiness to everyone I care about."

"I'll gladly take the blame for that, but go easy on poor Mason."

Quinn pulled into the parking space designated for Dr. James and turned off the car. "You've planted the seed. That's all you can do."

"Of course there's much more I *could* do, but I hear you. I'll restrain my desire to sprinkle fairy dust and plant food on Mason and Jordan."

"You're more than welcome to sprinkle your fairy dust on me any time you'd like."

Mallory laughed and reached for him, placing her hand on his face, turning him in her direction so she could lean across the center console to kiss him. "Thank you for all this. Our life is like a dream to me. I sometimes still can't believe it's actually real."

"It's very real, and it's the best dream I ever had." He kissed her back with the kind of passion they usually reserved for the privacy of their own home, rather than the parking lot at work where anyone might see them. "And PS," he said when they finally came up for air, "I should be thanking *you.*"

"We can call this one a draw. We're both thankful as well as old enough and wise enough to know a good thing when we've got it."

His brows furrowed. "Who you calling old?"

"Countdown to forty-one is on, Doc." They shared the same birthday on August ninth.

"We need to do something awesome that day. Like get married."

They'd been so busy at work that they hadn't taken the time to actually plan a wedding. "That would be kind of awesome."

"Right? What better way to turn forty-one can you think of?"

"I can't think of anything better, but let's make it chill. Not a big deal—just like our engagement." He'd put a ring on her finger one night in bed and said, "Let's do this forever." She'd been more than happy to agree to his plan.

"Sweetheart, I hate to tell you, but inviting your family alone makes it a big deal."

"True, although I refuse to be annoyed by that, because I spent my entire life wishing for the family I have now."

"I get it, and we need them all there. Maybe we can borrow Mac and Maddie's yard and have a cookout and a wedding?"

"That's an idea I can get behind. For sure. I'll ask them."

"So we're really going to do this on our birthday?"

"We're really going to do it."

He caressed her cheek and gazed into her eyes. "I can't wait."

"Me either."

AFTER BREAKFAST, Mason reported directly to Eastward Look, where his team was taking another look at the damage in the daylight. The roof was crawling with people when he pulled up, wondering if he would see Jordan while he was there. And why was he wondering that? Because of Mallory and her big ideas.

The last thing in the world he needed was her involved in his love life, not that he had a love life, per se. Which was the problem Mallory was trying to fix with her well-meaning meddling.

Near to the chimney, he could see a large scorched spot on the roof that hadn't been visible the night before.

Mason parked next to another fire department SUV, removed his sling and tried to bend an elbow that wasn't having it. "Ugh." Fucking thing hurt like a bastard. He got out of his SUV and walked over to talk to Dermot Smith, one of his lieutenants. "Morning. How's it going?"

"Hey, Chief. How's the elbow?"

"Hurts like hell."

"Dislocations are the worst. Will take a few weeks."

Mason didn't want to hear that. "What's going on with the roof?"

"I wish I could tell you, but we can't figure out what sparked the fire. The residents, Nikki and Jordan Stokes and Riley McCarthy, confirmed they haven't had a fire in the fireplace in more than a week, so it didn't start in the chimney. It's baffling."

"I had a thought. Have we checked the neighboring houses to see if anyone else had a fire or used a fire pit? Yesterday's wind might've been enough to carry a spark."

"I suppose that's possible, even if it sounds like a stretch."

"I agree. It's a long shot, but worth looking into. The wind was out of the north, so check the neighbors to the north and see if any of them had fires."

"Will do." Dermot went off to see to Mason's orders while Mason headed inside to get a closer look at the fireplace as well as the smoke and water damage.

Trip, one of the younger firefighters on his team, was working on cleanup. He stood up a little straighter when he saw Mason coming. "Morning, Chief."

"How's it going?"

"Good. I've managed to mop up most of the water, but the rug and furniture are a total loss. They'll never get the stink of smoke out of them."

"I'm sure they'd say that's a small price to pay for saving the rest of the house."

"Yes, sir. How's the elbow?"

"Hurts."

"I dislocated my shoulder once playing hockey. Hurt like a motherfucker."

"That about sums it up," Mason said, amused.

"How come you aren't out of work?"

"Because I don't need to be."

"Hell, I'd be on the beach with a beer if I were you."

"And that, my friend, is the difference between you and me. I gotta show up regardless."

"That kinda sucks. I don't ever want to be chief."

Mason laughed. "You probably don't need to worry about that." Honestly, these kids were too much. They had hardly any ambition and needed constant supervision. "Finish in here, and then check with Lt. Smith to see what he needs."

"You got it, boss man."

Mason sighed. "It's *chief*. Not boss man. *Chief*."

Trip flashed a shit-eating grin. "You got it Chief Boss Man."

Exasperated, Mason turned to go back outside as Jordan, Nikki and Riley were coming in. Mason's gaze landed on Jordan. He was relieved to see some color in her cheeks this morning.

"Ladies, Riley." Mason forced himself to sound normal when he felt anything but. How could one tiny woman have such a huge impact on him? "How're you feeling, Jordan?"

"Much better, thanks." She offered him a small, shy smile that made him want to beat his chest and protect her from all harm. And what the fuck was that about, anyway? "How's your head and elbow, and what happened to the sling?"

"I'm fine, and the sling was pissing me off."

"You need to do what they told you. Put it back on."

Her bossiness was insanely arousing. "I, um, okay. I will."

Nikki and Riley watched them with thinly veiled curiosity that Mason could almost feel coming from them.

"I'll get out of your hair."

"Would you like to come back for dinner?" Nikki asked. "We're cooking Jordan's favorite—pasta with veggies—as well as chicken Parm for us nonvegetarians, garlic bread and salad. It's the least we can do to feed you after you saved my sister's life."

He glanced at Jordan and found her watching him with those big eyes that made him want to stare at her sweet face for the rest of his life. *For fuck's sake.* He was off his freaking rocker, and it was all Mallory's fault for putting ideas in his head that didn't belong there. "Um, sure, thanks. That'd be nice."

"Great!" Nikki clapped her hands. "It's a date."

Jordan rolled her eyes at her sister's exuberance.

Mason loved that she could be sarcastic even when she didn't say a word.

"Does six thirty work for you?" Nikki asked.

"Sure does. I'll see you then. Oh, what can I bring?"

"Just yourself," Nikki said. "We'll take care of the rest."

"Thanks. I'll see you later."

They moved to let him go past toward the front door.

"Put that sling back on," Jordan called after him.

"Yes, ma'am." He walked out the door smiling like a fool, which was always a bad sign that he was about to be played for one.

Dermot met him as he came outside. "You were right, Chief. The next-door neighbors to the north had a fire pit last night. Best we can tell, sparks from their pit landed on the roof and sparked the preliminary blaze. That put off sparks that were fueled by the wind that possibly landed in the chimney and ignited the creosote. I'll be damned if I can come up with another explanation for how that chimney ignited."

"It's as good a theory as I've heard yet. Keep working the scene, and let me know what else you find. I've got a budget meeting with the mayor in twenty minutes that I need to get to."

"I'll see you back at the barn and will keep you posted."

"Thanks, Derm."

Mason got back in his SUV, put the sling on as Jordan had directed and headed for town while thinking about her, even as he told himself he had no business thinking about her. Women were a constant source of mystery to him and rarely behaved the way he expected them to. He'd been through so many heartbreaks that it was a wonder his heart still beat normally. And yet, he'd managed to somehow remain hopeful that someday he might meet a woman who wouldn't stomp all over his heart.

In all likelihood, Jordan Stokes wasn't going to be the one who changed his track record. She would be here only a short time before returning to her far more exciting real life. He couldn't allow himself to be drawn in by her only to be left once again.

He'd had enough of that bullshit.

CHAPTER 6

"*L*et's get you upstairs to bed," Nikki said after Mason left. When Jordan would've protested, Nikki added, "I promised David I'd keep you quiet today, and that's what I'm going to do."

Because David had released her only on Nikki's assurances, Jordan allowed her sister to usher her up the stairs, away from the pervasive smell of smoke that had hit her the second she crossed the threshold. After all the work Riley and Nikki had put into the place, to have it smell like that was heartbreaking to Jordan. She could only imagine how Nik felt.

"How bad is the damage?" Jordan asked.

"Not bad at all. A rug, the sofa and chairs will have to be replaced, but that's nothing compared to what could've happened."

"You leave me alone for one night, and I nearly burn the place down."

Nikki steered Jordan into the room that had been hers since they were girls. "*You* had nothing to do with it."

Not much had changed in there since then, which was actually comforting. Throughout a turbulent childhood in which she and Nik had been the subject of a fierce custody battle between their feuding parents and the many changes in the rest of her life, this place had remained constant.

The pink-and-white-striped wallpaper she'd chosen when she was ten matched the white eyelet duvet cover and the pink throw pillows she'd ordered from a catalog their grandmother had given them to decorate their bedrooms. She'd said they could have anything they wanted to make their island bedrooms feel like home. Gran had succeeded in her mission. Nowhere else had ever felt more like home to Jordan and Nikki than Eastward Look did.

"What're you thinking about?" Nik moved around the room, picking up discarded clothing from the floor and folding it into neat piles the way she did every chance she got. Despite being identical twins, they certainly had their differences. Nikki was a neatnik, and Jordan was not.

"About decorating our bedrooms here with Gran."

"I still get that catalog. They have the best stuff."

Jordan changed into a tank and leggings and got into bed. Dr. David and Katie had checked on her repeatedly throughout the night, so she'd slept sporadically. She couldn't remember the last time she'd been this tired. No wait, that wasn't true. She did remember, and it had been the last time she got released from the hospital, after Brendan had beaten her up and broken her arm.

"Sorry to keep doing this to you, Nik. It's not intentional. I swear."

"Oh, stop. I know that. Shit happens."

"It happens far too often to me."

"You've had a rough few months. It's going to get better from here. I know it."

"I've had a rough few *years*, and the hits keep on coming with a visit from my old friend asthma."

"That was caused by smoke inhalation. The asthma is *not* back."

"You sound awfully sure of that."

"Think about it, J. You haven't had an attack in more than seven years. You only had one because you were breathing *smoke*."

"I know, but I'm anxious about it anyway."

"Totally understandable. Riley is going to pick up your new inhaler

49

at the pharmacy, and you'll just keep that with you in case you need it. But you won't."

"Nik."

Nikki stopped straightening Jordan's room and turned to look at her, brow raised in inquiry.

Jordan patted the other side of her bed. "Come here."

Nikki sat on the edge of the bed.

"All the way."

Huffing with pretend annoyance, Nikki stretched out next to Jordan. "I'm here. What do you want?"

"I want you to stop folding my clothes and freaking out."

"I'm not freaking out."

"Yes, you are."

"No, I'm not."

Jordan raised a brow the way Nikki had done to her.

"Okay, maybe a little," Nikki said with a sigh, "but it's not about me. It's about you and making sure you feel better and have your meds and—"

Jordan gently placed her hand over Nikki's mouth. "It is about you, because I know how much what happens to me affects you, too." She removed her hand. "And you want to know how I know that? Because everything you do affects me. That's how we roll, and I'm painfully aware that my shit has been giving you way too much to worry about lately. That's going to stop. I promise."

"You're being way too hard on yourself. You had no way to know the chimney was going to catch on fire and give you an asthma attack. That's not your fault."

"Maybe not, but some of the rest of it could've been avoided if I'd listened to you."

"We can't rewrite the past. It's done. All we can do is move forward."

"I know, and it's time for me to figure out my shit and stop giving you constant reason to worry about me. You and Riley didn't even get one night on the mainland without me screwing it up."

"Are you spoiling for a fight about what's within your control and what isn't?"

"Not at all. I just feel really, *really* bad that your night away got screwed up and that you were in a panic about me—again."

"Well, you can stop feeling bad, because Riley and I have every night together, and it doesn't matter where we are. Every night with him is a good night. And I'll always panic when you're hurt or sick or anything other than perfectly fine. That's just how I'm wired."

"I want off this merry-go-round I've been on for far too long."

"You were feeling much better before the fire, and we'll get you back to that point again. You just need to rest and give your body the chance to recover."

"I'll pay for anything that needs to be replaced, as well as any damage."

"Don't worry about it."

"I will worry about it. I'm paying to fix it."

"Fine, whatever."

"By the way, what're you up to inviting Mason to dinner?"

"Just what I said. I want to thank him for saving you."

"And that's *all* you want?"

Nikki's brows furrowed into a confused expression. "Um, kinda engaged to Riley and wicked happy about that. Not sure what you're getting at."

"I'm wondering if you might be playing matchmaker, so quit being obtuse."

"The thought never entered my mind."

Jordan cracked up laughing. "You are the worst liar *ever*. Why do you even try?"

Nikki scowled at her. "Okay, it might've crossed my mind for a second, especially since he couldn't seem to take his eyes off you the whole time we were talking to him. But I mostly invited him because I do want to thank him for saving you. Although, at the moment, I can't recall exactly why I was so thankful about that."

Jordan poked her in the ribs. "You love me. And he was *not* looking at me. We were talking."

51

"He *was* looking. Trust me."

Jordan wasn't sure how she felt about that. "We had a good time last night, all things considered, but he was just being nice. He stuck around because I was alone at the clinic until you guys got there."

Nikki propped herself up on her elbows. "Think about what you just said. The *fire chief* of *all* of Gansett Island hung out for *hours* at the clinic because you were alone."

"That's what I said."

"How can you be so dumb sometimes and smart as a whip other times?"

"How am I being dumb?"

"The man *likes you*, Jordan. Why else would he have volunteered to be the one to keep you company at the clinic when he probably had a million things to do after a *fire* on the island?"

Jordan thought about that and couldn't come up with anything better than, "He was being *nice*, Nikki. Don't make it into something more than that." But there'd been that moment when she'd realized his lips were on hers, sending air into her lungs and electrifying the rest of her. Silliest thing ever, when it came right down to it. He'd probably done that a hundred times before, so it was ridiculous to make anything of something so foolish. He'd been saving her life, not coming on to her.

"I'm going to invite Finn and Chloe to come to dinner. Is that okay with you?"

"Of course. I love them. You know I do. Invite Kevin and Chelsea, too, if you want to. Make it a party."

"I haven't seen baby Summer in *three days*," Nikki said. "I'm going through withdrawals."

"We can't have that."

"You're really okay, J? You swear?"

"Swear to God, hope to die, stick a needle in my eye." Jordan called on the saying they'd used as kids when a situation called for the big guns. As children caught between feuding parents, they'd often needed the big guns.

"Call me or text if you need anything. I'll be downstairs." Nikki leaned over to kiss Jordan's forehead and got up off the bed. "Get some rest."

"Hey, Nik?"

She turned back. "Yeah?"

"Love you bestest."

"Love you bestest, too." Nikki smiled and left the room, closing the door behind her as she went.

Nikki had given her their standard reply, but Jordan knew it was no longer true. Nikki loved Riley bestest now, and that was how it ought to be. As she closed her eyes and tried to quiet her mind so she could get some sleep, Jordan wondered if she would ever love anyone the way Nik loved Riley.

MASON WAS late for the budget meeting with Mayor Upton, who was a stickler for punctuality.

The mayor's admin, Mona, greeted Mason with a friendly smile. "Go ahead in. Chief Taylor only arrived a minute ago, so don't worry."

"Thanks, Mona. You're the bomb dot-com."

She glowed with pleasure at the compliment.

He tried to think of a new way to compliment her every time he saw her, because she was, indeed, the best. The mayor, on the other hand...

When Mason walked into the office, Chet Upton was off on one of his favorite tangents—the length of Police Chief Blaine Taylor's hair. "You're setting a terrible example for the people who work for you with that hair."

"My wife likes it," Blaine said, nonplussed by the mayor's outrage. He sat with his booted feet on the mayor's conference table, as if he didn't have a care in the world, when he had far more cares this time of year than even Mason had. "It's staying."

"Now listen here," Upton sputtered.

"Nope. I listened to you, now you can listen to me. I work ninety hours a week for three months straight without so much as a day off. If you're unhappy with my job performance, feel free to let me know.

53

But my hair is off-limits. I thought we were here to discuss the budget anyway?"

Mason somehow managed to hold in the laugh that was busting to get out as he took his usual seat at the conference table across from Blaine. He loved the hell out of Blaine Taylor, who was a great colleague and friend. Mason thoroughly enjoyed the way Blaine refused to take Upton's shit.

He and Blaine busted their ass for the island and its residents, a fact that Upton never quite seemed to realize.

Upton did a double take when he saw the bandage on Mason's forehead and his arm in a sling. "What happened to you?"

"I crashed my bike."

"Oh." The mayor seemed relieved to hear the injury wasn't work-related, because that would've meant extra paperwork for him. "Is it broken?" His wary expression conveyed concern, but only for the possibility that Mason might have to be out of work—God forbid.

"Dislocated."

Blaine winced. "Ouch."

"Thank goodness that's all it is," Upton said.

"I'm fine," Mason said. "Thanks for your concern."

Blaine sputtered with laughter as Upton looked at the two of them like they were insane. He was often oblivious to the ways they insulted him to his face, which was a constant source of entertainment to the two men.

"Good of you to join us." Upton frowned, probably realizing they were busting his balls even if he didn't get the joke. "The meeting started ten minutes ago."

"I'm aware of that. I was out at Eastward Look, where my department saved a house from burning to the ground last night."

"And Mason saved one of the residents from certain death by running into the house and bringing her out—while his elbow was dislocated." Blaine glanced at Mason. "Well done, by the way."

"Thanks," Mason said, embarrassed by his colleague's praise.

"Yes, good job," Upton said, almost reluctantly.

Blaine rolled his eyes at Mason, who again tried not to laugh.

"Now, about the budget." Upton handed each of them a packet that had been stapled in the corner. "Both your departments are already trending to be over budget on overtime, and it's only June."

They had this same discussion every year around this time when the season kicked into high gear and took the overtime budget with it as the summer shit hit the fan.

As always, Blaine and Mason didn't reply. They'd learned to let Upton have his say about the overtime and not interrupt the tirade. If they didn't debate, but rather let him think he was reading them the riot act, they got out of there quicker.

Thirty minutes later, after being thoroughly chastised by the mayor, the two men emerged into bright sunshine and a cool breeze blowing in off the ocean.

"We again survived the midyear budget meeting," Blaine said. "This calls for a celebration. Lunch is on me."

"Yes, please. Lead the way."

"Let's go to the Wayfarer."

They walked from town hall down the hill to the newly renovated shore-dining-hall-style beachfront restaurant, bar and hotel that the McCarthy family had brought back to life.

"We'll take a table outside," Blaine said to the young woman working the hostess stand.

"Right this way."

They followed her through the sparsely populated interior to the back deck, where nearly every table was taken. On weekends, the place was overrun with day-trippers and tourists who came to party. Mason and Blaine had worked closely with the McCarthy family and Nikki, the Wayfarer manager, to discuss crowd control and other concerns as the Wayfarer reopened for business after being closed and abandoned for years.

"Thank God they hired their own security for this place," Blaine said when they were seated at a table with an unobstructed view of the ocean. On the way to their table, they waved to a few people they knew from town. The whole place had perked up at the sight of the two men in uniform.

A navy-blue-and-white-striped umbrella kept the sun off them while they perused the menu. The waitress, a young woman named Carly, came to their table. Her name tag indicated she was from Mystic, Connecticut. "Welcome to the Wayfarer. Have you been here before?"

"Yes, we have," Blaine replied. "I'll have the turkey club and soda water with a lemon, please."

"Since he's paying, I'll do a cup of chowder and a grilled chicken sandwich, hold the fries."

"Coming right up," Carly said as she took off to put in their order.

"What're you holding the fries for? That's the best part."

"Gonna be off the workout circuit for a week or so."

"Honestly, Mason, you don't have an extra pound on you, and you work out more than anyone I know. Have the fries."

"I'll have a couple of yours."

"Like hell you will."

Mason laughed. "How about Upton? What a windbag."

"Right? At least he's predictable. We can deal with him. They say the devil you know is always better than the one you don't know."

"True. So when are you getting your hair cut?" Mason asked, smiling.

"When I fucking feel like it, but it'll be at least three weeks longer than it would've been if he hadn't mentioned it."

"What I don't get is why he can't see that every time he comes at you about it, you just dig in deeper."

"Because he's an idiot. But that's why we love him. He leaves us alone most of the time, which is key. Since he can't find anything else to bust my balls about, he comes at my hair and my overtime budget, even though I budget for overtime."

"I actually followed that logic."

"Well, it's true," Blaine said, laughing. "We both budget for over-time, we rarely go over budget, and he *still* has to go off on us every year in June like clockwork."

"He probably sees it as his way of ensuring we're keeping an eye on it, which we are."

"Eh, whatever," Blaine said, waving a hand. "He's gotten enough of my mental energy for today. So what happened last night?"

"From what we can tell, sparks from the fire pit at the house next door ignited the roof at the Hopper place and then somehow ignited the creosote that had built up in the chimney."

"Can that even happen?" Blaine seemed as surprised as Mason and his team had been when they put the pieces together.

"Normally, no. But the wind was pretty strong last night, so that changes the game."

"I guess so. I heard you got Nikki's sister out of there in the nick of time."

"I'm glad I saw the flames and smoke."

"So how did you bang yourself up?"

"I crashed my bike after seeing the flames and getting distracted on a jump out at the bluffs."

"Jeez, Mason. You're lucky you didn't land on your head and break your neck."

"I know. I haven't crashed like that since I was a kid jumping ramps on my BMX."

Blaine laughed. "Ah, yes, the BMX Olympics. My brother and I did some of the craziest shit on those bikes. We should probably be dead."

"Right there with you. We had this neighbor with a pool."

"Oh God, you did not."

"We did! We set up this elaborate jump over a picket fence into the shallow end of the pool."

"Please tell me there's video of that."

"Somewhere, I'm sure."

"Did anyone ever miss?"

"We all did at one point, but this one kid ended up *on* the picket fence."

Blaine winced. "No."

"Yep, right between the legs."

"I can't." Blaine covered his ears. "Stop. I'll have nightmares."

Mac McCarthy approached their table, but didn't seem to see them until Blaine, his brother-in-law, called out to him. "Oh, hey, you guys. What's up?"

"Not much," Blaine said. "Want to join us?"

"Wish I could, but I've got to keep moving. I came over to check a few repairs that need to be made here, and I've got to get back to the Curtis house. We're taking the roof off today."

Mason didn't know Mac as well as Blaine did, but even he could see the guy looked troubled. "Everything okay?"

"Yeah, just busy as hell, per usual this time of year." In addition to his construction business, Mac also helped to run his family's marina in North Harbor. "Rain check on lunch?"

"You got it," Blaine said. "See you later."

"Take it easy."

"He seems tense," Mason said.

"Yeah, everyone is worried about him after he collapsed in the clinic. They said it was a major anxiety attack brought on by Maddie's pregnancy with the twins and staring down his busy season. He's supposed to be chilling out, but it doesn't look like he is. I'm going to text Tiffany to see if we can have them over for dinner to give them a break."

"That's a good idea."

A second later, his phone beeped with a reply. "She said let's do it at their place so Maddie doesn't have to go out. She's supposed to be mostly on bed rest until the twins arrive in September."

Mason grimaced at the thought of being inactive that long. He'd go mad. "Even better. I'm sure they'll appreciate it."

Ned Saunders, the island's resident land baron-taxi cab driver, stopped by to say hello. "Heard ya made a helluva rescue out at the Hopper place last night."

"I was glad to be in the right place at the right time."

"Very well done. The grandmother's good people. The sister, too. Sure they appreciate what ya did."

"Just doing my job."

Ned put his hand on Mason's shoulder. "Whatcha do means a lot ta us. Doncha ever think otherwise."

"Thanks, Ned. Appreciate that."

"Have a good day."

"You, too."

"Such a great guy," Blaine said after Ned had moved on. "Best father-in-law a guy could ever hope to have." Ned was married to Tiffany's mother, Francine.

"People like him make this job worth all the crap."

"For sure."

Their food arrived, and they dug in like they hadn't eaten in weeks.

Mason had something he wanted to ask Blaine, but it sounded so stupid in his own mind that he couldn't imagine saying it out loud. Still, he had to know, and Blaine was the only person he'd dare to ask. He forced a bite past the tightness in his throat, which happened only when he was nervous. It was ridiculous, really. Blaine was one of his closest friends. He had nothing to be nervous about with him, and yet this was still embarrassing to admit, even to him. "Can I ask you something kind of weird?"

Blaine ran a fry through ketchup and popped it into his mouth. "Yep."

Mason had no sooner posed the question than he regretted it. There was no way he could ask such a thing without sounding like a goddamned fool. "Never mind. It's nothing."

"Oh, come on! You've got me all curious."

"If I ask you this, you have to forget I asked ten seconds after, you got me?"

"Ah yeah, I guess."

"It's so ridiculous."

Blaine sat back in his chair and grinned at Mason. "This is gonna be good. Lay it on me."

Mason felt like he'd returned to middle school. "Have you ever, when doing mouth-to-mouth without a shield, has it ever been like, well…"

"Like what?"

"Kissing?"

Blaine stared at him for a long moment before he blinked. "Uh, no.

59

Usually, I'm grossed out by having to put my mouth on someone else's when I don't have a mouth shield handy. Why? Did that happen to you?"

"Nah, it was just this weird thing. Forget it."

"No way. Who were you... Oh! *Jordan Stokes?*"

"Shut *up*, will you?" Mason glanced around to see who might be hearing that he'd felt like he was kissing Jordan Stokes when he blew air into her lungs.

"You felt like you were *kissing her?*"

"Not exactly, it was just this strange thing. I don't know. It's stupid. I never should've said anything."

"You felt something when you..." Blaine rolled his hand to encourage Mason to continue.

"I don't know what it was exactly. But it was something."

"I've never had that happen. Usually, I try not to think about anything other than getting air to lungs that need it and then finding the Listerine."

"Same. Nothing like this has ever happened before. It was so bizarre, but her lips kinda moved, like she was trying to get more."

"Stop it. No way."

"Yes! I'm telling you. It was nuts."

"Wow." Having apparently lost interest in his fries, Blaine appeared to give Mason's revelation considerable thought.

That was the last thing Mason wanted. "Forget it. It was nothing."

"What if it wasn't nothing?"

"I wish I'd never said anything. I already feel stupid enough even thinking it was something, so don't make it worse."

"I'm not. I'm just saying that stranger things have happened than connecting to someone during an emergency."

"That's not what this was. We didn't 'connect.' I got her breathing normally again."

"And she tried to kiss you. But other than that, nothing happened."

Mason signaled for the check, eager to get out of there now that he'd made the huge mistake of mentioning it to Blaine.

Blaine cracked up. "I'm not busting your balls. I swear I'm not. I just think maybe you shouldn't discount it as nothing."

Mason tried to retrieve his wallet, but his arm protested the movement. "I'll take that under advisement."

"Mr. Saunders picked up your check," Carly told them. "He said to tell you thanks for your service."

"That's so nice of him," Mason said.

"He's the best."

"Don't repeat what I said about Jordan. I can't have something like that getting out."

"I won't say a word."

"Even to Tiffany."

"Even to Tiffany. Let me know how it goes with Jordan."

Mason rolled his eyes and got up to leave. "Let it go, Blaine. Seriously." He walked away as Blaine, that bastard, was still laughing. He hoped he hadn't made a huge mistake by sharing such a thing with him. And why had he, exactly? Stupid fucking move that he'd regretted almost the second the words had been out of his mouth.

He should've just chalked up the thing with Jordan to a weird second and forgotten about it.

Except, he could still recall how her lips had moved under his and how she'd seemed to want more.

As he returned to the barn, and they called the fire side of the public safety building, he vowed to put the matter out of his mind so he could concentrate on work. And then he remembered he'd been invited to dinner with Jordan—and her enticing lips.

"*Fuck.*"

CHAPTER 7

$\mathcal{M}$ ac left the Wayfarer with a short list of minor repairs that needed to be made. A leaking window, a strange hum in the exhaust vent in the kitchen, a rough spot on the bar that had caught a lady's sweater. He'd send Riley and Finn over there tomorrow to deal with it. Nothing they couldn't handle, he thought as he headed back toward the Curtis place, a Gothic-style house his team was renovating ahead of a family wedding in October.

Which meant they were under the gun. Again. Always.

These days, he felt like he lived his whole life under the gun, espe-cially at this time of year. But he'd promised Maddie and his parents and the rest of his family that he'd take a gigantic chill pill after he'd collapsed and scared the hell out of them. He could still recall coming to and seeing Maddie's sweet face, awash in tears and panic that he'd caused. He hated when she cried, especially over him.

Thankfully, it had "only" been an anxiety attack, like the one he'd had several years ago when he'd still lived in Miami. Back then, his life had been nothing but stress. Now he had Maddie and their family and a million reasons to take care of himself.

In keeping with the promises he'd made to her and his other loved ones, Mac pulled his truck off the road at the Southeast Light and parked in a spot with an awesome view of the lighthouse and the coast. He opened the window to let in the warm late-spring air and shut off the engine. His to-do list had a million things on it that needed his attention, but he took a few minutes to slow down, decompress and just breathe.

Closing his eyes, he focused on breathing the way he'd learned from a meditation video he'd watched on YouTube at Maddie's request. She'd read about how meditation could slow the mind and heal the body, so she'd encouraged him to give it a try. He hated that his stress was causing more for her as she carried their twins.

They just had to get through the summer and the delivery of the twins in September, and then things would get somewhat back to "normal," or whatever that would look like with five children, aged six and under.

It was better for his anxiety if he didn't think too much about what it would be like when they had *five* children. Three were killing them. What in the world would five be like? He and Maddie were due to meet later that afternoon with an au pair who'd come highly recommended by the agency they'd reached out to after Maddie had been put on bed rest. She was exhausted all the time, could never seem to get enough sleep, even now that she was on bed rest. Their mothers, fathers, sisters, sisters-in-law and friends had been pitching in to help with the kids now that Maddie had been ordered to stay off her feet, but that situation wasn't sustainable long term.

Mac had his hopes pinned on the au pair, a young woman named Kelsey, who'd be on the three thirty boat. She wasn't sure how she felt about living on a remote island, especially in the winter. Mac hoped he and Maddie could convince her to take them on. He'd arranged for her to have the apartment that Kara Torrington had once occupied at a property near the marina and was prepared to meet her salary requirements plus a bonus after the first year if she agreed to come to work for them.

Desperate times.

Breathe, Mac. Just breathe. He could hear Maddie's voice in his head, reminding him to stay calm, not to let the stress get the better of him the way it had before he collapsed and scared her—and himself—enough that he was heeding the warnings Dr. David had laid on him that day. This time, it'd been anxiety, David had said. The next time, it might be a heart attack. Mac had far too much to live for to allow himself to let stress get the better of him, so he was determined to combat it every way he possibly could. The idea of not being around to watch his kids grow up was unfathomable to him.

His phone chimed with a text from Maddie. He'd set up a special chime and ring tone so he'd never miss a call or text from her.

Blaine and Tiffany want to bring dinner over tonight and invite the family. Are you up for that?

He wasn't, really, but he knew how much she missed getting out and being with their wide circle of friends and family since her activity had been restricted. *Sure, sounds good. I'll be home with Kelsey after the 3:30 boat lands. Fingers crossed.*

Fingers and toes. Are you breathing?

Funny enough, I just took a break to do some extra breathing.

Good! Everything is fine and everything is going to be fine.

Keep reminding me.

Any time you need to hear it.

Love you.

Love you more.

Not possible.

For once, she let him have the last word and left him with a smile on his face as he contemplated the many ways his glass was more than half full. Yes, he had a lot on his shoulders, but he also had much to be thankful for, including his amazing, beautiful, courageous wife, three healthy children and two more on the way. His parents were healthy, his brothers and sisters were happy and so were his cousins. Everything was fine.

Keep telling yourself that, Mac. Maybe one of these days, he'd actually believe it.

· · ·

JORDAN SLEPT the day away and awoke late that afternoon feeling somewhat back to normal. Only a residual ache in her chest remained to remind her of yet another brush with death. Her grandmother used to tell her she was like a cat with nine lives. She'd used up most of them in the first twenty years of her life and had cashed in another chip last night. To hear that she'd been "barely breathing" when Mason arrived was terrifying.

What if he hadn't seen the flames? She'd probably be dead.

Tears filled her eyes and spilled down her cheeks when it registered with her that she'd had a very close call, perhaps the closest yet in a life full of breathing and other emergencies. She wiped away tears that made her feel weak and stupid for being so emotional, but near-death experiences tended to have that effect on people.

Jordan couldn't remember much about the events of last night, but she distinctly remembered the feel of Mason's lips on hers and how she'd tried to get closer to him. Totally mortifying! The man had been saving her life, and she reacted that way?

It was all so confusing.

And in the clinic, he'd been so *nice* as well as funny, helpful and generous about getting food for both of them, even though he'd been injured, too.

She'd liked talking to him.

There. She'd admitted it and was just as quickly back to confused. A few short months after a disastrous end to a disastrous marriage, the last thing she needed to be thinking about was the sexy fireman who'd rescued her. At least he was nothing like Brendan, who was half Mason's size and pale as a ghost most of the time.

Mason, by contrast, was one of the tallest guys she'd ever met and clearly took good care of himself, if his bulging biceps were any indication of what the rest of him looked like. Not to mention, he already had the equivalent of a late-summer tan and warm, kind eyes that had drawn her right in during their time together at the clinic.

After being married to Brendan, the only man she'd ever even dated, she was so starved for kindness, she'd overreacted to a man who was just doing his job by hanging with her while the clinic staff was busy. It would be just like her to read more into it than it warranted.

She'd had a health crisis.

He'd done his job.

End of story.

Jordan sat up and took a minute to get her bearings before going into the bathroom that adjoined her room to shower. She stood under the hot water for a long time and washed her hair twice, hoping to rinse away the stink of smoke. After conditioning her hair and washing up, she got out of the shower and had to sit for a minute on the closed lid of the toilet. If her past track record was any indication, the attack would leave her feeling depleted for the next few days.

Determined to soldier through, Jordan dried her hair and applied some mascara that made her feel human, even when she wasn't going anywhere. It was a habit she'd fallen into as a teen. "Mascara before coffee" was her mantra. And yes, she knew it was a silly mantra, but a girl had her needs, and mascara was one of Jordan's.

It was on her to-do list to find real purpose in life, something that didn't revolve around stupid things like mascara and social media and vanity and celebrity and all the things she'd once embraced before they turned to shit along with her marriage. She'd loved doing her show and connecting with fans. If only that was all there was to it, she would've done it forever. But the downside of celebrity was something no one could imagine until they'd experienced it for themselves. Now that she'd had firsthand experience with the downside thanks to her husband's outraged and crazy fans, she wanted nothing more to do with any of it.

Gigi, who had replaced Nikki as her manager—not that Nik could be replaced—had been badgering her to make some decisions about what was next. Ironically, the interest in her had gone way up after the hotel room incident, but that was just further proof of how depraved the celebrity lifestyle could be. They wanted her more because her celebrity husband had put her in the hospital?

Disgusting.

No, after five years of life in the fast lane, it was time to find some other more productive use of her time than chasing Twitter and Instagram followers and living her life "out loud" online. Since she'd gone "dark" after the incident in Charlotte, her fans had been hungry for updates. She planned to give them one once she figured out her life.

At the moment, she was no closer to finding that life than she'd been the night things blew up with Brendan. The one thing she knew for certain was that she wanted to be on Gansett with Nikki for a while longer, even if she felt like a third wheel with her and Riley. They'd both said they wanted her to stay, so she would take them at their word and give it at least another month in her favorite place before she had to confront The Future.

She felt like those words should be up in lights on a marquee somewhere since they hung over her like bright beacons, reminding her she was off course without a compass to guide her back to a path that made sense. Nothing made sense anymore, except her sister, who'd been by her side always—until she wasn't and everything fell apart.

Not that she blamed Nikki for that. She didn't. Not at all. When Jordan had decided to give her marriage one more chance, Nikki had strongly objected. So much so that Nikki had quit as Jordan's manager because she'd had enough of the toxic waste dump that Jordan's marriage had been. If Jordan had one thing to do over, she would've let her sister talk her out of joining Brendan on his tour to try one more time to save something that hadn't been worth saving.

She knew that now. Hell, she'd known it then and had done it anyway. She had to own that, not that she blamed herself for how it had ended. However, she'd put herself in that hotel room that night with a man she knew was unstable and addicted to Xanax and God only knew what else. It'd been a fool's errand to try to bail the *Titanic*.

The only reason she had for trying one last time was that after having grown up in the midst of a nasty divorce, the last thing she wanted was the same for herself. So she'd tried to save that which could not be saved. One thing she'd learned was that marriage took two people to make it work, and if one of those two people was unwilling to do the bare minimum, it was never going to last.

That was what she'd said to Brendan that last night in Charlotte. That she couldn't keep them going all on her own. He had to want it, too, and if he didn't, that was fine. But she couldn't go on anymore with the way it had been, competing with his fans, his groupies, his phone, his bros and his drugs for bits and pieces of his attention like a pathetic dog looking for a bone from someone who had no fucks to give.

Apparently, that'd been the wrong thing to say, because the fight had turned physical after she'd said that, and the next thing she'd known, his manager, Davy, had been punching Brendan while someone else got Jordan out of there until EMS came.

And thus her disaster of a marriage had come to a swift and dramatic end that the entire world had seen unfold on social media and the entertainment sites that had gone crazy over Zane's arrest and subsequent trip to rehab. His rabid fans had blamed Jordan for all his troubles, claiming he'd never had drug issues until she came along, which was one hundred percent false. He'd had a reliance on Xanax for as long as she'd known him, which she'd naïvely believed was no big deal. It wasn't heroin, right?

Well, it might as well have been for the damage it'd done to his life and their marriage. What'd started out as an occasional use to combat anxiety and insomnia had spiraled into a thirty-pills-a-day habit that involved a lot of enabling by the people around him, who'd seen to it that he got his pills when he needed them—or else.

Jordan had witnessed him fire a longtime employee who'd balked at getting him more pills after he'd filled a prescription the day before. She'd never seen that guy again, and the others around Brendan had learned to go along or suffer the same fate. So they'd done his bidding until it'd gotten so bad that he was slurring his words and staggering around when he wasn't onstage. They timed his intake to keep him sober to perform. The rest of the time, he was out of it.

She'd been shocked to realize how bad his dependence had gotten when she caught up with the tour in Houston following the publication of the sex video that had left her completely devastated and had led her to leave him for a time. He'd apologized profusely for making the tape she hadn't known about in the first place and for something so private between them being made public. He said he'd done it only to try to get her back, which was ludicrous reasoning. With the benefit of hindsight, she couldn't believe she'd given him another chance after that nightmare—and all because she hadn't wanted to be divorced.

Everything about him, the video, his addiction and her life as a celebrity wife, was ludicrous, and it was all in the past now, where it would stay.

A shrink would have a field day with how she'd satisfied her need for male attention with a malignant narcissist drug addict star to fill the void left by a father who'd never given her or Nikki much of anything other than heartache.

To make matters even worse, she'd allowed her husband's fame to propel her from small-time model to big-time reality TV star, which had seemed like such a great idea at the time.

Brendan had encouraged her to take the offer to helm an inside look at the life and marriage of a rapper's wife. "It would give you something to do while I'm on the road," he'd said, striking at one of her deepest insecurities—what went on when she wasn't with him. She'd reached the point where she simply couldn't bear to travel two hundred days a year and had expressed a desire to be home more often.

He'd acted like the show would solve all their problems, when in fact it had only made them worse. They hardly ever saw each other, and when they did, they were unable to recapture the connection that had brought them together five years earlier. Back then, when they'd both been starting out in the business as models, they'd relied on each other to get through the lean times and had quickly formed what Jordan had assumed was an unbreakable bond.

She knew better now, and was determined to do better, if not for herself then for Nikki, who'd suffered through more drama than any sister deserved.

Jordan walked to the window that overlooked the coast and the ocean in the distance and thought about the last few disastrous months.

Her whole life, she'd been searching for the kind of family so many of her friends had, the kind with two parents who loved each other and their kids more than anything. She'd never had that, and it was what she'd wanted to build with her husband. But there was no room in his wild, carefree life for a wife or kids or a home. He was too busy chasing the music and the money and the fans and the women and the drugs. She had few illusions about what he'd been up to when she wasn't with him on the road. Especially in the end, when the drugs had taken him over. He wouldn't have had the wherewithal to resist the massive temptation he encountered every night.

The day before it ended in spectacular fashion, his tireless manager, Davy, had subtly suggested she might want to go home until things "settled down" with her husband. Of course she hadn't taken his advice, because she'd still been so certain she would be the one to "fix" him, to bring him back from wherever it was he'd gone the last couple of years.

Now she knew better. The only person who could fix the man who'd become Zane was Zane. And though she missed her sweet Brendan, the man he'd been before the birth of Zane, she was wise enough now to know that her Brendan no longer existed. He was gone, possibly forever, and the last few months had been about finding a way to accept that.

Nikki had once told her that the definition of insanity was doing the same thing over and over and hoping for different results. She'd tried insanity—repeatedly—and that hadn't gotten her anywhere but bruised, battered and brokenhearted.

It was time to get off the crazy train and find a new plan. If only she knew what that plan might be.

A knock on the door preceded Nikki into the room. "Thought I heard the shower. How're you feeling?"

"Better. The sleep helped."

"Glad to hear it. Riley picked up your prescriptions." Nikki put the bag on the bedside table. "Can I get you anything?"

"No, thank you. I'm fine. I'm sure you have better things to do than babysit me on a rare day off."

"I'm not just babysitting you. I'm also making dinner and doing some cleaning. It's all good."

"Get whatever you want to replace the furniture and carpet, and put it on my card. You still have it, right?" Nikki was making a "regular" salary these days compared to what she'd earned as Jordan's manager, and she didn't want her sister to have to pay for the damage.

"I do, but—"

"No buts. It would make me feel better to take care of that after everything you've done for me. You and Riley invested so much time and money in this place that we all enjoy. The least I can do is make this right."

"If you insist, but no one is blaming you for the freak thing that happened when you were here alone. It wasn't your fault. In fact, Riley is blaming himself for leaving the flue open and not burning a chimney-cleaning log at the end of the winter like he should have."

"It's not his fault."

"Right, and it's not yours either. It happened, and we should focus on how lucky we are that Mason saw the flames and got here as fast as he did." Nikki's voice caught, and she waved a hand in front of her face. "Sorry. I just can't stop thinking how close I came to losing you."

Jordan went to her sister and hugged her tightly. "I'm fine, and it looks like I'll be causing you headaches for some time to come after all."

"Thank goodness for that." Nikki clung to her. "Still love you bestest."

"No, you don't, but that's okay."

"Yes, I really do, J. I love Riley *so* much, but there'll never be another Jordan, another peanut butter to my jelly."

"I thought I was the jelly," Jordan joked, relieved when Nikki laughed. She hated seeing her indomitable sister brought low by Jordan's overly dramatic life.

"You can be the jelly if you want to be. Whatever you want."

"I need to take full advantage of you while you're still thankful I didn't die."

"Too soon, bitch."

Jordan laughed and hugged Nikki for another full minute. "It's not going to happen again. I promise."

"I should hope this particular scenario will never happen again."

"None of it is going to happen again. I'm done with disasters that bring you running from whatever you were doing to deal with me. Those days are over."

"Okay, so I hear what you're saying, but just for the record, the last two disasters weren't your fault."

"I'll accept that the fire wasn't, but me being in that hotel room with *him*? One thousand percent my fault." She placed a finger over Nikki's lips to stop her from objecting. "I should've listened to you. The video should've been the end of it. I'll always regret that I let you go so I could have him. That shouldn't have happened. He wasn't worth that level of sacrifice, not the last couple of years, anyway."

"You didn't sacrifice anything where I'm concerned. I'm still right here with you where I've always been and where I'll always be. Nothing can ever change that. And by leaving you, I found Riley, so it worked out the way it was meant to. I'm just sorry you've been so hurt by someone you loved. That's what never should've happened."

"Very true, and I'm done with him and the madness that came with him."

"What about the show?"

"Gigi is trying to get me out of the contract."

"Is she still repping *him*?" Nikki asked.

"For now. I told her not to dump him on my account, although she wanted to. From what she's heard from his camp, he's taking rehab seriously and is determined to repair his reputation and his career."

"As long as he stays the hell away from you, he can do whatever he wants."

"Agreed."

"So, you're done with him and the show. What's next for you?"

"I have no idea. There's like this gigantic question mark hanging over any thoughts of the future."

"You don't need to decide anything right now. If there's one benefit to becoming a huge star, you've got plenty of money in the bank. Take the summer to rest, relax and think about what you want to do."

"I guess that's what I'll have to do, since I have nothing else to do."

Nikki put her hands on Jordan's shoulders and looked her in the eyes. "You've worked your ass off, made a lot of money, had a lot of heartache. You deserve a break. You've earned it. Settle in for the summer and just relax. The answers will come to you when you're open to them."

Jordan smiled at her sister. "When did you get so wise?"

"Around the time I chucked my life with you to come home to Gansett for a vacation and found my purpose—and my love."

"You really love running the Wayfarer, don't you?"

"I do. It's a huge challenge—not unlike running your career was—and it's something new every day. Plus, I get to be with Riley and support his family's business. I couldn't ask for anything more."

"I'm so glad it all worked out so well for you."

"It will for you, too. I know it."

"You'd really tell me if you and Riley wanted the house to yourselves?"

"No, I'd never tell you that, because this is your home as much as it is mine, and we both want you here. I talked to Gran this morning, and she's planning to come for a visit after the benefit she's throwing for a local children's organization next week. She wants to see us both and meet Riley."

"I can't wait to see her. It's been too long."

"She asked why you let the security go. I told her you didn't feel you needed them here."

"No one even knows I'm here."

"For now they don't. All it will take is one tourist spotting you out and about for that to change. I'm not comfortable with you not having security as long as *his* fans are still blaming you for his problems."

"Hopefully, he'll be out of rehab soon and can address the rumors. Davy agreed to stay on as his manager until he's out of rehab and is aware of what's going on. He's promised to deal with it as soon as he can talk to him. In the meantime, I refuse to live my life surrounded by security. It's no way to live. Especially here."

She could tell that Nikki wanted to object but chose to let it go. Jordan had no doubt the subject would come up again, especially when their grandmother arrived. "When's dinner? I'm starving."

"It'll be ready soon. Brownies are in the oven for dessert."

"Yum." Jordan hugged Nikki. "Thanks for spending your day off tending to me and cooking when you were supposed to be on a getaway with Riley."

"Riley and I have the rest of our lives together. We're right where we wanted to be today."

"Whatever I did to deserve you, I'm glad I did it."

Nikki laughed. "What you did was share a womb with me."

Jordan released her and made a disgusted face. "Ew. Don't say it like that."

"Well, how should I say it?"

"You could say I was born with you and stuck with you for life?"

Nikki gave her a gentle push toward the door. "I wouldn't have it any way other than being stuck with you, and you know it."

CHAPTER 8

*M*ason couldn't believe he was actually nervous about going to dinner at Jordan's house. He also couldn't figure out *why* he was nervous. It was just dinner, for crying out loud. Dinner with people who were grateful to him for doing his job. How had he managed to blow it up into something to be nervous about?

And why in the hell had he told Blaine about the mouth-to-mouth thing?

So stupid.

Now someone else knew that he'd felt, for a second, like he was kissing Jordan when he was trying to save her life.

Ugh.

This was why he'd all but given up on women and dating and all the nonsense that went along with it. He couldn't remember the last time he'd been out with anyone, because he'd grown tired of the dance and the endless cycle of getting his hopes up about someone only to have them dashed. He'd been through the full gauntlet—from a wedding called off one month before the big day, to promising first dates that never materialized into second dates, to no-shows, ghosting and everything in between.

It was a wonder he wasn't drooling in a corner somewhere, hiding from the world. But rather than do that, he'd simply stepped off the merry-go-round and focused on other things, such as ramping up his fitness routine so he was back in the best shape he'd been in since his competitive weightlifting days. He was also devoted to his work, his friends, his sobriety and the community he served, keeping himself so busy, he rarely had time to feel lonely.

Some people weren't meant for happily ever after. Maybe he was one of them. He had an uncle who'd never married and had led a rich, fulfilling life without having had a family of his own. Mason was determined to do the same if that was his fate. He'd be thirty-six this year and was more aware of time passing him by than he'd ever been before, especially as many of his friends welcomed their second and third children.

Blaine had told him last week that Tiffany was expecting their second child together and the third in their family. Blaine was completely smitten with his stepdaughter, Ashleigh, who had him firmly wrapped around every one of her cute little fingers. His friend was a lucky man to have a wife and children and an extended family that loved him.

Mason hadn't been lucky in that regard. So what? Not everyone got lucky that way. He had a good life that satisfied him, and he refused to get maudlin about what hadn't happened. He much preferred to focus on the good things. The incident with Jordan had thrown him off his stride. That's all it was. He'd be ludicrous to act on something that had been completely involuntary on her part. She hadn't actually kissed him. She'd been having an asthma attack, for crying out loud. Yes, he'd enjoyed talking to her last night at the clinic, but allowing himself to get *nervous* about going to dinner at her house was just plain ridiculous.

By the time he pulled into the driveway to Eastward Look, he'd talked himself out of the nerves. It was just dinner—food and conversation with nice people. Blowing it up to something more than that was what had made him nervous in the first place. He was better after working it out in his mind, the way he did when things confounded him. Lights were on inside and over the front door, making the house look warm and welcoming. Mason reached for the flowers he'd bought for Nikki and Jordan and got out of the SUV. As he headed for the door, Jordan appeared, and suddenly, he was nervous again.

She opened the door for him. "Hi there."

He drank in the details of her stunning face. "Hi. How're you feeling?"

"Much better after sleeping half the day away." Her long dark hair was down around her shoulders. She wore an oversized Gansett Island sweatshirt and pink sweats. Other than the shadows under her expressive dark eyes, you'd never know she'd been through such an ordeal the night before. He liked that she hadn't felt the need to dress up for him or put on excessive amounts of makeup other than the mascara that made her extravagant lashes more so. Despite the many reasons he shouldn't be attracted, her fresh, natural, unadorned look appealed to him like nothing had in a very long time.

"Sometimes, that's just what you need." He felt like a hulking giant next to her in the vestibule. She was tiny compared to him, more than a foot shorter.

She didn't seem to feel crowded, though, as she looked up at him, her gaze taking a thorough inspection, or that's how it seemed to him, at least.

He'd gone home to shower and change before dinner. He was wearing jeans and an untucked light blue button-down shirt and had removed the bandage that had covered the cut on his forehead. Feeling self-conscious, he rubbed his face. "Did I cut myself shaving or something?"

She smiled up at him. "No, I was just noticing how different you look out of uniform."

"You saw me out of uniform last night."

"I know, but today I saw you *in* your uniform, and I thought it looked really nice on you."

"Is that right?"

"Uh-huh. You know how you expect someone to always look a certain way, and then they look different, and it's like you're meeting them all over again? That's how I felt seeing you in your uniform today."

Could she be any more sweet or adorable? "How is it possible that I actually understood that?"

Her smile got even bigger. "Where is your sling?"

"I can't stand it. I threw it out the window on the way over here."

"You did not!"

"I did."

"That's littering."

"Some animal will find it and use it to line their nest. That's the only thing it's good for anyway."

She gave him a skeptical look. "Isn't it against the law for the chief of the fire department to litter?"

"Are you going to report me?" Were they flirting? Is that what this was? If so, he was rather enjoying it. As if the conversation he'd had with himself on the way over had never happened, he leaned against the doorframe, settling into the conversation.

"Maybe." She nodded to the flowers. "Are those for me?"

"And your sister. For having me over." He handed the two bundles to her. "You can pick which one you like the best."

Jordan appeared to give the choice some considerable thought before settling on the pink roses over the mixed assortment. "Nikki will like these," she said of the second bouquet.

He thought it was sweet that she made her choice based on what her sister would prefer.

"Jordan! Let Mason come in, will you?"

Jordan's sheepish little grin twisted him up inside, minutes after he'd lectured himself about swearing off women and the drama that came with them. Drama was this woman's middle name. She'd made a profitable career out of courting and exploiting it, which was contrary to what he wanted for himself. He had no business finding her adorable or wishing he could actually kiss those sweet lips that formed the cutest smiles.

As he followed her into the house, he told himself not to look, but found his gaze traveling over her anyway, which didn't do a thing to support his "don't get involved" campaign. Despite the oversized clothing, she was still one of the sexiest women he'd ever met. Her sister was equally attractive, but standing in the kitchen with both of them, his gaze sought out only one of them.

"Glad you could make it, Mason," Nikki said. "What can I get you to drink? We have beer, wine, vodka, soda, water."

His mouth watered from the scent of garlic and spices. The stench of smoke had been largely eliminated by the removal of the living room furniture and rug. "I'll do a cola or ginger ale if you have it."

"Are you on duty?" Jordan asked.

"Nope, but I don't drink anymore. I've been in recovery for thirteen years." He was always transparent on the subject of why he avoided alcohol, preferring to share his truth rather than try to hide from it. That, too, helped him stay sober.

"Oh." Jordan sat at one of the stools at the counter and gestured for him to join her. "That's cool."

As he slid onto the stool, he could tell she wanted to ask more about it but didn't. "I'm an open book on that topic," he said as he accepted a glass of iced ginger ale from Nikki, "so don't be shy if you want to know about it."

"It's none of my business," Jordan said, "but good for you. That's an amazing accomplishment."

"Thanks. It's something I'm proud of."

Nikki put both bouquets in water and placed them on the countertop. "Thanks for the flowers, Mason. They're gorgeous."

"The pink ones are mine," Jordan said, flashing that sly, sexy little grin at him again.

"I like these better anyway," Nikki said of hers.

Jordan winked at him, as if to say, *Told you so.*

Mason was dazzled by her, and all the warnings in the world couldn't stop him from wanting more of her or from doing something that would probably lead to even more heartache than he'd experienced in the past. She was the kind of woman who could truly ruin him, which was all the more reason to keep his distance. But as he sat next to her in the cozy kitchen, a feeling of rightness and completion came over him that made him feel even more ridiculous than he had earlier.

He was smitten.

No fool like an old fool, he thought, having been down this road so many times, he knew the routine by heart. He could name every pothole and detour that was waiting to derail him, and yet he couldn't bring himself to care about any of that now that he was sitting a foot from her, steeped in the rich, fragrant scent of her hair and on the receiving end of her sweet, sexy smiles.

All he wanted was more of her—any way he could get it.

JORDAN COULDN'T STOP STEALING glances at Mason. Everything about him fascinated her, from his towering height, to the blond streaks in his brown hair, to his tanned skin and the way his large hands cradled the icy glass of soda. And that he'd come right out and told her he was a recovering alcoholic gave him mad points in her book. Most of the people she knew would never admit to being anything less than perfect and certainly wouldn't have owned their alcoholism the way he had. That was definitely something else about him to be admired, especially in light of what she'd been through with Brendan and his addiction issues, not to mention her mother's struggles with drugs.

She liked the deep timbre of his voice and how handsome he looked in the light blue dress shirt that he'd rolled up to reveal strong forearms covered with golden hair. He wore a fancy-looking silver watch with complex dials and gauges.

And he smelled really good.

For fuck's sake, Jordan, knock it off. You're technically still married to Brendan and have no business cataloging another man's features, even if his features are hella sexy.

She pulled herself out of her own silly thoughts to tune in to what he and Nikki were talking about.

"Where're you from originally?" Nikki asked him.

"Upstate New York. I grew up in the Syracuse area and came to

Rhode Island for college. I worked in Worcester, Massachusetts, before I came here."

"Is your family still in Syracuse?" Nik asked.

"Two of my older sisters still live there with their families. My parents retired to Florida a couple of years ago, my younger sister followed them south, and my older brother is in Seattle."

"Ever been married?" Nikki asked.

"Nik!" Jordan said. "Stop with the inquisition!"

"It's not an inquisition. I'm getting to know Mason."

Mason laughed at their bickering. "It's fine. I almost got married once, but it didn't work out. So no, never been married. What about you guys? Where'd you grow up?" Mason took a cracker and a slice of cheese from the plate Nik had put out.

"We mostly lived in the LA area growing up," Nik said.

"Just the two of you?"

Jordan spoke up to answer that one. "We have numerous half siblings, but we aren't particularly close to them. They're a lot younger than we are."

"We were the subject of a rather bitter custody battle that raged on for years," Nik added.

"Yikes, that must've sucked."

"That's one word for it," Jordan said. "Our family is pretty much each other, our amazing grandmother and our mom, who's remarried and living in France, so we don't see much of her."

"I'm sorry you guys went through that."

"It was a long time ago now, but suffice to say we were pretty thrilled to reach our eighteenth birthday," Jordan said.

"Best day ever," Nikki added.

"So it went on that long?" Mason asked.

"Right up until literally the day before we turned eighteen," Nikki said, "and they haven't spoken a word to each other in the nearly ten years since, which is fine with us. They put us through a nightmare."

"Sounds like it. Thank goodness you had each other."

"We say that all the time," Jordan said, smiling at her sister. "My luckiest break ever was being born a twin."

"Same," Nik said. "Which is why I've never been more thankful to anyone than I am to you, Mason, for seeing the flames last night and acting so fast. I'll never have the words to properly thank you for saving my sister."

He glanced at Jordan. "I was in the right place at the right time, thankfully."

She met his gaze and couldn't look away, recalling the feel of his lips on hers as he revived her.

"I'm, ah, going to check on Riley," Nikki said. "He's taking a long time in the shower." She left the room in a hurry.

Subtle, Jordan thought, suddenly unnerved to be left alone with the sexy firefighter.

"After dinner," he said in a low, intimate tone that set her heart to racing, "do you want to go for a ride?"

"I do, but I, um, I should tell you that I'm still married."

"Oh. Okay." Did he seem disappointed, or was that her overly active imagination?

"Not for much longer, but technically." She shrugged. "I'm waiting for him to get out of rehab so I can serve him with papers."

"There's no chance you'll go back to him?"

"No chance in hell."

"Then going for a ride shouldn't be a problem, right?"

Jordan swallowed hard, wondering if *going for a ride* was code for much more than that. She nodded, unnerved by the intense way he looked at her. It'd been so long since her husband had paid her any real attention. She could barely remember what it had been like to feel the heady sort of anticipation that came with understanding that a man was interested in her. And that she was equally interested.

"I'm kind of a red-hot mess, Mason, and you seem like a really nice guy. Things have been complicated and…" The words died on her lips when his big hand covered hers, infusing her with warmth that seemed to touch her everywhere.

"We're just going for a ride, okay?"

Now she felt foolish for blowing it up into more, but he had a right to know her marital status in light of the attraction between them that couldn't be denied. "I'm looking forward to it," she said, smiling because she wanted him to know she meant it.

"Me, too."

"And we're going to find that sling."

Before he could reply, Riley and Nikki came down the stairs with loud footsteps and conversation that had Jordan rolling her eyes at an amused Mason.

"Could they be any more obvious?" she whispered. Nikki must've tuned in to the sparks flying between them, or she wouldn't be acting like such a loon.

Then again, Nikki would be thrilled to see Jordan attracted to anyone who wasn't Brendan. Mason was so different from him that he might as well have been from another planet.

Riley followed Nikki into the room, his dark hair still wet from the shower. He shook hands with Mason. "Glad you could make it for dinner."

"Thanks for asking me."

"Where's your brother?" Nikki asked Riley. "Dinner is almost ready."

"I'll text him." Riley pulled out his phone. "Dad texted to send their regrets. Summer is fussy, and Finn said they'll be here in ten minutes."

"Text your dad to come get dinner to go," Nik said. "I made a ton. I'll box it up for them."

Riley typed in the text. "He said you're awesome, which of course we knew, and he'll be over in a bit."

"Congrats on your new baby sister," Mason said to Riley.

"Thanks. She's so cute." Riley called up some pictures on his phone and handed it to Mason.

Jordan leaned in for a look and immediately wanted to get even closer. This silly little crush on Mason was absurd, but after her near-death experience—not to mention the nightmare with Brendan—she didn't care if she was being absurd or ridiculous. Last night was a good reminder that life was a gift that could be taken away without any warning. She'd been given a second chance, and being around him made her feel *alive*, and not just because he'd saved her life. It was also because of the way he looked at her and listened to her. And, well, he smelled *so* good.

Brendan smelled like sweat, cigarettes and pot most of the time in the last few years.

Mason was the polar opposite. His scent was fresh and clean and spicy and suited him. Everything about him was strong and masculine and endlessly appealing. Twenty-four hours ago, she hadn't met him yet, and now she was tripping into serious crush territory. Probably because he'd saved her.

But no, it wasn't just that.

Her thoughts were interrupted when Finn and Chloe came in, apologizing for being late.

"It was totally my fault," Chloe said. "My last client took forever."

Jordan thought Chloe was one of the coolest, hippest women she'd met in a long time. She was lean and sexy with dark hair streaked with hot pink and a sleeve tattoo on one arm. Jordan admired the other woman's resilience as she battled the ravages of rheumatoid arthritis while still occasionally working as a hairstylist.

"Thought you weren't cutting anymore," Riley said as he poured her the one glass of wine she allowed on occasion and got a beer for his brother.

Jordan wondered if it was hard for Mason to be at events where other people were drinking alcohol.

"I rarely cut anymore, but Cindy had a migraine today, so I filled in for her."

"Which Cindy is working with you?" Mason asked.

"Cindy Lawry, Owen's sister."

"Ah, right. I hadn't heard she was staying for the summer."

"She is," Chloe said, "and thank goodness for that."

Finn put his arm around her and kissed the top of her head.

Chloe leaned into him, arms crossed and hands tucked out of sight, as she did when she didn't want people to notice the redness and swelling. Nikki had told Jordan about Chloe's RA and the impact on her hands in particular. Chloe was now overseeing the design of the McCarthy family's new spa, which would be built over the coming winter at their hotel in New Harbor, while Cindy ran Chloe's Curl Up & Dye salon in town.

The bond between Finn and Chloe touched Jordan every time she was with them. From what Riley had told her, Finn had rallied to the cause by finding out everything he could about RA and how he could support her. Like his brother, Finn was a great guy, and Jordan had been envious more than once of her sister and Chloe.

Where had men like them been when she'd been falling for a malignant narcissist?

Mason nudged her with his good elbow. "You okay?"

Jordan realized she'd spaced out of the conversation—and he'd noticed. "I'm good. Just thinking."

"You looked sad. Are you?"

Surprised by the insightful question, she tried to decide how to answer him. "I'm wondering what the secret is," she said in a low tone that only he could hear as the others chatted with each other the way they did whenever they were together. The four of them had become close, and Jordan had been happy to know that Nik had made such great friends on the island.

"The secret to what?"

She nodded toward the two happy couples. "That. What they have."

"Ah, *that* secret. If I knew, I'd tell you, but I'm clueless."

"Glad I'm not the only one." Jordan helped herself to cheese and a cracker, which she then handed to him before getting another for herself.

"You're definitely not the only one."

"Do you believe that some people get lucky and others don't?"

He appeared to give that some significant thought. "I haven't really considered that before, but I suppose it's possible. Why does one person find their soul mate and another never does?"

"Right, exactly. There's an element of luck to that, wouldn't you say? Take Nikki, for instance. She met Riley because the roof leaked, and he came to fix it. What if the roof had never leaked? Would they still have met?"

"That's an interesting question. Perhaps the universe intended to bring them together, and if the roof hadn't leaked, it would've found another way for them to meet."

"Do you really believe that?"

"I don't know. Like I said, I haven't given it much thought."

"I have. I've thought a lot about why some people click with each other and other people never click like that with anyone. Chloe cuts the hair of hundreds of people in a year, so what made Finn stand out the first time he came into her shop for a haircut?"

"I'm not saying I find him handsome, but from what I've been told, women tend to like him."

Jordan laughed. "He's not exactly tough on the eyes. I'll give you that. But I'm talking about the *click*. That thing that sets him apart from every other guy she's ever met. That's the intangible part that fascinates me. Why him? Why not one of the hundreds, if not thousands, of other guys whose hair she's cut?"

"You didn't have the click with your husband?"

"I thought I did. At first, but things changed and…" She shrugged as she glanced at the others. "I didn't have that. Not even close. And the funny thing is, until Nikki met Riley and I got to see them up close, I didn't even fully grasp that my relationship with him wasn't what it could've been. How's that for a deep confession?"

"That's pretty deep."

"It's sad. That's what it is. I wasted years with a guy who didn't deserve me."

"Well, at least you know it now."

"Yeah." Jordan rested her head on her upturned hand. "Sorry for the deep thoughts by Jordan."

"Don't be sorry. You raised interesting questions."

"You ever had the click?"

"Thought I did once, but it didn't work out."

Jordan wanted to ask what'd happened, but she didn't want to make him uncomfortable. "That must've been tough."

"It was a long time ago."

Something in the way he said that indicated it might've been a long time ago, but the pain of it had stayed with him. She understood that. Some things could never be outrun, no matter how much time went by. Like the way her father had betrayed them and their mother by having a whole other family with another woman—while still married to their mother. And then the court had given him custody over their mother, who had mental health and addiction issues.

"Everything is ready." Nikki's announcement burst the intimate little bubble Jordan had been in with Mason while the others carried on without them.

She'd liked being inside that bubble with him and looked forward to spending more time with him later. Whether she ought to be anticipating more time with any guy right now was neither here nor there. Nothing could keep her from going for a ride with the sweet, sexy firefighter who'd saved her life.

CHAPTER 9

*D*inner was fun and entertaining with the McCarthy brothers in attendance. The two of them were always good for laughs, and tonight was no different, but Jordan could hardly think of anything other than how much she wanted to continue the conversation she'd been having with Mason.

He sat next to her at dinner, so she couldn't really see him without everyone noticing if she looked at him.

"Jord?"

She glanced at Nikki. "Sorry. What?"

"Chloe asked how you're feeling."

"Oh, sorry. I'm good. My chest aches a bit the way it always does after an asthma attack, but otherwise, I'm fine. And I'm very thankful to Mason."

"We all are." Nikki raised her wineglass. "Here's to Mason. We owe you an eternal debt of gratitude."

Jordan glanced his way in time to notice that Nikki's toast embarrassed him, which she found endearing.

His gaze met hers, sending a shocking jolt of awareness through her that had her scrambling to hide her reaction from everyone else.

"I'm glad I was in the right place at the right time," Mason said.

"We all are," Riley said.

"How's your elbow, Mason?" Nikki asked.

"It's fine. Just a little stiff and sore, but that's to be expected."

"What happened?" Finn asked.

"I was riding my bike out at the bluffs when I saw the flames over here. Took my eye off a jump for one second and landed hard. Cut my forehead and dislocated my elbow."

"Ouch," Finn said. "I did that once playing hockey. Remember that, Ri?"

"Ah yeah, how could I ever forget the way you screamed like a banshee when they put it back where it belonged?"

"That hurt worse than being stabbed," Finn said. "No kidding. Worst pain I ever had."

"It was pretty bad," Mason said, "but it immediately felt better after they reset it."

"I can't believe you carried Jordan out of here with a dislocated elbow," Nikki said.

"I was operating on adrenaline. I hardly even remembered it was messed up until after."

"Not sure how that's possible," Finn said. "I couldn't breathe until mine was fixed."

"He cried like a baby," Riley added as only a brother could.

"Fuck off. You would've, too!"

Having gotten the rise he wanted out of his brother, Riley lost it laughing.

Chloe shook her head at Nikki. "How old will they be when they finally stop pushing each other's buttons?"

"We'll be dead years old when that happens," Riley said emphatically.

Finn raised his beer bottle to touch it to Riley's. "You said it, brother."

Mason laughed right along with the other guys, and a feeling came over Jordan that was all new to her, something she couldn't readily identify. Whatever it was, she liked it and wanted more of it.

The moment was lost when Nikki stood to begin clearing dishes, and Jordan got up to help her.

"No way, missy," Nikki said sternly. "You're supposed to be relaxing. Riley will help me."

"I will, too," Chloe said, standing.

"Nope." Nikki took the salad bowl from Chloe. "You're off duty, too. Go light the fire pit, Riley."

Jordan wanted to tell them not to do that, but she'd feel silly protesting something they did all the time. A few random sparks from the neighbor's fire pit had nearly led to disaster last night. That didn't mean it would happen again. What were the odds of it happening in the first place? She'd ask Mason that when they went for their ride.

She followed Nikki to the sink. "I'm going for a ride with Mason to find his sling."

Nikki gave her a perplexed look. "To find his sling? Where is it?"

"He lost it on the way over here."

"How did he lose it?"

"He threw it out the window. He's supposed to have it on, so I'm going to help him find it."

"You sure you feel up to going out?"

"We're just going for a ride. I'll be fine." She kissed her sister's cheek. "Thanks for a wonderful dinner."

"You're welcome. Thanks again for not dying."

"Happy to still be here."

"I hope you mean that, Jord. I know things have been rough, but it's going to get better. I just know it."

"Nowhere to go but up."

"That's right. Good luck finding the sling. Or is that a metaphor for other plans?"

Jordan laughed. "We're really going to find it. He's supposed to wear it for a week, and he got pissed and threw it out the window. Be back in a bit."

"Okay. Have fun looking."

Mason came over to them. When he was standing right next to

her, the top of her head came to the middle of his chest. She wondered how it would be to... *Okay, stop it. Right now.*

"Thanks for dinner, Nikki. It was delicious."

Nikki hugged him. "Happy to have you. You're welcome here any time, Mason. Open invite to come by for dinner any time you're hungry."

"If you knew me better, you'd never make such an offer. My appetite is somewhat legendary."

"I mean it. We owe you everything. Least I can do is feed you."

"That's very nice of you. Thanks again for having me."

Jordan nudged him toward the door before the others could come back inside and waylay them. She wanted to go for that ride with him in the worst way. "Let me just grab a jacket," she said when they were in the foyer. "Be right back."

"I'll wait for you outside."

"Okay." Jordan went up the stairs slower than she wanted to, but only because this would be a bad time to trigger another attack. She was always more susceptible after a recent incident. She grabbed a white denim jacket, put the new inhaler in her pocket, just in case, and ducked into the bathroom to brush her hair and teeth. Then she went downstairs and out the front door into the cool air.

It took until late June or even into early July before the evenings warmed up on Gansett. The breeze off the ocean kept the nighttime temperatures cool for most of summer.

Mason was standing by his SUV, waiting for her. He opened the passenger door for her.

"We're going to find that sling."

"If you say so."

"I do. I say so. And you're putting it back on."

"Are you always this bossy?" He sounded amused as he drove the SUV down the driveway.

"Only when it's important. Your arm can't heal properly if you're using it all the time."

"How do you know that?"

"I looked up dislocated elbows online and found out it's a serious injury. You're supposed to keep it immobile for one to three weeks if you want it to heal properly."

"You looked it up online?"

"Did you hear the rest of what I said?"

"I heard it. I just can't believe you actually looked it up."

"Why not? I was interested."

"Well, I was interested in the treatment for a severe asthma attack, and from what I read, you're supposed to still be in the hospital."

Jordan laughed. "Touché. Dr. David let me go home because my breathing was almost back to normal, or I'd still be there. You, on the other hand, are not back to normal. Put the bright lights on. We're going to find that sling."

He turned the high beams on.

"Where were you when you tossed it?"

"I don't remember."

"Yes, you do. Where were you?"

Chuckling, he said, "About half a mile from here."

"Are you lying?"

"Nope."

"Which window did you throw it out of?"

"Passenger."

Jordan leaned forward, scanning the roadside brush. "If we can't find it, I'm going to make one for you."

"Thanks for the warning."

Jordan smiled, pleased by his sarcasm. "Slow down. We don't want to miss it."

"Yes, we actually do."

"No, we actually don't."

"Stop!"

Mason hit the brakes.

Jordan released her seat belt and jumped out to grab the sling from around a bush. Standing in the bright glare of the headlights, she held it over her head and did a little victory dance before getting back in the SUV. "Now put it back on."

Mason was smiling widely as she handed it over to him. "What if there're bugs in there?"

"Put it back on."

Mason did as he was told, grimacing as he worked his injured arm into the sling. "There. Happy now?"

"Yes, as a matter of fact, I am. You can take it off to shower and get dressed. Otherwise, you need to have it on until David says otherwise."

He shifted the SUV into Drive and continued along the road. "Let me ask you this—do you do everything you're told, or do you occasionally throw the sling out the window?"

"I've never actually thrown a sling out the window."

"How about an inhaler?"

Jordan bit her lip as she thought about that. "That might've happened. Once."

"Ah-ha!"

"Easy. I was nine at the time, not however old you are. How old are you, anyway?"

"Thirty-five."

"There you have it. I was nine when I chucked my inhaler. You were thirty-five when you chucked your sling. See the difference?"

"Nope."

Jordan laughed as she tried to remember the last time she'd had this much fun with anyone.

"How old are you?"

"Twenty-eight. I'm surprised you didn't look that up online, too."

"Maybe I did."

Jordan's good mood shriveled up and died at the thought of him looking her up online. Knowing what was out there for him—or anyone—to find was something she tried not to think too much about out of fear of losing her sanity. "You shouldn't have done that."

"Why not? I was interested in you after meeting you last night."

"And now you know all sorts of sordid things." She kicked off her flip-flops and pulled her knees up, wrapping her arms around them, wishing she hadn't come on this ride with him.

"I only found out how old you are because I was actually afraid you were, like, twenty or something."

"You were not."

"Yes, I was!"

"Why were you afraid of that?"

"Because I really liked hanging out with you last night, and if you were only twenty, that would make me feel like a dirty old man. But seeing as you're an old lady at twenty-eight, then I don't feel so silly."

"About what?"

"About being nervous about going to dinner with you and wishing we could hurry through dinner so we could go for our ride or whether I have any chance at all of convincing you to maybe hang out with me again sometime. That kind of stuff." He pulled into the parking lot at the town beach and shut off the engine.

"You were nervous about coming to dinner?"

"Yep."

"Why?"

"I don't know. I just was."

"Because of me?"

"Well, I wasn't nervous because of Nikki."

"Why were you nervous about me?"

Mason didn't answer right away, but she noticed he tightened his grip on the wheel. "I had fun last night, which is kind of weird when you figure I was injured and you were struggling to breathe." He shrugged. "And yet, it was fun."

"I had fun, too, despite the circumstances."

"You did? Really?"

"Yes," she said, laughing. "You couldn't tell?"

"I wasn't sure if it was just me."

She turned toward him. "It wasn't."

He glanced at her. "You want to go for a walk?"

"On the beach in the dark?"

"That was kind of the idea."

"My grandmother always told us to stay off the beach at night."

"I'll keep you safe."

Four little words that meant so much to her. "You only have one working arm. How will you keep me safe?"

"I only need one arm to fend off the dragons. They're scared of me because I'm so tall."

And he was delightful. "All right, then. Let's walk."

They got out of the SUV and walked the length of the wooden boardwalk that delivered them to the sand. The full moon cast a glow upon the beach as they walked toward the water, which lapped gently against the sand.

"The wind really died down," he said of the flat-calm water that stretched out before them, seemingly into infinity.

"Without the wind last night, we wouldn't be standing here right now." Jordan wasn't sure where the thought came from or why she'd shared it with him.

"No, we wouldn't, but you also wouldn't have almost died."

"Do you believe in things happening for a reason?"

"Not usually, but I'm wondering if I should reconsider."

"It's funny that a leaking roof brought Riley to Nikki, and the same roof catching on fire brought you to me."

"That is funny."

She'd no sooner said that than she felt silly for comparing them to Riley and Nikki when they were on a whole other level.

But as they walked slowly along the shoreline, Jordan felt peaceful for the first time in longer than she could remember. The ocean had always had a calming effect on her. Apparently, her companion did, too. "So you almost got married once?"

"Yeah, she called it off a month before the wedding. Kinda sucked at the time, but I've come to see it was a blessing. We weren't meant to be."

"I'm sorry that happened to you."

"Like I said before, it was a long time ago. Feels like another lifetime, really."

Jordan sensed he didn't want to talk about it, so she changed the subject. "Did you spend time by the ocean when you were a kid?"

"My grandparents had a place on the coast of Maine. We went there every summer. What about you?"

"We lived about an hour inland from the coast in LA and much closer in the summer when we got to be here."

"Did you come every year?"

"Yep, the day after school ended, we were on a plane."

"Mrs. Hopper was your mother's mother?"

"Right, and she provided the sanity in a chaotic childhood."

Mason's cell phone rang, and he twisted awkwardly to pull it from his back pocket. "Fucking sling."

Jordan laughed at his contortions. "You need a hand?"

"Haha. Very funny." He glanced at the screen. "Sorry, I've got to take this."

"No problem."

"Hey, what's up?" After a pause, he said, "How bad?" Another pause. "I'll be right there." He ended the call and stuffed the phone back in his pocket. "My team is working a pretty serious accident in town. I need to run over there."

"That's fine."

As they started walking back to the parking lot, Jordan could tell he was making an effort to match his stride to hers when, normally, he'd be walking much faster. "The thing is, I don't really have time to take you back to the house first."

"No problem. I'll just go with you."

"Sorry to mess up our walk."

"It's really fine, Mason. I know you're always on call."

"I am, and that sucks at times like this."

"At times like what?"

"When I have something else I'd much rather be doing."

He sounded truly annoyed to have had their time together interrupted.

"How about we take a rain check and do it again some other time?"

"You want to do it again?" he asked as he held the door for her.

She laughed. "Why do you sound so surprised?"

"I guess it's been a while since I had a second date."

96

"Oh, was this a date?" she asked, her brows raised.

He blew out an aggravated huff and shut the door. While he walked around to the driver's side, Jordan laughed while she had the chance. Why was it so fun to push his buttons? And why wasn't it awkward to be pushing the buttons of a guy she'd only just met?

CHAPTER 10

She was doing this on purpose, Mason decided as he flipped on flashing emergency lights and headed for town. Winding him up in knots for the fun of it.

"I'm very sorry for teasing you," she said after a few minutes of silence.

"You're not one bit sorry." She was fun to be around. That much was for certain.

Her low snort of laughter confirmed her lack of contrition. "I'm a little bit sorry."

He glanced at her, struck again by how naturally beautiful she was. "No, you're not."

"I am!"

"So this was a date, then?" He cringed to himself at how stupid he sounded. That he'd even had to ask.

"Sure, we can call it that if you'd like."

"I can do better than a walk on the beach in the dark."

"Is that right?"

"That's right."

"I'm intrigued."

"Tomorrow night?"

"Let me check my schedule." She pulled out her phone and pretended to peruse her calendar. "It appears I'm free."

"Good," he said, amused by her even when he should be annoyed by the way she was yanking his chain. "I'll pick you up at six thirty."

"Where're we going?"

"You'll find out."

"What do I wear?"

"Whatever you want."

"That's not enough information."

"That's all you're getting." He'd never sparred with a woman this way, especially one he wanted the way he wanted her. And yes, he wanted her, even if his better judgment was still urging caution. He'd heard all the reasons his better judgment had come up with for playing it cool with her. And then, within thirty seconds in her presence, his better judgment had been thoroughly overruled. He'd have to be dead not to want her, especially after the way she'd tried to kiss him when he was saving her life.

Speaking of that… No, he wasn't going to play that card. Not yet.

In town, they arrived at the scene of the crash, where numerous other public safety vehicles had already converged. "I'll try to be quick." He parked his SUV off to the side so it wouldn't get hit while Jordan waited for him.

"Take your time. I hope everyone is all right."

"Me, too." If they were, he could get back to her that much sooner. He stepped out of the SUV and crossed the street toward the island's one rotary, the scene of many a crash over the years. He and Blaine had tried for a while now to get the town to consider putting a light at the intersection, but so far, they'd been unsuccessful in making that happen. The islanders liked their rotary and didn't want any stoplights on their unspoiled island. So the crashes continued.

"What've we got?" he asked Blaine, who was also in street clothes.

"Oh, hey, sorry you got called in. I could've handled it." They did that for each other often—one covered so the other didn't have to. "Three injured, one seriously. I called the chopper for him." He gestured to where Mallory and another paramedic nicknamed Boner were doing CPR on a man in the street. "I called David to let him know we're bringing in two others."

"Tourists or local?" He didn't recognize the cars.

"Tourists hit a local."

"Fucking rotary."

"You said it."

They went their separate ways to supervise their subordinates. Blaine saw to traffic control while Mason ducked his head into the back of the ambulance where Shorty, one of the firefighter-paramedics, was with a woman who appeared to be about fifty. "What've you got?"

"Head lac and possible fractured wrist," Shorty said.

"Is Jeff all right?" the woman asked. "No one will tell me."

"Is Jeff your husband, ma'am?"

"No, my boyfriend. He was driving, and I can't get anyone to tell me what's wrong with him."

"I'll check on him." Mason went to talk to Mallory.

"He suffered a cardiac event." She was breathing hard from the exertion of performing CPR. "We're not sure if it was before or after the accident, but we've been working on him for ten minutes already. No heartbeat yet."

"Crap."

The roar of the approaching helicopter drowned out everything else as everyone took cover while it landed in the middle of the normally busy street. His personnel loaded the patient onto a gurney, hustled to the chopper and turned him over to the paramedics on board. They'd have him at a level-one trauma unit in Providence within minutes.

As the chopper took off again, Mason made his way over to the ambulance. "Ma'am, your friend has suffered a cardiac event and is being transported to the mainland."

"Oh God. Oh no. *Jeff.*"

"Please try to stay calm, Carol," Shorty said in a soothing tone. "He's in the best possible hands."

The woman broke down into tears as she nodded to acknowledge what Shorty had said.

"Where's our other casualty?" Mason asked.

"Still in the car."

Mason went to look in on the young woman, who'd been given an ice pack to hold against a bump on her head. "How're you doing?"

"I'm okay. Just bumped my head."

"I'd like to get you to the clinic to be sure it's just a bump. Is that all right?"

She nodded. "My mom is coming. She'll be here in a minute. That other car, it just cut me off, and there was nowhere to go. I don't know what happened."

"We think he might've suffered a possible heart attack."

"Oh, well, that explains why he was in my lane."

Mason waited with her until her hysterical mother appeared on the scene to take her daughter to the clinic.

"Write it all up and get me a report by the morning," Mason said to Carl, his other lieutenant.

"Yes, sir."

"Call if you need me."

"Will do."

With everything under control, for the moment, anyway, Mason returned to his own vehicle. The alluring scent of his passenger was the first thing he noticed after he closed the door.

"Is everyone okay?" she asked.

"Two are. The guy in the helicopter isn't so good."

"Is he going to die?"

"I don't know."

"How do you deal with this stuff every day? I'd be a mess."

"Believe it or not, you get used to it and become a little numb to it after a while. That doesn't make you less compassionate for people in crisis, but you don't take them all home with you the way you do at first."

"I suppose you'd have to become a little numb to it or go mad."

"Some people don't last in public safety because they can't deal with the stuff they see. I never blame anyone who can't handle the job. It's not for everyone."

"How'd you end up the fire chief on Gansett Island?"

Mason pulled into traffic, following the direction of the officer who was guiding vehicles around the accident scene. He took a right turn that would eventually lead them back to Eastward Look, but he took the long way around the island so he could have more time with her. "I went to college for criminal justice, planning to be a cop. I applied all over but didn't get picked up, so I started applying for fire department jobs and was hired in Worcester before I finished college. I spent nine years there, working my way up to lieutenant. When I heard about this job, I applied thinking I didn't have a snowball's chance in hell of getting it—and at first, I didn't."

"What do you mean?"

"They hired someone else, who couldn't handle the winters or the isolation. He lasted four months. The mayor called to ask if I was still interested. I've been here four years this December, and I love it."

"Isn't it boring after working in a big city?"

"It can be, but I was never going to be chief in Worcester. I would've been lucky to make captain there."

"And you wanted to be chief?"

"It's nice to be the boss," he said, winking at her.

He loved her smile, would do anything to make it happen, especially when it was directed at him. "I see how it is."

"Then again, sometimes being the boss sucks, such as when you're doing something fun and you get called into work, which happens far more often than I'd like."

"So you have a lot of *fun*, then?"

He looked over at her, wishing he could see more of her face. "Not this kind of fun."

"What kind of fun is this?"

"The best kind."

"Is it?"

"Uh-huh. At least it is for me."

"It is for me, too. The most fun I've had in a long time."

Her revealing statement filled him with an unreasonable amount of hope. The many reasons why he shouldn't be letting himself become enthralled by a woman who was still married to someone else failed to matter in the face of all that hope. "Are you in a rush to get home?"

"Not really. Why?"

"There's something I want to show you."

"Where have I heard that line before?"

Mason laughed. "No, I really want to show you something. Trust me?"

"Since you saved my life, I suppose the least I can do is trust you."

"Gee, thanks."

"You're welcome."

He grinned like a loon, thankful for the darkness that made it impossible for her to see how delightful he found her, how refreshing and special. When they reached the access road that led to his favorite place on the island, he took a left turn and navigated the bumpy dirt road that wound through a dark thicket of trees.

"And then they found her body two weeks later."

Laughing, he said, "Your imagination is creative."

"This is how every episode of *Dateline* begins. A woman goes for a ride with the burly fireman, and only one of them comes back."

"You think the fireman is burly?"

"Duh. Like you don't know you are."

"I've been called a lot of things. Burly ain't one of them."

"What else have you been called?"

"Stretch was my nickname growing up. My grandfather called me that. My brother calls me Roid from the days when I lifted competitively, and PS, I never once took anything other than vitamins."

"Your brother is funny, and hello, you lifted competitively?"

"For a couple of years, until life kicked in and I had to get a real job —you know, the kind that paid actual money."

"I know what that's like. That's how I became a model."

"You were a model?"

"For years."

"What kind of model?"

"Mostly underwear. I did pretty well because my look is nontraditional, or so they used to say."

"I bet you were in *hot* demand."

And yes, he emphasized the word *hot*, which had Jordan wondering if he thought she was hot. *Why do I hope he does? Maybe because I find him insanely hot in a tall, strong, muscular, incredibly competent sort of way? I've seen him three times, and I already know there's not much that rattles him, certainly not fire or smoke or car crashes or women who aren't breathing.*

Since just about everything rattled her, Jordan had mad respect for people who kept their cool in a crisis.

"Wait for it," he said as he navigated another bend in the dirt road. "This is what I wanted to show you."

When they cleared the last curve in the road, they were treated to a view of the water, which was brightly lit by the full moon. It was truly one of the most beautiful things Jordan had ever seen. "Wow."

"Right?"

"How'd you find this place? I've been coming here all my life and never knew this was out here."

"Technically, this road isn't open to the public, but we had a brush fire out here one night on a full moon. Now I come out here every time there's a full moon."

"Ah, I see. It's part of your date formula, right?"

"What's a date formula?"

"It's when a guy has a reliable 'wow' package of things he does on every first date that's guaranteed to leave an impression. I had a friend in LA who always got tickets to either the Lakers or Dodgers, depending on the season, with dinner either before or after at the same place every time, followed by a drive up Mulholland to cap the night off with panoramic views of the city. Worked like a charm for him. He got a lot of second dates."

"Huh, well, I've never had a first-date formula, and I've never been here with anyone else for the full moon."

Jordan gave him the side-eye. "Really?"

"Really," he said, laughing. "You're so jaded."

"Wouldn't you be if your husband released a video of you having sex so the whole world could see what you look like when you come?" The words were out before she took even a second to consider what she was saying—or who she was saying it to. They'd been having a nice time, and she had to go and ruin it. "Sorry, that was a bit intense."

"I'm sorry that happened to you, and I don't blame you for being bitter."

"Did you watch it? When you looked me up before, did you watch the video?"

"I didn't and I won't. I swear."

"Good." She released a deep breath full of relief. "He took down the original, but there're bootleg copies all over the place. It's like a game of whack-a-mole. We get one taken down, and another pops up. I've begun to accept that this is my life now."

"I can't think of anything worse than someone I loved violating my trust that way."

"It's part of the toxic cocktail that was our marriage. And I went back to him after that." She shook her head, her expression regretful. "That was the breaking point for Nik. She was my manager before I went back to him." And why was she telling Mason this crap? What did he care about the shitshow her life had become? "Anyway..."

Mason reached over and placed his big hand on top of hers, infusing her entire body with warmth. "I'm sorry for what he put you through. You deserve better."

Jordan appreciated that he expressed only regret, not pity. She couldn't bear to have him pity her. "Some of it was my fault. I put up with it way longer than I should have. I got caught up in the nonsense that comes from being famous for no good reason. It was fun and exciting at first, and then, it wasn't. So here I am with millions of followers on Twitter and Insta and no idea what to do with them."

"What do you want to do?"

He didn't remove his hand, which was fine with her. She liked the way his hand enveloped her much smaller one. He made her feel safe, which was such a relief after the unpredictable man she was married to. "I have no idea, which is my biggest problem at the moment, now that I've been given this second chance at life thanks to you. I'm contracted to do another season of my show, but I really don't want to. I can't see how the show works anymore without me married to *him*. He was the reason the network wanted me."

"It wasn't just about him. They wanted you for you, too."

She looked over at him. "How do you know that?"

"I told you. I've seen the show."

"I still can't believe that. You're not exactly my target demographic."

"How do you figure?"

"My show appealed to shallow young women who're mostly about their phones, their look, their social media accounts."

"And men who like to watch sexy women be sexy."

Jordan thought nothing he could've said would've shocked her more than to hear he'd watched her show, but then he managed to top that. "It was silly."

"It was fun—and funny and interesting."

"Come on. You're joking, right?"

He turned in his seat so he could better see her. "I'm one hundred percent sincere. I enjoyed the show the few times I caught it. You and your friend Gigi were funny to watch."

"Because she's certifiable. She'll say anything."

"And you were the sensible one."

"She'd be in jail if it wasn't for me, even if she's a lawyer. We're not sure how that actually happened, but she swears her law degree is legit." She turned toward him. "I can't believe you watched the show."

"I read that you had between six million and eight million viewers. Why wouldn't one of them be me?"

"You make a good point. Listen, the show is dumb. I always knew that, but I was proud of it. We made something from nothing."

"You should be proud of it, Jordan. Millions of people enjoyed it."

"I think half of them have emailed or hit me up on Insta and Twitter to ask when we'll be back. The network is pressuring me." She shrugged. "All that feels like a million years ago since things blew up with my husband."

"You should do whatever you want now. You're a star in your own right, separate from him. People responded to *you* and to Gigi on the show. It wasn't about him. Maybe they were interested in the show at first because of your connection to him, but that's not why they kept coming back."

"You're very good for a girl's fragile ego."

"Your ego has absolutely no reason to be fragile."

She turned her palm up to connect with his and wrapped her fingers around his hand. "Your hands are huge." Placing her palm against his, she realized his hand was easily twice the size of hers.

"I've heard that before."

"Did you play basketball?"

"All the way through college."

"I bet you were good."

"I was okay. I lacked the fire in the belly you need to make something of it. I preferred weightlifting, much to my basketball coach's dismay."

"Can I ask you something else?"

"Anything you want."

"Last night, when you were, you know, saving me, did something weird happen between us, or was that just me?"

CHAPTER 11

Under normal circumstances, Maddie McCarthy loved nothing more than being surrounded by family and friends. However, there was nothing normal about anything these days. Being confined to bed or the sofa while the world, including her three young children, went on around her, Maddie was going slowly insane from inactivity. Not to mention, she was certain that looking at the cupcakes Syd had brought was putting more weight on her that she'd never be able to lose after the twins arrived.

If that wasn't enough, her sweet husband, Mac, was about to spontaneously combust, despite the breathing and meditation exercises he'd been doing religiously since an anxiety attack had caused him to collapse at the clinic in the single most frightening moment of her life. The strain of her pregnancy was getting to them both, and nothing they did to alleviate it seemed to help. Even having the family over for a dinner they didn't have to cook.

If they hadn't lost their son Connor the way they had, they'd probably be coping with this unexpected pregnancy better than they were. But between losing him and this unexpected pregnancy with twins, the stress had swelled to dangerous levels for both of them. The fact that they couldn't have sex only added to the pressure cooker they were living in.

Something had to give.

Maddie just wished she knew what to do. With the summer to get through until the twins arrived, she and Mac would be in pieces long before then, even with the wonderful new au pair they'd hired earlier in the day. Kelsey had been terrific with the kids, who'd taken to her right away. She'd be back in the morning to help out, providing a much-needed lifeline.

Maddie's sister, Tiffany, came to sit with her while the others raised hell on the deck. Maddie had come inside when the lounge had begun to hurt her back.

"What's up?" Tiffany asked.

"A whole lot of nothing. You?"

"Other than 'morning' sickness that lasts all day, nothing much."

Maddie winced. "That's a drag."

"Eh, it's nothing compared to full-time bed rest."

"It's not nothing."

"Blaine is out of his mind over it. 'How can this be normal?' he asks every day as I'm puking my guts up."

"He wishes he could do something to help."

"I know, and he's a huge help with Ashleigh and Addie. I couldn't cope without him."

"Maybe you should tell him that. It'll make him feel less useless when you're sick."

"I probably should. What about you? Tensions are running high around here."

"You can tell?"

"Honey, everyone can tell."

"I don't know what to do for him. He's so stressed."

"Kelsey seems great, and the kids loved her."

"Yes, she's agreed to give us the summer to see how she feels about island life, so that's a relief."

"We'll make sure she loves it."

Mac's sister Janey came in from the deck and sat in a chair next to the couch. "Did you ask her yet?" Janey said to Tiffany.

"Working up to it."

"Ask me what?" Maddie said.

"We have an idea," Janey said. "We want you and Mac to get out of here for a while, just the two of you."

Maddie shook her head. "We have three children, Janey."

"I know that, Maddie, but hear me out. We can all see that you two are having a tough time of it. So get in the car, take the ferry to the mainland and stay at Joe's place for a few days to recharge."

"Mac would be stressed being unable to get to the kids. I would be, too." If there was a downside to island life, that was certainly at the top of the list.

Tiffany looked at Janey. "Did you ask your mom?"

"I did, and she said they can make it work."

"Make what work?"

"We had a feeling you might not want to go off-island and leave the kids here, so I checked with my mom, and she's holding a room at the inn starting tomorrow afternoon through Friday. It's all yours."

"It's so lovely of you guys to want to do this for us, but the kids…"

"Between Kelsey and Mom and Ned and Mac's parents and the two of us, we've got you covered, Maddie," Tiffany said.

"You're puking all day," Maddie reminded her sister.

"I can puke at your house as easily as I puke at mine."

Though she was touched by her sister's generosity, Maddie shook her head. "You don't feel up to having my kids on top of yours. Besides, you're so busy at the store."

"It's fine. I want this for you. We all do."

"Mac will never take the time off," Maddie said. "Not at this time of year."

"We arranged for Shane to cover the construction stuff, and Luke's got the marina along with Dad," Janey said. "They were more than happy to help because they've noticed how tense he is, too. Mom and Francine are fully on board, as are Abby, Steph and Grace," Janey said of their sisters-in-law. "Go to the hotel. Have a couple's massage.

Sleep all day. Get breakfast in bed. Relax while we take care of everything here. You need it, Maddie. You both do."

Maddie's eyes filled with tears that made her feel silly, but pregnancy hormones were a bitch that way. "Everyone is stressed this time of year. We're no different."

Janey stared at her, astounded. "You *are* different. You're expecting twins and are on full-time bed rest after having suffered the tragic loss of Connor. None of us is in that boat."

Tears spilled down her cheeks as she swept them away. "It's too much to ask of you all."

"You're not asking," Tiffany said. "We're offering. Blaine and I would move in here with our girls, and the others would help. It's all arranged. All you have to do is agree to it."

"Agree to what?" Mac asked when he came to check on her as he had every ten minutes since she relocated to the sofa. "And what's wrong? Why're you crying?"

He had purple circles under his eyes and a pinched look to him that hadn't been there a few months ago.

Maddie held out her hand to him. "Come see me."

Tiffany relocated to a chair so he could sit with his wife.

Mac took Maddie's hand and sat on the sofa. "What's going on?"

"Ladies." Maddie gave the floor to Janey and Tiffany. This was their big idea to sell to him.

"We want to give you and Maddie a few days alone together," Tiffany said.

Mac shook his head. "Too busy."

"I know," Janey said, "but we've got everything covered here and at work."

Mac glanced at Maddie, who shrugged. "What's this about?"

"You're stressed," Tiffany said. "Both of you. We're worried about you, and we've been talking about you behind your backs. We came up with a plan to give you a break, and we hope you'll take it in the spirit in which it's offered." She stopped short, took a deep breath, covered her mouth and said, "'Scuse me," before running for the bathroom.

Janey picked up the ball for her partner in crime. "As she was saying, we see how tense you both are and thought you could use a break."

"It's very nice of them," Maddie said.

"Yes, it is, but we won't go off-island without the kids."

"I had a feeling you'd say that, so I talked to Mom about a room at the hotel," Janey said. "You're all set for tomorrow through Friday." In-season weekends at the McCarthy's Gansett Island Inn were booked a year in advance, but the weekdays weren't as busy.

Maddie watched Mac as he processed the information. Had he ever looked more tired and drawn than he did now? Not that she'd seen. He tried so hard to keep his turmoil hidden from her, because he always put her ahead of himself. "We gratefully accept," Maddie said before he could come up with a reason to decline their generous offer.

Janey clapped her hands. "Excellent."

Tiffany rejoined them. "What'd I miss?"

"They said yes."

"Well, Maddie said yes," Mac said.

"I can't do it without you." She gestured to the sofa, as if either of them could forget the restrictions she was living under. "And I really want to go."

Mac nodded, as she'd known he would when she said she wanted to go. He went out of his way to do whatever it took to make her happy. In this case, taking care of himself would make her happy.

Janey pulled a folded piece of paper out of her pocket and handed it to Maddie.

"What's this?"

"Check it out."

Maddie unfolded the paper to find a gift certificate for a couple's massage at the hotel's spa. Over the next winter, Mac's company would build an even bigger spa for the hotel in one of the adjacent buildings on the property.

"That's from all of us," Tiffany said. "We want you to relax and enjoy and not worry about a thing."

"Thank you so much, you guys," Maddie said, feeling tearful again.

"Yes, thank you," Mac said, but his face was still pinched, and his eyes were weary.

Hopefully, the time away from their responsibilities would help.

"I mentioned our plan to Kelsey before she left," Janey said, "and she's also on board to help in any way she can."

"All you need to do now is pack and enjoy," Tiffany said.

Maddie smiled at her sister. "I can't wait." Hopefully, Mac would come around in time to enjoy their unexpected break.

MASON DIDN'T SAY anything for such a long time that Jordan worried he thought she was crazy to have asked such a question. Of course nothing had happened for him when he'd been saving her. He'd been doing his damned job.

Then they both spoke at once.

"I'm sorry, I shouldn't—"

"Yes, something happened."

"Oh," she said. "It did?"

He nodded.

Jordan dug deep to find the courage she needed to ask more about it. "Has that, um, happened to you before?"

"Not once ever."

"Oh."

"Yeah."

"So, um…"

"I felt like I was kissing you," he said.

"I felt that, too."

"I thought maybe it was just, you know, a random thing."

She stared at him in the moonlit darkness. "It wasn't? Random, I mean?"

"I'm not sure."

"What do you mean? It was either random or it wasn't."

"There's really only one way to find out."

She thought she knew where he was going with that but wasn't completely sure. "What one way?"

"I could 'save your life' again."

Jordan tipped her head to gauge his meaning.

His gaze became laser-focused on her lips. *Oh.*

"I'm feeling a bit breathless," she said in a teasing tone.

He flashed a dirty grin that did wondrous things for his arresting face. "Are you now?"

"I am. Do you know what to do about it?"

"I have a few ideas. Come with me."

Wait. *What?* "Come with you where?"

"You'll see."

Jordan got out of the SUV and joined him at the front of the vehicle. "Is this the part where you chuck me off a cliff?"

"You have a very fertile imagination. Why would I have bothered to save you last night if I was just going to chuck you off a cliff tonight?"

"How should I know? I have no insight into sociopathic logic."

"Is that a thing? Sociopathic logic?"

"I made it up."

She really liked his smile and the straight white teeth it revealed. "So what's your plan now that you've managed to lure me outside the safety of the car?"

He put his good arm around her and lifted her onto the hood of the SUV.

"Oh." She wasn't sure how she felt about the way he effortlessly put her where he wanted her—with only one working arm, no less. Hello, *weightlifter.* Even with the advantage of the vehicle under her, he still towered over her, but she didn't feel at all intimidated. A shiver of excitement caught her by surprise. When was the last time anything had excited her?

"Last night, something happened that's never happened to me before."

Mesmerized by the intense way he seemed to study her face, she said, "What was that?"

"I can't describe it, but it started when I did this." He touched his lips to hers. "You remember that?"

"I remember," she said, truly breathless now for reasons that had nothing at all to do with asthma.

"All day today, I kept thinking, that couldn't have actually happened." He continued to gently rub his lips against hers. "But it did, didn't it?"

She nodded, eager for more of his sweet kisses.

"I need this freaking arm out of my way for this." He removed the sling and tossed it aside.

"Only for a minute."

As if she hadn't said anything, he got closer to her now that his injured arm was out of the way. "Strangest thing," he whispered as he tipped her chin to improve the angle.

She wound her arms around his neck and buried her fingers in his hair, which drew an urgent-sounding groan from him that made her feel powerful in a way she hadn't before with a man.

His hands slid down over her back, cupping her ass to lift her off the hood of his SUV and into his arms.

Jordan wrapped her legs around his waist and opened her mouth to his tongue, which teased and flirted with hers. Only when she felt her chest tightening from the lack of oxygen did she pull back to draw in a deep breath.

"Sorry," he muttered, his lips pressed now to her neck and sending shivers spiraling through her.

"I'm not sorry."

Against her neck, she felt his lips curve into a smile. "We need to make sure you can breathe."

"I'm breathing just fine. How's your arm?"

"Jordan."

"Yes, Mason?"

"I, uh, I wasn't expecting this."

That drew a laugh from her. "Me either."

"So, um, what should we do about it?"

She moved her hands to frame his face, encouraging him to look at her. When she had his attention, she kissed him, teasing him the way he'd teased her with soft sweeps of his lips that had him leaning in so he wouldn't miss anything.

Mason turned to sit on the hood, keeping her on his lap. "Stop teasing me."

"Why? It's fun."

"I didn't realize you were so mean."

"Now you know."

The low rumble of laughter that came from him thrilled her. She loved making him laugh.

He grasped the back of her head and anchored her lips to his, taking control of the kiss, and holy moly, the man could kiss.

She liked that he didn't grope her or do anything other than kiss her and pull back after a minute to check on her.

"Are you breathing?" he asked, sounding a little breathless himself.

"Not as well as usual."

He studied her face intently, taking a visual inventory. "Are you okay?"

"Yes." She laughed at the concerned expression that had his brow furrowing. "It's you that's making me breathless. Not the asthma."

"Oh, well, that's good."

"Uh-huh."

He nuzzled her neck and held her even closer, if that was possible. "You want to take this somewhere more comfortable?"

She wished she felt ready for that, but she needed a minute to process this unexpected development with the sweet, sexy fire chief who'd saved her life. "I don't think so."

"Oh. Okay."

"I didn't say never. Just not tonight."

"I shouldn't have even asked. You were in the clinic last night."

She kissed the words off his lips. "I'm glad you asked. It's nice to feel wanted."

He pushed the impressive length of his erection against her core, sending a jolt of heat zinging through her. "You're definitely wanted."

They kissed again, the rush of desire leaving her spinning as he made her feel very, *very* wanted.

Jordan began to question her decision to call a halt before things went any further.

He ended the kiss in slow increments and then held her until they both were breathing normally again. "So tomorrow night, then? Yes?"

"Absolutely."

CHAPTER 12

*J*ordan woke early the next morning, and the first thing she did was take a deep breath to check to see if her chest was hurting less than it had the day before. It was much better, but her lips were sore from kissing the face off her sexy rescuer. Smiling, she ran her fingers over her sensitive lips, recalling the wild desire he'd inspired in her. Knowing he wanted her so fiercely had done amazing things to her self-confidence, which had suffered a hard hit lately.

She reached for her phone to call Gigi.

"Oh my God, bitch," Gigi moaned when she accepted the FaceTime call. "It's four thirty in the morning here!"

"Whoops."

"Don't whoops me. You knew that."

"I also knew that you'd take my call no matter what time it was."

"Yeah, yeah. Clearly, I've spoiled your ass."

They'd been best friends since grade school and had been through everything together. Jordan considered herself lucky that Gigi had stuck with her through the Brendan mess, because she, too, had been furious when Jordan went back to him after the video nightmare.

"What's up?"

"Where are we with the divorce?"

"Still on hold. I talked to Davy yesterday about the timeline. He said Z is due to be released from rehab in the next few weeks, and he'll get the papers to him then."

"I want it to happen sooner. Why do we have to wait for him to be done with rehab?"

"Davy said he's doing really well, and the divorce papers might be a setback for him."

"I honestly don't care if it causes a setback for him. I'm done putting his needs before mine. I want a divorce, and I want it now."

"Whoa, what's brought this on?"

A hot, sexy firefighter with the softest lips she'd ever experienced. "You really have to ask me that?"

"No, but why the sudden increased urgency?"

"I'm ready to move on with my life, and I can't do that while I'm still married to him."

"And that's all it is?"

Freaking Gigi knew her as well as Nik did. "There might be a guy."

"Ah-ha! I knew something was up. Do tell, and leave nothing out."

"I thought you were busy sleeping?"

"I was, but I'm awake now, and I want to hear all the dirty details."

"The details aren't that dirty. Yet."

"Oh, this is very interesting. How'd you meet him?"

"By nearly dying."

"What? What the hell, J?"

Jordan told her the story of the fire on the roof, the smoke in the chimney, the asthma attack and Mason's rescue, leaving out the part about the sizzling connection they'd both experienced when he'd saved her life.

"Damn, J. You just scared the living fuck out of me. Are you okay?"

"I am now, but the asthma attack freaked me out a bit. It's been years since I last had one."

"I remember how terrifying they were."

One attack had occurred during a sleepover at Gigi's house. That'd been a bad one that had put Jordan in the hospital for a week.

"Does the doc think the asthma is back?"

"Not necessarily. He said it was almost definitely triggered by the smoke."

"So fucking scary. Are you sure you're okay?"

"I'm sure. Mason saved my life. He said I was barely breathing when he showed up after seeing the flames when he was out riding his mountain bike. And get this, when he saw the flames, he got distracted and crashed his bike. He rescued me with a bleeding head wound and a dislocated elbow."

"Wow. A true hero."

"Yep."

"What's he look like?"

"He's six and a half feet tall."

"Holy cow! He must tower over you."

"He does, and he's a former competitive weightlifter, so he's very fit and muscular. He's got brown hair that's streaked by the sun and warm brown eyes."

"He sounds dreamy."

"He's very handsome and sweet, and he makes me laugh."

"Aw, Jord. This is the best news I've had in years."

"Don't get too excited. I've only seen him a couple of times."

"Maybe so, but it sounds like those times left a big impression—emphasis on big. If he's six and a half feet tall, imagine how big he must be everywhere else."

"Gigi! Stop!"

Gigi snorted with laughter. "Oh, please. Don't act like you haven't thought the same thing."

Jordan didn't mention that she'd been up close and personal with his "bigness" last night.

"After the dickless wonder, you're gonna be getting you some of the good stuff with this one. That's just what you need. A good, thorough f—"

"Shut it," Jordan said, shifting to address the throb between her legs as she imagined where Gigi had been going with that.

"Have you kissed him?"

"Maybe."

"Oh, I'm really loving this. I'm gonna have to come to your quaint little island in the middle of nowhere to check this guy out."

"You know you're welcome to come visit any time you want." Jordan and Nikki had tried to get Gigi to come to the island with them for years when they were growing up, but she'd always said she'd be bored senseless in the middle of nowhere.

"I might have to finally take you up on that."

"We'd love to have you. Gansett would never be the same with you here."

"You know it. I'll get that place rocking."

Jordan laughed at the image of Gigi and her stilettos, fake lashes and fancy everything taking Gansett by storm. The place wouldn't know what hit it. She was as LA as LA got. "Hey, Geeg?"

"What, honey?"

"Get me out of that marriage, will you please?"

"I'll do everything I can."

"Thank you." They chatted for a few more minutes about the negotiations Gigi was handling with the network about the show, as well as other endorsement offers that had come in over the last few weeks.

"Do you think the network is going to let me go?"

"Eventually. They're fighting back because the show is such a big hit for them, but as I said to them, your situation has changed, which would change the format of the show. I told them, you want what you had before, but after everything Jordan has been through, she's not the same person she was."

"And that's entirely true."

"They asked if you'd consider retooling the show to change up the format to better suit your new life."

"They'd have to come to Gansett Island to shoot."

Gigi laughed. "Can you even imagine that?"

"Gansett is beautiful. It would be a great place to set a show."

"Good luck selling them on that. One thing we need to talk about before too much longer is posting something to give your fans news about how you're doing. They're going crazy speculating."

"I'll work on that this week."

"Any more issues with the crazies?" That was the word they'd assigned to Brendan's fans who'd threatened Jordan.

"Nothing recently, but I'm not monitoring the online shit."

"I have been, and it seems to have died down."

"That's a relief."

"It is, but it doesn't mean it's over and done with. You still need to be vigilant, especially since you let the security go."

"I'm safe here. Don't worry."

"Keep that sexy firefighter close. He'll keep you safe."

Jordan felt warm all over as she remembered the way he'd lifted her onto the hood of his SUV and kissed her. The encounter had been one of the sexiest and most thrilling of her life, making her see that more than one thing had been missing in her marriage. As much as she'd loved Brendan, especially before he'd become Zane, he'd never set her on fire the way Mason did. And then she laughed to herself about the sexy firefighter setting her on fire.

"Nothing to say to that?" Gigi asked.

"I'm trying not to get too far ahead of myself on this, but I really like him."

"That's a good place to start."

"It is, but I just wonder..."

"What?"

"Where can it go, Geeg? He lives on Gansett. He's got a job and a life he loves here. My whole life is in LA."

"Not your whole life. Nik is on Gansett, which is your favorite place in the world."

"To visit in the summer. Not to live here all the time."

"How do you know that until you do it?"

"Are you trying to get rid of me?"

"Not even kinda. But it's been a long-ass time since you liked any guy who wasn't what's-his-fuckface. I want to meet this six-and-a-half-foot-tall firefighter of yours and kiss him on the lips for giving you something new to be excited about."

Jordan laughed. "Keep your lips and every other part of your sexy self away from my firefighter."

"And you're already territorial where he's concerned. I love this so much."

"Am I crazy to like this guy, G?"

"No! I say go all in with him. It might be the best thing you could do for yourself."

"But will it be the best thing I could do for him? He's a really nice guy. Part of me wants to protect him from the shitshow that's my life."

"Your life *was* a shitshow. It's not anymore."

"I'd like to think that."

"It's safe to move on, J. I promise. We're going to get you a divorce and figure out something to make the network go away. It's all good. You do you. I got you covered over here."

Jordan released a long deep breath. "Love you."

"Love you, too. Keep me posted on the firefighter. I can't wait to hear how big his di—"

"Gigi! Shut up!"

Gigi died laughing. "You want to know as bad as I do. Later, bitch."

"Later."

Jordan ended the call, laughing at Gigi's outrageousness, which had always been part of her personality. It had only gotten worse over the years, and she was a big reason why the show had been such a hit. The fans freaking loved her and how she had zero filter. Gigi had been almost as important to Jordan as Nikki, who was also friends with Gigi. The three of them had been a squad, as they'd referred to themselves, taking LA by storm. They'd had tons of fun and gotten into more than a bit of trouble together. If Gigi said she had Jordan's back, then her back was well covered.

Her phone chimed with a text from Mason, who'd given her his number last night when he brought her home after the best "ride" she'd ever taken with a guy. *Thinking about you and counting the hours. Is it tonight yet?*

Jordan's heart gave a happy lurch at hearing he was thinking of her. She quickly typed in her reply. *Can it be tonight before tonight?*

Groan. I've got a full day, but I might be able to sneak out early. Will let you know.

She replied with the fingers-crossed emoji. And then added, *Are you wearing the sling?*

Yes, ma'am.

Good. Don't take it off.

How you feeling?

Very, very good today.

That's nice to hear. I'll hit you up in a bit.

I'll be here.

I can't wait to kiss you again.

Same.

UGH, I hate my job!

No, you don't.

Today I DO!

Jordan sent laughing emojis. *Hurry up and get your work done.*

I'm hurrying.

Jordan sighed as she put down the phone. This reminded her of high school and the heady excitement of first crushes, only this was so much better than that had ever been. Mason was a real man, a sexy, thoughtful, sweet, funny man who made her feel things she never had before. Today, she didn't want to think of any of the problems waiting for her back home in LA. She didn't want to think about Brendan or the divorce or anything other than how long she had to wait before she could see Mason again.

Suddenly, he was the only thing that mattered.

MASON WASN'T GOING to survive this day. He'd been hit with one challenge after another since arriving at the station after an AA meeting. One of his newer firefighters had called out sick—again—another had the flu, and a third was showing signs of coming down with the same thing. The mayor had already called twice about his most recent payroll report, which had shown higher-than-normal overtime for this week in June. They'd responded to three calls, and it was only noon.

His plan to get out of there early wasn't going so well. In spite of the chaos, he couldn't stop thinking about Jordan and the time they'd spent together last night or how much he'd loved kissing her.

It was really hard to focus on incident reports and personnel training with thoughts of Jordan and her sweet lips occupying his every thought.

The clock seemed to move in reverse as he participated in a training Dermot ran on responding to alcohol-related incidents and the signs of alcohol poisoning, both of which were nearly daily occurrences during the summer months.

Mason was making progress on an early getaway when they were called to the bluffs to rescue a hiker who'd taken a bad fall. That was another thing that happened several times each year, people getting too close to the edge and having the land beneath them give way. A man had been paralyzed after a similar fall two years ago and others grievously injured in similar incidents.

In this case, the man had fallen about thirty feet and was clinging to a root that was the only thing stopping him from falling an additional hundred feet to the rocky coast below. His hysterical wife or girlfriend had been leaning over the edge of the bluff when they arrived. Pulling her back had been their first order of business.

They could get their equipment only so close to the edge of the land, which made these rescues that much more difficult and risky for his team. As he supervised the delicate operation, he wanted to scream with frustration because he couldn't do a goddamned thing to help except supervise, thanks to his injured arm.

Dermot rappelled down the cliff to assess the man's injuries and to get a line on him so he couldn't fall any farther. "He's got a possible broken right ankle," Dermot reported by radio, "as well as a laceration on the back of his head." Next, he put a cervical collar on the man and got him strapped onto the board that would be used to raise him. All this was a delicate and painstaking process that both Mason and Dermot had done many times before.

When the man was strapped in, Dermot gave the signal to begin winching both men back up the side of the cliff. As the backboard cleared the edge of the bluff, the man's significant other ran over to him.

Mason held her back with his good arm. "It's very important that we don't move him any more than necessary until we can fully access his injuries."

The young woman had a wild look to her tearstained face. "I just need to kiss him. Please."

Mason nodded to Chris, the paramedic who was assessing the victim.

Crying hysterically, the woman kissed her partner, who was also in tears.

They'd had a close call that had been entirely preventable if they'd only adhered to the signs warning people to stay back from the edge.

Mason often wanted to ask them if the selfie had been worth the near disaster, but he bit his tongue so as not to pile on in the midst of a crisis. But he had the thought every time they rescued someone out there.

"What're you thinking?" he asked Chris, who was assessing the patient.

"Not thinking we need the chopper. Let's get him to the clinic and see what Dr. David thinks."

The ambulance left with the man and his partner a few minutes later.

Dermot, who was still wearing the harness he'd donned to rappel down the cliff, approached Mason. "A matter of inches once again."

"We've got to put more pressure on the town to get some sort of fence up out here."

Residents had objected to doing anything that would impair the raw beauty of the rugged coastline, but something was going to have to happen to keep people from falling off on a regular basis. "I'll broach it again with the mayor."

"Good luck with that."

No one was more opposed to the fence than Mayor Upton. "He's not the one out here risking his own neck to save people who are too dumb to heed the warnings."

"I'd hate to think that someone is going to have to die before they act," Dermot said.

Though they'd had many close calls, they hadn't lost anyone at the bluffs. Yet.

"I'm going to approach this another way," Mason said. "We'll get it done. Will you run by the clinic to check on how he's doing and write it up?"

Dermot stepped out of the harness. "Will do."

"Great job, Derm."

"Thanks." The younger man grinned. "A good rappel always gets the blood pumping, especially when we save someone from certain death."

"Makes it worth getting up in the morning, for sure."

"That it does. See you back at the barn."

Mason headed for his SUV, thankful for colleagues like Dermot who were willing to risk their own safety to save others. Being a first responder could be heartbreaking and exhilarating—often both at the same time. Knowing they had made a difference for the couple on the bluffs today made all the long hours and difficult moments worth it for people like Dermot and Mason, who'd become first responders because they wanted to help others.

As he drove toward North Harbor, Mason put through a call to Big Mac McCarthy.

"Hey, Mase. Heard you saved another one out at the bluffs."

"You heard right. Are you at the marina?"

"Yep."

"Mind if I stop by for a minute?"

"Course not. Come on over."

"On my way." He ended the call and hoped he wasn't about to endanger his job by appealing to the president of the Gansett Island Town Council to do something about the increasingly more dangerous situation at the bluffs. Going around the mayor was never a good idea for a department head, but if the suggestion came from

Big Mac rather than Mason, it was more likely to gain traction with Upton.

Playing politics was never his idea of a good time, but then, neither was fetching people who'd fallen off the side of a cliff. The metaphor wasn't lost on Mason, who was clinging to his own cliffside in this situation with Jordan. But even if he was on his way to an awful fall, he couldn't seem to resist the danger she represented.

Danger had never been so much fun.

CHAPTER 13

*H*e was almost to North Harbor when he took a call from Blaine on the Bluetooth. "What's up?"

"Heard you pulled another one back from the brink."

"Yep. As Dermot said, it was a matter of inches. Again. I'm on my way to the marina to talk to Big Mac. Upton isn't going to do anything about it, but maybe if it comes from the council rather than us, that'll make a difference."

"Good call. Let me know how it goes with him."

"I will."

"I wanted to let you know that I got roped into helping out with my niece and nephews while Mac and Maddie take a break. I'll be at their house but available if you need me for the rest of the week."

"Yikes. Five kids."

"And a wife who's puking all day."

"Damn."

"It's for a good cause. Mac and Maddie are super stressed out, and it's really getting to them. Tiffany and Mac's sister Janey hatched a plan to give them a break from it all."

Mason had heard about the baby they'd lost a couple of years ago.

"Good of you guys to do that. I'm around if anything comes up. Take care of your family."

"Thanks, Mase. I'll talk to you later, I'm sure."

"No doubt." They talked multiple times a day in season and covered for each other whenever one of them needed time off or had to be off-island for whatever reason. If there was one thing Mason knew for certain, it was that he wouldn't want to do this job without Blaine Taylor as his partner in all things public safety.

He was fairly confident Blaine felt the same way. He was also thrilled to have added Blaine's brother Deacon to their team when he joined Blaine's department as the summer harbor master. Deacon was a seasoned law enforcement professional who'd brought a wealth of knowledge to the island after having worked for the Boston Police Department. And, not for nothing, the brothers were hilarious together, as they constantly pushed each other's buttons.

Mason pulled into the parking lot at McCarthy's Gansett Island Marina, which was quiet for a weekday in June. By Friday, just about every spot in the marina would be filled with boats and people looking forward to a weekend on Gansett.

With his distinctive mop of gray hair, Big Mac McCarthy was easy to find. At six-four, he was one of the few men Mason encountered on a regular basis who was almost as tall as him. Big Mac spotted him coming and walked toward him from the main dock, where he'd been conversing with a boater. He wore a faded Gansett Island T-shirt with khaki shorts, boat shoes and sunglasses.

He reached out to shake hands with Mason. "Always good to see you, Chief."

"Likewise."

"How's the arm?"

"It's a pain in the ass."

Big Mac laughed. "Worst thing I ever went through was having to keep an arm immobile for weeks on end."

Mason would never forget the day they'd nearly lost Big Mac in an accident at the marina. "I'm hoping it heals quickly, because the sling is a drag."

"Can I buy you a coffee?"

"I won't say no to that." He followed Big Mac into the marina restaurant and stirred cream into the coffee Big Mac poured for both of them. "Doughnut?"

"Don't tempt me. I'm not working out while my arm is screwed up."

"You can have one. Doctor's orders." He brought a plate of the marina's famous sugar doughnuts to a table and sat across from Mason. "What's going on?"

Mason told him the details of the latest rescue at the bluffs.

Big Mac swore under his breath. "What is wrong with people that they get close enough to the edge to fall off?"

"I believe it's directly related to the selfie craze."

"Stupidest thing I ever heard."

"Agreed, but it's happening so often that Blaine and I think the town is looking at a real liability if we don't do something sooner rather than later to limit access. As you know, the mayor is adamantly opposed to putting any kind of fence out there. We were hoping we might call upon you to try to talk some sense into him. It's only a matter of time before someone is killed. The guy today was inches away from certain death."

"Jeez." Big Mac took a big bite of a doughnut and pushed the plate across the table toward Mason, who was powerless to resist when it came to McCarthy's sugar doughnuts.

He took one and bit into the fried deliciousness. "Goddamn, that's good."

Big Mac laughed. "Damn right they are." He wiped the sugar off his lips with a paper napkin. "I get the argument about preserving the natural beauty of the bluffs, but we gotta do something."

"Please, before we lose one of our guys saving some tourist who can't read. Blaine and I have discussed it in depth. If we did some sort of wire fence, you'd hardly notice it."

"That's a good point. I'll bring it up with the council."

"And you'll leave our names out of it?" Mason asked, speaking for himself and Blaine.

"Of course. No worries."

Big Mac certainly knew how Upton could be, and Big Mac could be trusted, which was why Mason had come to him in the first place. "Appreciate it."

"Whatever you guys need. That's my philosophy. Not one of us would want to do your jobs, especially this time of year, so we've got to keep you well supported."

"It does get sporty round about this time every year," Mason said with a grin. "As Dermot said, it keeps the blood pumping."

"I imagine so."

"How's the family?" Mason asked.

"Everyone is great. We're about to have a baby boom the likes of which this family has never seen. My daughters-in-law Maddie, Abby, Grace and Stephanie are all pregnant, as is Maddie's sister. And Maddie's having twin girls."

"That's a lot of babies."

"We can't wait. Linda and I canceled our travel plans for the fall and winter so we can be here for all the excitement."

"Not sure if this island can handle that many new McCarthys all at once."

Big Mac barked out a laugh. "Speaking of getting sporty."

"That's the best kind of sporty, I'd imagine."

"Indeed. We're thrilled to see all the kids so happy with their families. That's all we need to be content."

"Happy for you all."

Big Mac gave him a fatherly look. "Everything good with you?"

"Yeah, it's good."

"Heard you made one hell of a rescue out at Evelyn's place the other night."

"I did. Thankfully, I saw the flames before they could do serious damage."

"Which wouldn't have taken long with the way the wind was howling that night. Did you figure out how it started?"

"Best theory we've got is the sparks came from the neighbor's fire pit."

"What're they doing having a fire on a night like that?"

"Who knows? People don't think."

"Nope, they don't, and then you and your team get to clean up the mess. Thank goodness you were there to get Evelyn's granddaughter out. Jordan, right?"

Mason nodded and popped the last bite of doughnut into his mouth.

"Her sister, Nikki, is doing such a brilliant job for us at the Wayfarer. She's such a sweetheart."

"Jordan is, too." Mason realized his error when Big Mac's eyebrow arched upward.

"That right?"

"Uh-huh. Well, I'd better get back to the station. The paperwork doesn't take care of itself."

Big Mac walked him out and shook Mason's hand. "Thanks for all you do to keep us safe."

"Appreciate your support. Means a lot."

"Any time. You know where to find me—and my doughnuts."

Mason laughed. "Those things are dangerous."

Big Mac patted his still-flat belly. "Best kind of danger, my friend."

"If you say so."

Still smiling, Big Mac waved him off as Mason pulled out of the lot to head back to town. He glanced at the clock and saw it was nearly three thirty. He had another hour, maybe two, before he could escape and get to the best part of his day.

After he'd parked at the spot reserved for the chief at the station, he took a minute to text Jordan. *Trying to get out of here in an hour. Gotta go home, shower and change. I'll let you know when I'm headed your way.*

She replied right away. *Come get me before you go home.*

Will do.

That she wanted to see him as badly as he wanted to see her ramped up the urgency to get done with work so he could be with her. It'd been a very long time since any woman had ever made him feel like he was going to die if he couldn't see her as soon as possible. Only the woman he'd almost married had ever gotten to him this way, which made his growing obsession with Jordan that much more dangerous to a heart he'd patched back together more times than he cared to count.

He'd known her for two days, and he already knew she could crush him. Not to mention her life took place three thousand miles from where he lived and worked. But even being painfully aware of the many ways this could end badly for him, he couldn't stay away from her.

Mason rushed through the paperwork that absolutely had to be done that day, including submitting timesheets for payroll, a summary incident report for the mayor and making final preparations for a water safety training he was running for his team and Blaine's later in the week. He'd been coordinating that with Deacon Taylor, who would be presenting most of the material.

An hour and fifteen minutes later, he walked out of the station without a word to anyone. They knew how to reach him if they needed him. If he told them he was leaving, that would've slowed him down. He got into the SUV and texted Jordan.

On the way.

Hurry up.

Two words had never turned him on more than those did. *I'm hurrying.*

As MAC DROVE himself and Maddie away from their house in his truck, he tried not to worry about leaving the kids behind in the capable hands of their sisters and parents. Whatever came up, they could handle it, and if they couldn't, Mac and Maddie would be five minutes away.

"Are you feeling guilty about this?" Maddie asked as he brought the truck to a stop at one of the three intersections between their house and his parents' hotel.

"Super guilty."

"Glad it's not just me."

"Definitely not."

"It was nice of them to make this happen, though."

"Very nice. I just hope the kids don't make them regret it."

"I'm sure they will," Maddie said, laughing.

"They'll have a great time with their cousins."

"True."

Mac drove up to the hotel's main door a few minutes later. He'd gotten the room key from his mother earlier in the day so he could take Maddie directly to the room when they arrived. "Be right around for you, love."

"You shouldn't be hauling me around. If you throw your back out, where will that leave us?"

"I'm not going to throw my back out."

"And you know that how?"

Mac leaned across the center console and looked her in the eyes. "The day I can't carry my own pregnant wife around is the day I'm ninety-two and feeble."

"I will not still be pregnant when you're ninety-two, because you're getting that thing snipped."

"On behalf of my thing, we're offended, and don't talk about the snipping in front of him. It makes him shrivel up and die."

Maddie laughed, as he'd hoped she would. "He's of no use to us at the moment anyway."

Mac shot her a horrified look. "Speak for yourself."

His lovely wife was crippled with laughter.

Pleased to see her laughing, he got out of the truck and walked around to retrieve her. "Hold on to me, my love."

She curled her arms around his neck and held on as he lifted her out of the truck and into his arms.

One of the young bellmen opened the door for them. "Welcome, Mr. McCarthy. May I help with your luggage?"

"Yes, please," Mac said. "It's in the backseat."

"Very good. I'll bring it right up and take care of parking the truck for you."

"Thank you," Mac said, adding for Maddie, "The keycard is in my shirt pocket if you'd grab it for me."

She fetched it and held it up to the new electronic readers his parents had installed a year ago as part of their efforts to modernize the old hotel. Their room was on the second floor and had a balcony that looked out over the family's marina and the vast Salt Pond.

Mac deposited Maddie gently on the bed and went to open the drapes to let in the view.

"We should ask for a different room," Maddie said.

He turned to her, surprised. "Why?"

"You shouldn't be looking down at work while you're supposed to be relaxing."

"It's no problem. I'll pretend like the marina is someone else's problem while we're here. Besides, if my lovely wife is around to distract me, I won't even notice the place."

"Your extra-pregnant wife can't do much to distract you these days."

After accepting the luggage from the bellman and handing him a ten-dollar bill, Mac shut and locked the door and went to stretch out next to her on the bed. "That is absolutely not true. My lovely wife distracts me by being in the same room as me, by breathing, by looking at me with those eyes that remind me of melted caramel. She distracts me by being such a wonderful mother to our kids—the ones we already have and the two she's taking such good care of while they wait to join the party."

"You're very good at this."

"Good at what?"

"Making your wife feel better about not being able to do much of anything."

"Making my wife feel better about everything is my most important job."

"I miss being able to, you know…" She waggled her brows suggestively.

"Don't say it, or I'll want it. Don't even think it, or I'll want it."

"Don't say what? That I miss sex?"

Mac groaned, immediately interested in something they couldn't have for months yet.

"It's gonna be a really long summer."

"It'll go by fast," Mac said, praying that was true.

"I don't know about you, but ever since David told us we can't, it's all I can think about."

Mac covered his ears. "Don't tell me that either."

She rolled onto her side and studied him with those beautiful eyes that saw right through to the very heart of him. "Have you lost the bet yet?"

"I have not," he said, indignant that she would even ask.

Her brow lifted. "Not even once in the shower when no one was looking?"

Before her, Mac had never found eyebrows to be particularly sexy. Hers were. Everything about her was sexy to him. "Not even once, and I'm appalled that you'd even ask. What about you?"

Her snorting guffaw made him smile. "First of all, I couldn't reach it if I tried—"

"Try." Strangled by the epic surge of desire that crimped his windpipe, Mac pushed himself up on one elbow. "Right now. Let me see you try."

"I don't think that's a good idea."

"It's a fantastic idea. Do it."

"Mac."

"Please? I won't be able to think about anything else until I know whether or not you can."

She released a nervous-sounding laugh that only made him more determined to make this happen.

He slid closer to her, resting his hand on the huge baby bump. She was already as big as she'd been the day she delivered Hailey and Mac. "I've never seen you back down from a challenge. Don't start now."

"I'm not sure I can do *that* in front of you."

Words alone had never turned him on more than those did. "Maddie, sweetheart, if you don't do it, I'm going to *die* from wanting you to."

"Don't talk about dying after you recently had me thinking you were going to."

"Better safe than sorry."

She rolled her eyes. "I've never seen this manipulative side of you before."

"Yes, you have." He moved his hand to her leg, inching the hem of her dress up to her waist. Then he reached for her hand and brought it down to where he wanted it, noting that she could, in fact, reach.

"There. Now you know."

"Don't stop now."

"I have to! I'm not supposed to—"

Mac covered her hand with his and pressed it into the warmth between her legs as he leaned in to kiss her neck.

"We have to stop."

"I know," he said, panting, "but I so don't want to."

"You don't have to." She pulled her hand free of his grip and stroked his hard cock through his shorts. "David said no sex. He didn't say anything about this."

"Doesn't this count as sex?"

"Absolutely not."

"Right. This is like an appetizer. It's the main course he was concerned about."

She dissolved into helpless laughter at his metaphor. "If we could've been having appetizers all this time, why haven't we?"

"Because I was afraid to go near you. I'm really, really *starving* for the main course."

"I'm so sorry, Mac—"

He kissed her before she could finish that thought. "You, my love, have nothing at all to be sorry about. Look at what you're doing. You're growing two little ladies in there. You're a freaking badass goddess. Don't ever apologize for what we can't do while you're making babies."

"Well, since I'm not growing any more babies after this."

"Less talking." He kissed her as he covered her hand with his. "And more of this."

She continued to stroke him. "I like this."

"Me, too. It's gonna take nothing."

"Let me do it."

"Those words might be enough."

Maddie laughed as she pulled at the buttons to his shorts, her hand brushing against the tip of his impossibly hard cock.

For a second, Mac thought that alone would finish him off. Somehow, he managed to hang on until her soft hand was wrapped around his shaft. "*Madeline.*"

She squeezed and stroked. "Yes, Malcolm?"

That was all it took. He came so hard, his heart nearly stopped. "Holy crap." Mac opened his eyes to realize Maddie was laughing uncontrollably. "*What* is so funny?"

Between gasping bursts of laughter, Maddie said, "We suck at abstinence."

"We suck *so hard.*"

"Don't say suck."

"Because it rhymes with fuck?"

She lost it all over again, taking him with her until they were both helpless with laughter. They laughed harder than they had in a long time.

He reached over to wipe away her laughter tears, leaving his hand on her sweet face. "I hate to say my sister was right about something."

"Same. It goes against everything we believe in to confess such things. *However.*"

"They were right. We needed this."

"We need this, and we needed appetizers."

"I'm a *big* fan of appetizers," he said. "In fact, they're my new favorite food, and I can't wait to have more."

"I'm very happy to be able to just kiss you. That's all the appetizer I need for now." Maddie's smile was his favorite thing in the world, especially when it was directed at him. "Why did we ever think we could stay away from each other?"

"We tried. We really did."

"I hate feeling like I need to keep my distance from you. It's the opposite of what I want and need."

"Same, babe. It's torture to stay away from you. I actually think that's been adding to my stress."

"Me, too. So let's not do that. And forget the bet. If you need to take the edge off, I'm your girl."

"Yes, you are. My best girl."

"Remember the day we met when I kept trying to get you to go away?"

He chuckled as he recalled the most important day of his life. "You were very hard on my fragile ego."

"Oh, please. Your ego was and is robustly healthy."

"It took some hard dents that day."

"I just want you to know that I'm really glad you didn't listen to me."

"Even knowing you didn't want me around, I couldn't stay away from you or Thomas."

"I was afraid to want you around. I was so used to taking care of myself and Thomas that the idea of leaning on you, of getting used to having you around and then you leaving."

"You didn't know then that I'd never leave. How could I when everything I want and need is right here in one beautiful package who came with a son I love more than life itself?"

"I just hope you know that despite how I treated you at the beginning, I'm so, so thankful for you and this life and our family and everything we have."

He caressed her face and smoothed his hand over her soft hair. "I'm just as thankful to you. You're the one who makes it all happen."

"We make it happen together."

"Yes, we do." He slid his leg between hers and grasped a handful of soft ass cheek as he placed a series of strategic kisses on her neck. "How about some more kissing appetizers?"

Maddie shivered the way she always did when he kissed her right there. "I'm down with that."

CHAPTER 14

*A*fter Jordan told him to hurry, Mason grinned like the lunatic he'd become since he met her. He drove toward Eastward Look much faster than he should have, but whatever. There were few advantages to giving most of his awake hours to the town of Gansett. Speeding without consequence was definitely one of them. He resisted the temptation to flip on his emergency lights, laughing to himself over the idea of using his lights to get to a woman faster. That was a line he wasn't far enough gone to cross. Yet. It took eight minutes to get to Eastward Look when it probably should've taken fifteen.

He tore into the driveway like a man possessed, and that was probably a fitting description. Because what other explanation could there be for a thirty-five-year-old man who certainly knew better to be losing his mind over a woman?

Jordan came out of the house, her dark hair down around her shoulders, her eyes big with excitement and her smile even bigger as she came toward his vehicle.

Mason kept himself perfectly still as he took in every detail of the frilly top and tight cropped jeans she wore. But it was her stunning face that was the showstopper. He should've gotten out to hold the door for her, but she was in the car before he had the thought, bringing the distinctive scent of expensive fragrance with her.

She grinned at him. "Glad to see you and the sling."

Mason could only stare at her. How was this incredibly beautiful, smart, sexy woman interested in him?

"You okay?" she asked, her brow furrowing.

"I think so."

"You think so? What's wrong?"

"Nothing," he said gruffly. "Not a goddamned thing."

Her smile got even bigger. "Is that right?"

"Uh-huh." Mason's brain had been scrambled by the sight of her, and he had to pull himself out of his dazzled state to put the SUV in Reverse, to drive, to remember where he was going and what his own name was. Shit, this was bad, and getting worse by the second. Ask him if he cared.

"Where're we going?"

He had no fucking clue. "I need to run home to change, and then we can decide what we feel like doing. Okay?"

"Sure."

"I have no idea what condition my house is in."

Jordan's low sexy laugh was like a lightning rod of desire that electrified every cell in Mason's body. Christ have mercy, she would be the very death of him at this rate. "Are you a slob?"

"I wouldn't say I'm a slob, per se, but things get messy when I'm working all the time."

"I'm a slob. Just ask Nikki. It drives her crazy. She's a neat freak. The way I see it, life is too short to be worried about cleaning all the time."

"Agreed, but I don't do dirty."

"In general, or are we still talking about housekeeping?"

Mason released a long deep breath. "You're doing this on purpose, aren't you?"

"Doing what?"

"Being so sexy you make my head spin while pushing my buttons and tossing out suggestive one-liners that make it so I probably shouldn't be driving in my current condition."

"What current condition?"

"I can't discuss it."

"Why not? Is the subject too *hard*?"

The low growl that escaped from his tightly clenched teeth made her laugh hysterically. "You're such a brat."

"So I've been told all my life."

"Why do I suspect you take that as a compliment?"

"How else should I take it?"

"You must've been a holy terror as a kid."

"I kept things interesting."

Mason laughed, delighted by her and thrilled to be with her even as he reminded himself that the last time he'd been delighted by a woman, he'd ended up flattened and heartbroken. That'd been years ago, but he'd never forgotten the way it had felt to be left by the woman he'd loved.

He wanted to think Jordan was different than Kayla had been, but he was smart enough and wise enough to know that he was taking a huge risk by getting so excited about a woman whose life took place on the other side of the country. "Could I ask you something?"

"Sure."

"How long are you here?"

"I don't know."

Mason tightened his grip on the wheel as he tried to figure out what he should say to that.

"Why?"

"I'm just wondering if I'm on a dangerous mission here."

"How do you mean?"

Mason took a right into his driveway and pulled up to the barnlike garage where he was restoring a vintage Mustang in his "spare" time. He hadn't touched the car in weeks. After cutting the engine, he turned in his seat to look at Jordan, who was looking right back at him with big brown eyes that slayed him. "I like you. I like this, whatever it is, we're doing here. I liked last night—a lot. But what I

143

wouldn't like is to let this go on only to be left crushed when you go back to your real life."

Jordan pondered that, appearing to give his concerns serious consideration. "I hear what you're saying, and I'd be the first to tell you that getting involved with me is a risky proposition, especially right now. My life is a bit of a mess at the moment. I'm still technically married to a malignant narcissist and could get sued by my production company unless I continue my show when I really don't want to. So yeah, I hear what you're saying."

She glanced at him, looking madly vulnerable, and held his gaze as she continued. "But the thing of it is, Mason, I really like you—and not just because you saved my life. I like talking to you and pushing your buttons and kissing you. I like how I feel when I'm with you."

"How do you feel when you're with me?" He called himself ten kinds of fool for asking, but he had to know.

"Comfortable. Safe. Entertained. Amused. Aroused."

Mason closed his eyes, took a deep breath and held it for a long moment before releasing it.

"Those are things I hadn't had with my husband in a very long time. Some of them I've never had."

"Which ones?"

"I never felt particularly safe with him, and he stopped being entertaining quite some time ago. I've been uncomfortable around him for years, and it's very difficult to be aroused by someone who makes you nervous about what he's going to do next. I don't mean to compare you to him, because there's no comparison. I'm only saying that this, with you, is more in a few days than I had in years with him."

"Why'd you stay, sweetheart?"

"I told you about how I was raised, shuttled between divorced parents who were fighting over us. I didn't want to be divorced. I hate that word and everything that comes with it. When I married Brendan, I thought it was forever. I really did. He knew how important it was to me that I not end up divorced. But then his career took off, and I couldn't compete with everything that came with it."

"You shouldn't have to compete with anyone or anything. He should've put you first."

"For a while, he did, but we both got swallowed up by the celebrity life. I won't lie to you. It was fun for a while. We liked being Jane, which was the stupid couple name the press gave us. We liked the money and the perks, and I loved the clothes and the photo shoots and the endorsement deals. I take my share of the blame for getting swept up in superficial things and letting the marriage get away from me. I woke up one day and realized I didn't even know him anymore, and I'm sure he felt the same way about me."

"What happened at the end was in no way your fault. Tell me you know that."

"I do. I didn't do anything to deserve a broken arm or a concussion or a split lip that took weeks to heal."

Mason fumed at the thought of her being so badly injured at the hands of the man she'd once loved. "Which arm did he break?"

"This one." She pointed to her right forearm. "I'm told it was a clean break, but it hurt like nothing ever has."

"Did they make you wear a sling?"

The side of her face lifted into a small, sad smile. "No, because it was my forearm, it didn't need to be completely immobilized. It only required a cast that ended before my elbow."

Mason reached across the center console to rest his hand over the place on her right arm that had been broken by her husband. "How'd he do it?"

"He grabbed my arm, and when I tried to get away, the bone snapped."

"I'd snap his neck the same way he snapped your arm if he was here."

She covered the hand of his that was still on her arm, the warmth of her hand permeating the chill that had overtaken him at hearing how her husband had broken her arm. "He's not worth you spending the rest of your life in prison."

"It'd be worth it to know he could never hurt you again."

"He'll never hurt me again, Mason. I won't allow it. I shouldn't have gone back to him after the video."

"If you blame yourself in any way for any of this, that's not going to make me happy."

"You're very sweet when you're pissed off."

"I'm pissed off at him, not you."

"I know that." She glanced at him. "So to answer your original question, I'm kind of a mess and my life is a wreck, but I really like you, and I couldn't wait to see you today."

"I couldn't wait to see you either. I left work hours earlier than I normally would."

"Will you get in trouble?"

"I don't give a flying fuck if I do."

She smiled. "All righty, then."

"You want to come in?"

"Uh-huh."

They hadn't decided anything, but he'd learned more about what she'd been through with the asshole she'd been married to. He hoped that guy never showed his face around here, because Mason wouldn't trust himself not to actually snap the fuckwad's skinny little neck.

After hearing about Jordan's childhood and how it had been splintered by an ugly divorce, Mason already understood the things that would matter to her—loyalty, faithfulness, peace, harmony and unconditional love. How could the man she'd married not have known those things about her?

Is this you keeping things cool and protecting yourself from devastation? The voice inside him, the voice of reason, was pissing him off as he walked with Jordan toward the door to his home. Most people who lived on Gansett didn't bother to lock up their homes, but he did because he interacted with a lot of people at their worst moments. He didn't want one of them seeking him out at home to cause trouble. Blaine felt the same way.

He stepped around Jordan to unlock the door and then ushered her in ahead of him. "Make yourself at home. I'll be right out."

"You need help getting changed?"

"I think I've got it this time, but you can help next time." In truth, he needed a minute to get himself together, because this situation had spun so far out of control so quickly that he could barely keep up. While she wandered to look at the framed photos and books on the shelves that lined the walls on either side of his fireplace, Mason went into his bedroom, closed the door and leaned back against it to collect his thoughts.

She'd all but warned him off by telling him her life was in an uproar. But then she'd told him how she felt around him, and that had been his complete undoing. That she felt safe and comfortable and aroused. Without a doubt, she was the sexiest woman he'd ever met and so far out of his league as to be laughable.

However, he wasn't laughing.

He shed the sling, grimaced as he tried to get his elbow moving and began unbuttoning his uniform shirt. Frustrated when his numb left hand refused to cooperate, he pulled the white shirt up and over his head. He shook his hand to try to get some feeling back in it as he fumbled with his belt, the button to his pants and work boots. By the time he was dressed in a T-shirt and shorts, he was thoroughly annoyed and in pain from the effort it took to do the simplest things. Maybe he should've let Jordan help him.

No, he shouldn't have.

So what's your game plan here, sport?

He had no fucking clue. All he knew was he wanted to be with her and would take whatever he could get. If it turned into yet another in a long line of romantic disasters, he'd deal with it when it happened. There was no way in hell he wasn't going to enjoy every second he had with her while it lasted. The future would have to take care of itself, because he had much more important things to take care of in the present.

Eager to get back to her, he opened the door and emerged into the living room, coming to a dead stop at the sight of her completely naked and reclined on his sofa.

"I thought of something we can do."

.   .   .

FOR A SECOND, Mason thought he might've actually swallowed his tongue as his brain raced to catch up with what was happening. He was so captivated by bare breasts and miles of smooth, tanned skin that he couldn't find any other thoughts in his brain that didn't involve breasts and skin and legs and the come-hither look on her face.

She was the devil.

That thought snuck past the others as he moved toward her like a metal object being pulled by the strongest of magnets.

She held out her arms to him.

Before he accepted the many invitations she was putting out, he whipped the T-shirt over his head and came down on top of her, taking care not to crush her since he was easily twice her size.

"Hey," she said.

"What's up?"

She pressed her pelvis against his erection. "You tell me."

He had things he wanted to say, such as this was happening way too fast, that once they did this, they could never undo it. Not to mention she was still married. However, with her naked in his arms and sexier than any woman had a right to be, he said none of those things. Rather, he followed her lead straight into another of the scorching kisses from last night that had kept him awake for hours afterward imagining what was happening right now.

The feel of her breasts against his chest made him want to whimper and howl, and he was so hard, so fast, he felt light-headed. If someone had told him five minutes ago that he'd have her nipple in his mouth now, Mason would've said they were crazy—or that his overly active imagination was getting ahead of him.

But the only thing that had gotten ahead of him was her, and now he was determined to catch up and make this good for her. "Hang on," he said, pulling back so he could see her face.

"I'm hanging on."

"Tighter." With her arms wrapped around his neck, he hooked his right arm under her and stood, bringing her with him.

"That's very hot, Chief."

"Is it?"

"Uh-huh." She bit down on a tendon in his neck, and the sensation went straight to his dick, which had been on the verge of exploding from the second he saw her naked on his sofa. "Where we going?"

"Somewhere more comfortable." Mason took her into his bedroom, where an extra-long king-size bed would give them room to spread out. He needed the room to make this unforgettable for her, to treat her the way she deserved to be treated. After hearing the way her husband had hurt her, he wanted to give her the kind of pleasure that would make her forget that scumbag had ever existed.

Maybe the other women he'd been with in the past had been the dress rehearsal, preparing him for this, the main event of his lifetime. Leaning on his right elbow, he reached out with his left hand to smooth a strand of hair off her face. For the longest time, he only looked at her, feasting his eyes on every beautiful inch of her. His hand moved from her face to her chest to caress full breasts and a flat belly.

"Wait, the sling, your arm…"

"Shhh, my arm is fine."

"Mason."

He kissed her, hoping to make her forget about his arm. No question, he needed both hands for this. The kiss quickly became desperate and needy as they both strained for more. "Easy, baby. Nice and easy." He kissed the graceful length of her neck, using his tongue on the tender hollow at the base of her throat before moving down to kiss along her collarbone and down the inside of her arm, causing goose bumps to erupt on the surface of her skin and her nipples to tighten.

"Are you doing this on purpose?"

"Doing what?" He inhaled the scent of her soft skin and kissed the small bump that marked the spot in her right forearm where the break had occurred.

"Making me crazy."

"Yes, I'm doing that on purpose."

She huffed out a laugh. "That's mean."

"No, it's not."

"Yes, it is."

"Shhh, relax. Close your eyes and just breathe."

"I can't breathe when you're doing that."

"Try." He cupped her breasts and dragged his thumbs over her tight nipples. "Let me see you breathe."

Jordan's body trembled as she took a shuddering deep breath and expelled it.

"Do it again."

After giving him a withering look, she took another deep breath.

"No asthma attacks allowed here, so keep breathing. I only want you breathless for all the best reasons." He continued to caress her nipples with his thumbs, making her squirm beneath him as he discovered what made her gasp and moan and dig her sharp little nails into his back. Bending his head, he drew her nipple into his mouth and spent long minutes licking, sucking and dabbing with his tongue while she writhed beneath him. Only the press of his hips against hers kept her anchored to the bed.

Then he switched sides and started all over.

Jordan cried out and nearly ripped the hair from his head with her enthusiasm. "Mason."

"What, honey?"

"You're torturing me."

"No, I'm not."

"Yes, you are."

He curled his right arm under her leg and lifted it to his shoulder. "Is this what you want?" he asked as he buried his tongue inside her sweetness. Lord but she was sweet and wet. His cock was so hard, it hurt, but he kept his focus on her. It was all about her.

"*Please.*"

The desperate tone of her voice thrilled him. That he could make a woman like her desperate was far more satisfying than sex with other women had ever been. "You need something, sweetheart?"

She uttered an inarticulate sound that was full of air. At least she was breathing.

Mason focused his attention on the tight knot of her clit, sucking it into his mouth as he drove two fingers into her. The combination had her coming with a scream that nearly took him right off the cliff with her—and nearly gave him a bald spot from the way she fisted handfuls of his hair.

As she panted in the aftermath, he got up to find a condom, dropped his shorts and rolled it on.

He leaned over her and pressed a kiss to her belly, making her jolt.

She opened her eyes to find him watching her, waiting for her to catch up to him, which was how he saw her eyes widen when she zeroed in on his erection. "That isn't going to fit."

CHAPTER 15

$\mathcal{M}$ason laughed as he kissed his way up to her breasts, giving them each more attention. "Yes, it will. How about I show you?"

"I, uh. I don't know. I figured you'd be big all over, but that thing is rather intimidating."

Mason shook with silent laughter. "He's offended to be called a 'thing.'"

"If you were me, what would you call it?"

"I'll let you come up with a better name after he's shown you what he's capable of."

"Okay, big man, do your worst."

"I'd much rather give you my very best." Mason hovered over her, trying to ignore the fierce pain coming from his left elbow as he framed her face with his hands and kissed her sweet lips, drawing out the suspense with more kisses while she raised her hips, looking for something he wasn't quite ready to give her. "You're awfully eager for someone who's so intimidated."

"That's your fault."

"Sweetheart," he said, laughing, "this is all *your* fault. Who's the one who went and got naked while I was off minding my own business?"

She raised a brow. "Are you complaining?"

"Not even kinda."

"Didn't think so. So are you going to talk all day, or are you going to show me what you're made of?"

The challenging tone made him even harder, not that she needed to know that.

She closed her eyes and made a snoring sound. "I'm growing old over here."

Mason pushed into her, and her eyes flew open, her expression conveying a hint of panic that made him slow down to let her catch up. "You were saying?"

"*Uh.*"

"What was that?" He gave another gentle push and met with tight resistance that made him see stars from the effort to hold back, to make this amazing for her. "Relax, love. Just relax and let me in."

"Trying," she said through gritted teeth.

Mason used his left hand to roll her clit between his fingers as he dipped his head for another taste of sweet nipple as he slid in deeper.

"That's all, right?" she asked on a gasp.

"That's half."

"Fucking hell, you've got to be kidding me."

Mason again rocked with laughter at the deer-in-headlights look on her face. "You're not going to wimp out on me, are you?"

She made an inarticulate sound that had him smiling as he continued to caress her clit and tug on her nipple, rocking against her repeatedly until he felt the telltale signs of impending orgasm. As she cried out, he sank the rest of the way into her as her muscles clamped down on his cock. If he'd ever felt anything better in his life than being inside her when she came, Mason would be hard-pressed to recall it.

Speaking of hard-pressed… As she came down from the high to find him still hard and still inside her, she looked up at him with a madly vulnerable look on her stunning face that touched him in places that had nothing to do with what was happening below. His heart ached and his muscles trembled from the effort it took to be gentle with her, to treat her with the reverence she deserved.

"You didn't…"

Mason shook his head.

"Fucking hell. You're going to break me."

"No, I'm not. Hold on to me."

She placed her hands on his shoulders.

"Put your knees up by my hips."

"Why?"

"Just do it."

She gave him what he wanted, opening herself for part two.

Mason's cell phone rang. He ignored it. The fucking house could be on fire for all he cared. Nothing, not even the biggest emergency Gansett Island had ever seen, could make him stop what he was doing to take that call.

"M-Mason, your phone."

"Ignore it. Look at me." He waited until her gaze collided with his. "Keep looking at me."

"Wh… what're you. *Oh.* Oh my *God.*"

He'd pulled almost completely out of her before plunging back in. He did that several times as she blinked and tried to keep her gaze fixed on his while he gave her his very best—over and over and over again until she was screaming and clawing his back and coming even harder than she had the first time.

He let himself go with her this time, the orgasm seeming to come from his very soul as he hammered into her, clutching her sweet ass with both hands as he came for what felt like an hour. *Holy shit.*

She'd just ruined him for any woman who wasn't her.

WAS that drool running down her chin? Jordan thought it might be, but she couldn't seem to get her hand to move to find out or to work up the wherewithal to care if she was drooling. With him still lodged deep inside her as she continued to have one small orgasm after another, she had far *bigger* things to contend with than a little bit of drool.

What the actual hell had just happened here?

He'd completely *owned* her and made her come *three* times. Her mind was racing to catch up to recent events and to process the fact that she had never in her life had sex that could compare to sex with Mason Johns.

Dear God. She'd be lucky to ever again walk normally after what'd taken place in his bed.

"Am I crushing you?" he asked.

Jordan tightened her arms around him. "No." She was almost afraid to let him go and to find out if the exit would be every bit the struggle the entry had been.

Mason's phone rang again. "Fuck. I have to get that."

Jordan let him go and tried to prepare for his withdrawal, but she couldn't help the sounds that came from her as her sensitive flesh reacted to him as if she hadn't just had *three* earth-shattering orgasms.

"Are you okay?" he asked, his brows knitted with concern.

"I don't know what I am."

Smiling, he wiped up the drool—yes, it was drool—from her mouth and chin and then kissed her gently. "Hold that thought for a second." When he got up to find his phone, she got an up-close look at the back of him, which was every bit as muscular as the front, including the tight butt cheeks that flexed when he bent to retrieve his shorts from the floor. "Johns."

He stood to his full, formidable height and walked into the bathroom as he listened to whatever the caller was saying. "I can't do that today," he said. "I don't care if Jesus himself is asking, that can't happen today. I'm off duty and away from the office. Tell him I'll get to it first thing in the morning, and don't let him give you any crap." He listened some more. "Thanks, Mona." After ending the call with a softly spoken, "Fuck," Mason closed the bathroom door and then flushed the toilet a minute later.

The whole time, Jordan stayed perfectly still in his bed, afraid to so much as move out of fear that she might very well be broken after taking on the biggest cock she'd ever seen.

He came out of the bathroom, giving her a bird's-eye view of the front of him, and returned to the bed, snuggling up to her with his injured arm stretched out across her middle.

For the first time, Jordan saw the dark purple bruises that surrounded his elbow. She ran her fingers lightly over the bruises. "Is everything all right?"

"Yeah. The mayor wanted some numbers that he can't have today."

"It's almost five thirty."

Mason grunted out a laugh. "Blaine and I think he doesn't own a watch or a clock or phone or anything that would tell him the actual time. He calls us at all hours and expects us to jump."

"Will you get in trouble for not getting him what he wants tonight?"

"I couldn't care less if I do. I'm off duty and have much better things to do tonight than think about him."

"Like what?"

His smile unfolded slowly across his handsome face. "Like proving that you're a stud."

"I think it's safe to say *you're* the one who's the stud."

"Nah, you're the badass who took it all and then some."

"And I may never walk again as a result."

"Are you hurt?"

She placed her hand on his face, smoothing her thumb over the frown line that replaced the smile she much preferred. "I'm fine. Just a little shell-shocked."

"How so?"

"Three times? That's never happened."

"No?"

"Nope."

He flashed the smug smile of a man who'd pleased his woman— repeatedly. Not that she was *his woman*, per se, but he'd sure as hell pleased her. *Three times!*

"Want to go for four?"

"Not yet, but thanks for asking."

"No problem. I'm available for stud services on a moment's notice."

Jordan laughed. "Good to know."

He flattened his big hand on her abdomen, reminding her once again—as if she needed the reminder—how big he was. "Just for the record, finding you naked on my sofa?"

She glanced at him. "What about it?"

"Sexiest fucking thing I've ever seen in my entire life."

"Was it?"

"Hell yes, it was. I think I'll probably recall every detail of how you looked on my sofa in the last seconds before I punch out of this life. And I'll never, ever look at that sofa the same way again."

"Want to hear a secret?"

"I want to hear all your secrets."

"I was freaking out waiting for you, hoping I hadn't misjudged you or this."

"If you were freaking out, you did a hell of a job hiding it. To me, you looked as cool as a cucumber, all naked and hot. Like a freaking goddess who'd been put there just for me."

"You're good for a girl's fragile ego."

"There's absolutely no reason whatsoever for your ego to be fragile. I know you went through hell with him, but he was the problem. Not you."

"How do you know that? For all you know, I was a screaming shrew of a wife."

He shook his head. "No, you weren't. That's not how you roll. When you get pissed, you probably go silent. You don't start screaming."

Stunned, she said, "How do you know that?"

"If I had to guess, you probably grew up with a lot of yelling, which means you'd gravitate to the opposite reaction when the shit hits the fan in your own life."

She stared at him, unnerved by his insight.

"Am I right?"

"Yeah, you are. I hate screaming and fighting, and believe it or not,

I hate drama for the sake of drama. That might seem funny to you after watching me and Gigi manufacture drama for the show, but that was all fake nonsense. In my real life, drama makes me sick. My stomach actually hurts when it happens."

"Has it always been that way?"

She nodded. "I had a teacher in first grade who was a screamer. I had stomachaches that whole year, and around the time my parents split, they got so bad, my mom took me to the hospital for it once. They couldn't find anything wrong."

He gave a gentle tug to bring her into his embrace. "That's because everything was wrong."

"It was, and it stayed that way for a very long time."

"How old were you when they split?"

"Eight."

"And they fought over you until the day before you turned eighteen." He shook his head in disbelief.

"Yep. My mom had mental health and substance abuse issues that she tried so hard to overcome. He never gave her a single break. When we were here in the summer, our grandmother had custody of us, not our mom. He's the one who had an affair, had children with someone else, and she's the one who was made to suffer while he had custody of us."

"You suffered, too. You had to live with him when you couldn't stand him."

"It was really nothing compared to what he put her through. He treated her like she was a junkie living on the street, when that was never the case. She went through hell due to her illnesses and battled her demons for years before she finally got clean and was put on the right meds."

"But that was too late for you and Nikki."

"We were happy that it happened when it did. It was hard to watch her struggle."

"You're due for a break, sweetheart."

"How'd you get me to talk about this shit, anyway? I never talk about this stuff." And certainly not with a guy she'd just met. This was supposed to be about fun and transitions and moving on, but in the scope of the last hour, it'd become so much more than that. The realization left her feeling unnerved. "I should probably go."

"Why? You got somewhere to be?"

"No, but…"

"What?"

"I… I don't know."

"I want you to stay. Unless you don't want to."

"I do want to."

"Why do I hear a very loud 'but' in there?"

"I feel like I need to keep telling you that my life is a mess, Mason, and you're a really, really nice guy. I'm afraid."

With his fingers on her face, he gently turned her to look at him. "Of what?"

"I don't want to hurt you."

"While I appreciate that more than you could ever know, I've got my eyes open here. I know things are in transition for you right now in more ways than one. All I can tell you is being with you is the most fun I've had in years."

"Same," she said, thrilled to know he felt the same way she did.

"And what just happened here?" He gestured to them and the bed. "Hands down, no contest, best I've ever had."

"Also same." Not that she had much to compare him to, but he was better at everything than Brendan had been.

"So it sounds like we're on the same page here." He tipped her chin up for another of the soft, sweet kisses that made her heart race and her blood boil. "Lots of fun, no worries."

After spending most of her life in some sort of an uproar, his plan sounded absolutely perfect to her.

"JORDAN ISN'T COMING HOME TONIGHT," Nikki said to Riley as he got into bed. "She's staying at Mason's."

"That's an interesting development."

"I guess."

"You don't like that she's hanging with him?" Riley asked.

"It's not about him. By all accounts, he's a great guy, and he'll have my gratitude forever for saving her. It's just that she's in such a weird place right now, and I worry about her."

Riley took her phone from her, placed it on the bedside charger and then wrapped his arm around her.

Nikki snuggled up to him, as she did every night. She couldn't recall what it'd been like to sleep without him.

"I know you're preconditioned to worry about her, and I get that she's given you ample reason to, but maybe this thing with Mason is just what she needs to reset, you know?"

"Maybe. I just worry about her getting hurt again."

"He's not going to hurt her, babe. He's not that kind of dude."

"Every dude is that kind of dude," Nikki said with a laugh. "He may not set out to hurt her, but don't pretend it's not possible that he could."

"Not every dude is that kind of dude."

Nikki heard the hurt in his softly spoken words. "Every dude but you, I should say."

"You're preconditioned to expect the worst, and I get why, but I wish there was some way to convince you that not everything will end badly. Some things," he said, kissing her, "are meant to last forever."

She felt terrible for speaking without thinking about how her words would be taken by him. "I'm sorry, Ri. You have to know I have no doubts whatsoever about you."

"I hope you don't. I'm all in with you. Forever won't be long enough."

Nikki blinked back the tears his sweet words brought to her eyes. "No, it won't be long enough. I know you're all in, and so am I. I wasn't talking about you. I swear I don't worry about any of that with you."

"I really hope not."

"I don't. But I do worry about Jordan. She's been through so much. I want to see her find what makes her happy the way I have. I want that more than anything."

"She will. She just needs to figure it out for herself the same way you did and I did and everyone else does. I know it's hard for you to see her struggling the way she has lately."

"It's not just lately. It's always. Starting when we were kids with the asthma and everything with our parents and then *him*. It's been a lot."

"Yes, it has, but maybe all that was meant to happen so that when the right thing came along, she'd know it."

"I suppose." She looked over at him. "Do you think Mason could be the one for her?"

"Stranger things have happened. Take you and me, for instance."

"Nothing strange about that."

"You don't think so? Hmm, well, from my perspective, a goddess moved to Gansett from LA and found this schlep who was fixing her leaky roof."

Nikki laughed and then turned on her side so she could kiss the words right off his lips. "Don't call my sexy, wonderful, amazing fiancé a schlep."

"Compared to you, babe, he's a schlep."

"No, he isn't."

"Yes, he is."

Nikki appreciated the way he'd managed to get her mind off her worries about Jordan, but they remained in the background as she began to doze off, steeped in the warmth and security of Riley's embrace. What had she ever done without him? The difficult months they'd spent apart after they first met seemed like a distant memory now that they lived together and spent every night together. "Thanks, Ri."

"What for?"

She grasped his hand, which was resting on her abdomen. "All of it. Everything. You make me so happy and have given me things I didn't even know I needed."

"Same goes, babe. I used to think my cousins were crazy for settling down with one woman, but now I get it. When it's the right one, the only thing you want is to be settled with her."

"Who is she, and how can I have her killed?"

Riley's laughter rumbled through his chest. "There's only one woman for me, and you know her very, very well, as do I. Which is how I know you suffer when Jordan suffers. But I have a good feeling about her and Mason. They could be great for each other for however long it lasts."

"I suppose so. As long as no one gets hurt." Jordan couldn't handle another big disappointment, and neither could Nikki. Because Riley was right—when Jordan hurt, Nikki did, too.

CHAPTER 16

*J*ordan had no idea where she was when she awoke in the dark with a heavy arm around her. As the events from earlier came rushing back to remind her of the best sex she'd ever had, she shifted her position and winced from the bite of soreness between her legs. The man was formidable in more than one way. Smiling, she thought about how sweet and tender he'd been with her even as he'd rocked her world right off its axis. How was it possible that a man she'd only just met seemed to "get" her in a way the man she'd been married to never had?

Unlike Brendan, who'd always been far more self-absorbed than he should've been, Mason didn't have a self-absorbed cell in his body. He was constantly tending to others, and when they were together, he seemed to actually *see* her rather than look through her the way Brendan had, even before he'd gotten crazy-famous. It was always as if he was looking for something better, something *more*, and it had driven her crazy that she felt like she was constantly trying to keep his attention on her.

She'd noticed the way Mason stayed focused on her that first night in the clinic. Even as others came and went, he never became distracted the way Brendan would have. Even after her husband had begged and pleaded with her to forgive him after the video debacle and promised her things would be different, it had been more of the same when she joined him on tour.

They rarely had a minute to themselves, and when they did, he didn't want to talk about their relationship or how they were going to get back on track. He was more than happy to have sex, but there was no sense of connection or true intimacy. It felt transactional, like something he was doing because he felt he had to or because he needed the physical release, not because he wanted to show her how much he loved her.

Truth be told, Jordan didn't think he'd actually loved her in quite some time. How could he when he was so consumed with love for himself and his music and his band and his groupies? Where was there anything left in that maelstrom for his wife? Then add his addiction issues to the mix, and you had a recipe for certain disaster.

Mason stirred, his arm tightening around her, bringing her in closer to him and making her feel safe with his big body curved around hers.

True confession—he was the second guy she'd ever slept with, and now she knew her husband had failed her in bed, too. She was lucky if she had an orgasm every fourth or fifth time with him, and usually it happened when she helped herself along. Because she'd never been with anyone else, she'd assumed the failing was hers. Now she knew better. It wasn't her at all.

"You okay over there?" Mason asked, his voice gruff from napping.

"I'm very okay."

"Very okay is good. You hungry?" The room had gone dark while they snoozed.

"I could probably eat something. What time is it?"

He raised his arm to check the digital display on the watch he wore to work. "After eight."

Jordan ran her hand over his arm. "Is it hurting?"

"Just aches a little. It's fine. Much better than it was." His hand slid from her abdomen to cup her breast. "What about you? Anything hurting?" He ran his thumb over her nipple and just that quickly had her straining against him.

"Not hurting so much as a bit sore."

"Sorry about that."

"Don't be. It was well worth it."

"Glad you think so. What do you feel like eating?"

"Doesn't matter to me. What do you want?"

"I'd go into town to pick something up, but I might get dragged into something for work if I show my face there."

"Let's order takeout."

"Mario's will deliver to me if I ask, but we've already done that."

"I love their big house salad, so that works for me if it does for you."

"Good for me, too." He kissed the back of her shoulder and got up to call in the order.

Jordan was disappointed when she noticed he'd pulled on boxer briefs before going to find his phone. She'd hoped for another look at his well-honed body. The deep rumble of his voice from the living room drifted into the bedroom as she relaxed into the pillow and tried not to overthink what was happening here.

She'd had a nice time—and amazing sex—with a great guy. It was tempting to read more into it than that, but doing so would be a mistake. Especially right now, with so many aspects of her life so uncertain. Besides, Mason had a good life that satisfied him on Gansett. Jordan was fairly certain she'd go mad living on the island full time. Gansett was a great place to visit in the summer, but to live there? No way, and she'd said as much to Nikki when she decided to stay.

Of course, Nik had Riley and his extended family to keep her entertained, so it made more sense for Nik to stay. It would make no sense for Jordan to stay. What would she *do* here besides go stir crazy? Although, after the last five years of absolute madness, the slower pace of Gansett wasn't without its appeal. For a little while, anyway.

Jordan shifted onto her back, wincing at the ache between her legs while wondering how long it would take her body to become accustomed to a guy of Mason's size. It would be fun to find out.

Mason came back into the bedroom and stretched out on the bed next to her. "Forty minutes."

"Let me pay this time. My purse is on the chair."

"Too late. I already paid. You can get it next time."

His use of the words *next time* gave her heart a happy lift that was contrary to the talking-to she'd just had with herself. It wouldn't be wise to let something like this become anything more than lighthearted fun, and she realized she needed to say as much to him. "Mason."

"Yes, Jordan?" He'd taken her hand and pressed her palm against his, reminding her once again that his was easily twice the size of hers.

"I just wanted to say…" She'd never done this before, never had to tell a guy not to get overly invested in her because it wouldn't be a good idea for him.

He turned on his side to face her, keeping his grip on her hand. "What's wrong?"

"Nothing is wrong. Tonight has been amazing."

"For me, too. I'll never forget it."

His sweet words made her smile. "I won't either. It's just that being with you is so much fun, but it really can't be anything more than that." She swallowed hard, suddenly feeling emotional for reasons she couldn't begin to fathom. "I'm not able to promise you anything right now."

"I get it, honey. Don't worry. I know the deal."

"I'll understand if you want to stop this before it goes any further."

"Is that what you want?"

"No, it's not, but I want to be fair to you. I'm technically still married, and I have no idea how long it will be until I'm not, among other things."

"What other things?"

"I'm still trying to get out of the contract for another season of the show, and if that doesn't happen, I'll have to go back to LA for a few months. Gigi is trying to get them to see that I'm in no condition to be stalked by cameras, but I'm also in no condition to be starting a new relationship."

"I hear you."

"I don't want to hurt you, Mason, or get hurt myself by getting attached to you and then having to leave."

"We won't let that happen. We'll hang out, have fun and maybe some more of this." He leaned over to kiss her. "And some more of this, too." Pushing the sheet down, he ran his tongue over her nipple.

Jordan buried her fingers in his hair, amazed by how quickly he'd woken up her entire body and put her on full alert. She'd said what needed to be said, told him the whole truth of her situation, and he'd heard her. Now there was nothing left to do but enjoy whatever time they got to spend together.

MASON WAS QUITE certain he was going to wake up any second to discover that he'd dreamt this whole thing, because surely there was no way Jordan Stokes was naked in his bed or pulling his hair as he licked her nipple or squirming under him, letting him know he was turning her on. God, she was sexy and sweet and utterly adorable.

Regardless of what he'd said to her before, he did have his hopes up where she was concerned. He didn't care that she lived in LA or that she was still married or that her life was in an uproar. How could he care about any of that when he felt such a genuine connection to her? Maybe it was ridiculous to feel that way so soon. Hell, he knew it was ridiculous, but damned if he could push the train backward now that it had left the station.

It had started with the odd reaction he'd felt while getting her breathing again and had continued with every subsequent encounter. The only analogy he could come up with was being with her felt the same way touching a live wire would—shocking, disruptive, attention-getting, life-threatening. She could turn his whole world upside down if he let her, and even knowing that, he couldn't stop himself from gorging on her while he could.

This would end badly. He had no doubt about that, and it would be even worse than it had been when Kayla broke up with him four weeks before their wedding. He'd loved her. He honestly had, but in three years together, he'd never felt the connection to her that he'd immediately experienced with Jordan. As he tended to the other breast and kissed his way to her belly, he acknowledged that he'd had the same feeling of connection every time he'd seen her.

"How's the soreness?" he asked, glancing at Jordan, who watched him with big brown eyes framed with extravagant lashes.

"Not so bad."

"Maybe I should kiss it better."

Raising her knees and spreading her legs, she said, "That might help."

She drove him wild with her blatant sexuality. It'd been a very long time since anything had truly surprised him the way she had earlier when he'd found her naked on his sofa.

Even as he acknowledged that this might be nothing more than fun and games to her, he already knew it was more than that for him. She was more than that. She was the kind of woman who could change a man's life and make him thankful for the earthquake she caused because he got her from it.

He propped her legs on his shoulders and set out to destroy her with his tongue and fingers and gentle suction on the tight nub of nerves. Perhaps if he ruined her for all other men, she wouldn't ruin him by leaving. Though he knew it was absolutely preposterous to hope for such things with a woman like her, he couldn't help but wish that there was something he could say or do to make her want to stick around to see what this might become.

Taking care to be gentle, he pushed a finger into her as he swirled his tongue over her clit.

Her hips jolted as she pulled harder on his hair.

He kept up the sensual torture until she was coming with a loud cry of completion that made him feel ten feet tall because he'd done that to her. Mason wanted so badly to follow up her pleasure with more of his own, but she was sore from the first time, so that would have to wait.

He rested his forehead on her abdomen, needing a second to get himself together.

"Mason."

"Yeah?"

"Come here." Her voice was throaty and sexy from screaming her way through the orgasm, and those two words from her made him even harder, if that was possible.

He moved so his head was next to hers on the pillow. "I'm here."

She turned on her side and kissed him as she wrapped her hand around his erection. "I can't get my hand all the way around it."

Hearing those words in her sexy voice made him crazy. He cupped her ass, his fingers digging into taut flesh as he tried not to blow his load all over her.

She gave his shoulder a gentle push. "Lie on your back."

God was she... Oh *fuck*, she was. "Jordan."

"Shhh, it's your turn." She fitted her lips around the crown and gave a gentle suck.

Mason bit back a pathetic-sounding whimper as he tried to think of the least-sexy things he could come up with. Only an image of Mayor Upton came to him, and that was enough to beat back the rush of desperation, for the moment, anyway.

She took him into her mouth, her lips stretching to accommodate him as she sank down on his shaft while her fingers cupped his balls.

Holy shit. "Jordan. *Sweetheart.*"

"Mmmm."

The vibration of her lips against his shaft was his undoing. Before he had even a second to warn her, he was coming as hard as he had earlier. If it was possible to see stars, he saw an entire fireworks show in the span of a few seconds. "Sorry about that."

"About what?" She used her tongue to mop up the mess he'd made and looked at him with those big doe eyes.

"I didn't give you any warning."

"I knew what was coming." She gave him a madly vulnerable look that tugged at every emotion he'd ever experienced. "It was okay?"

Mason huffed out a laugh. "You couldn't tell?"

"Just making sure."

"Everything about you is far more than okay, babe."

"That's nice to hear."

"It infuriates me that anyone would ever make you think otherwise." He let a strand of her hair slide through his fingers. "You have to know you're amazing and beautiful and sexy and funny and ballsy."

"Thank you, but I haven't felt very ballsy lately."

"Seriously? That move on the sofa earlier? *All* the balls."

Jordan giggled. "I was freaking out on the inside. I've never done anything even remotely like that before."

Mason loved that she was an intriguing mix of worldliness and innocence, that she often touched both ends of the spectrum in a single second. "You should do it all the time, but only for me." He no sooner said that than he realized he'd just crossed the line that she'd put in the sand earlier by asking him not to get overly involved. Before he could take it back or tone it down, his phone rang. "Hold that thought." He got up to retrieve the phone he'd left in the other room. "Johns."

"Hey," Dermot said, "wanted to give you a heads-up that we've got some overdue boaters. Deacon and Linc Mercer's Coast Guard team are out looking for them, but they're about to call it off until the morning."

"Anyone we know?"

"Haven't gotten names yet, but I'll text you when I know more."

"Let me know if you need me to come in."

"I think we're okay for now."

"Thanks for letting me know." Mason put down the phone and went to turn the light on for the delivery from Mario's that should be arriving any minute. He ran his fingers through his hair and thought about the revealing statement he'd made to Jordan, how he wanted her to get naked only for him.

Why did the thought of her baring that exquisite body for anyone but him already make him furious? This was what he did—dove in headfirst without knowing if there was water in the pool, and when he hit the bottom—hard—he usually had only himself to blame for being stupid in the first place.

More than at any other time in the past, this woman had the power to absolutely ruin him. There was no water in this pool, and he knew that before he dove in. He had to control the crash before he inflicted damage on himself that could never be undone. The only problem with that plan was that with her in his arms and in his bed, he was powerless to dial it back even when he knew he absolutely had to.

He didn't want to. He wanted to take the dive, regardless of how painful the crash would be in the end.

Jordan came up behind him and slipped her arms around his waist as she rested her head on his back. "What's going on?"

Mason placed his hands on top of hers and told her the truth as it stood right then and there. "We've got some boaters overdue."

"Do you need to go to work?"

"Not at the moment."

"So everything is all right?"

He gave her truth as he saw it right then and there. "Everything is just fine."

CHAPTER 17

*I*n the morning, as he drove Jordan home, Mason got a text from Dermot letting him know that the "missing" boaters had ended up in Martha's Vineyard without letting anyone know their plans and were safe.

"Does that happen a lot?" Jordan asked him after reading the text to him.

"More often than you'd expect. People don't think. They take off on boats, let cell phones go dead and get sidetracked while loved ones are frantically looking for them."

"Not to mention the first responders who have to risk their lives searching."

"Not to mention. I also got a text this morning that the guy in the car accident had a heart attack, but they got him back. He's in critical condition, but they expect him to recover."

"That's good news."

"Yes, it is. He got lucky." Mason reached for her hand. "Last night was awesome. I had the best time."

"Me, too. Thanks for having me over to visit."

"My pleasure," he said with a dirty grin. "Can you come out to play again tonight?"

"Let me check my busy schedule." She paused, tapped her chin and said, "Looks like I can."

"Excellent. I'll pick you up after work."

"Or I could borrow my sister's car, hit the grocery store, go to your place and make you dinner while you're working."

"Yes, please."

"You're sure that's okay?"

"I'm absolutely positive that's more than okay. There's a key under the flower pot on the porch."

"I promise I won't snoop."

"Snoop away. I have no secrets." He took the turn into the Eastward Look driveway. "Sorry to have to stop, drop and roll, but the boss can't be late, or he takes a ton of abuse from the troops."

"No worries. I'll see you later?"

"Yes, you will. I'll text you when I have an idea of what time I'll be free."

"Have a good day, dear."

Mason leaned across the console to kiss her. "You, too."

Jordan got out and waved him off before heading inside. Even though she'd been coming to this house all her life and thought of it as home, she still felt weird walking into what had become Nikki and Riley's home. "Put your clothes on," she called out. "The buzzkill is home."

In a scene too adorable for words, the lovebirds were seated next to each other at the breakfast table, the *Gansett Gazette* spread open as they drank coffee and read the paper.

"Did you give her permission to stay out all night?" Riley asked Nikki.

"I did not, and I think we need to ground her."

"Agreed. No boys for a week, young lady."

Jordan rolled her eyes at them and went to help herself to some of their coffee. "Spoken like the upstairs rabbits who make the bed squeak every night."

"We do not!" Nikki sputtered.

"Ah, yeah, we do, love."

173

"Shut *up*, Riley."

Jordan glanced at them over the rim of her mug. "I've got you fighting. My work here is finished."

"Get over here and tell us everything about where you've been, who you were doing."

"*Riley!*"

Jordan nearly choked on a sip of coffee. Her future brother-in-law was cute and funny. As she slid onto the bench across from them at the table Nikki had refinished, she gave Riley a pointed look. "None of your business."

"As long as you're living under my roof, young lady—"

Jordan looked to Nikki for help. "Will you please do something about him?"

"I've been waiting *years* to use my father's best lines," Riley said. "Let me have my fun, will you?"

"Did you have fun?" Nikki asked.

"Uh-huh." If she'd had any more fun, she might never have walked straight again.

Nikki was about to say something when her phone chimed with a text that had her knitting her eyebrows.

"What?" Riley asked. "Work trouble already?"

"No," Nik said as she typed a response. Her terse reply and the continued furrow of her brows put Jordan on edge.

"What's wrong?"

Nikki put down her phone and looked at Jordan. "*He* is out of rehab and wants to know where you are."

Jordan's stomach dropped and took her good mood down with it. "He *texted* you?" Nikki was the last person Brendan would ever text—and that was before the altercation in Charlotte.

"No, Davy did. He said the only thing *he* wants is to see you, and Davy asked me to tell him where you are."

"I hope you told him to fuck off."

"In so many words. We can get a restraining order."

Jordan shook her head. She wanted nothing to do with him, even to request the protective order, news of which would be all over

Twitter before the ink dried. "I don't want that. It would bring attention I don't need." Not when things had finally died down and she was
enjoying spending time with Mason. She didn't want anything to ruin
that, especially not the soon-to-be ex-husband who had hurt her so
badly.

"Tell Davy to pass this along to him. You ready?"

"Ready."

"This is coming directly from Jordan. She has nothing to say to
him now or ever. Now that he's out of rehab, he'll be receiving
divorce papers. She suggests he sign them to end this once and for all.
If he tries to contact her in any way, she won't hesitate to call the
police. It's over. Put *over* in all caps."

"Got it. Send?"

"Send it."

"Done." Nikki put down the phone and reached across the table
for Jordan's hand. "You okay?"

"I'm fine." Jordan refused to be anything other than fine. "How are
you?" She was also tired of being the center of attention all the time.

"Seeing you stand up to him makes me very proud of you."

"Don't be proud of me. I should've done it a long time ago. I need
to call Gigi and let her know he's out so she can get him served. It's
time to end this nightmare."

"Let us know if we can do anything, Jordan." Riley put his hand on
top of Nikki's. "And for what it's worth, I'm proud of you, too."

"It's worth a lot. Thanks, guys." Jordan got up, put her mug in the
dishwasher and headed upstairs to plug her dead cell phone into the
charger. As soon as it had enough of a charge to turn it on, she found
a text from Davy asking her to call him. Jordan was disappointed that
Davy was still working with Brendan. He'd said he was through with
him after Charlotte.

Ignoring his text, she instead called Gigi, even though it was crazy-
early in LA. She tried to ignore the low hum of tension that had every
muscle in her body on alert for imminent danger. That was Brendan's
legacy. He'd made her afraid, and she was done being afraid of him—
and his legacy.

"Wake up," she said when Gigi grunted into the phone.

"Girl, someone had better be dead."

"He's out of rehab."

"How do you know?" Gigi asked, now sounding wide awake.

"Davy texted me and Nik. He wants to know where I am."

"Did Davy say where *he* is?"

"No."

"Don't worry. I'll find out and have him served immediately. Should I also file for a restraining order?"

"If you do, it'll be all over the internet that I'm playing hardball with him. I don't need his crazies coming after me again. Once was more than enough."

"I don't give a rat's ass about his crazies. The only thing that matters is keeping you safe."

"I'm perfectly fine here. He has no idea how to find me, because he would never come with me when I came here. I doubt it would even occur to him that I'm here."

"That island is a postage stamp, J. If he wants to find you there, he will. How about we get back the security your grandmother hired?"

"No security. I'll lie low until it blows over. Just get him served so we can be done with this."

"I can't promise that his camp will keep it quiet that we've served him."

"I'll deal with that when it happens."

"Okay, I'm on it. We'll get this done ASAP, if I have to hunt down his skinny ass myself."

"Don't do that. He knows what you mean to me. Please don't risk yourself on my account. I wouldn't be able to take it if something happened to you."

"Girlfriend, I could kick his ass if I had to. Don't you worry about me."

"Just hearing his name makes me feel sick."

"I know. Leave it to me. We'll dispose of him like the trash he is."

"Thanks, G. Love you."

"Love you, too. Stay strong. We got this. I'll call you when I have news."

Seconds after she ended the call with Gigi, her phone rang. Seeing her grandmother's name on the caller ID, Jordan took the call. "Hi there."

"I saw on the news that he's left rehab."

"I know. Davy texted me and Nik to find out where I am."

"Oh Lord. You guys didn't tell him, did you?"

"Hell no. Nik told him for me that I want nothing to do with him and that he should sign the divorce papers he'll be served with imminently."

"Good for you, sweetheart. That's the way. I want you to have security for the next few weeks. Just until things die down again."

"No, I don't want them. I'm on Gansett. I'll be perfectly fine. You know how it is here. People don't even lock their doors. And he declined every time I asked him to come here with me, so he has no idea where the house is or how to find me."

"All that's true, love, but you know how crazy his fans can be and that they blame *you* for *his* issues." Evelyn took a deep breath and released it. "Please let me send them back to you."

"I'm doing really well, Gran. Things are good. Better than good, actually. Everything is okay. Gigi is going to make him go away, and I have faith in her."

"You're sure about this?" Evelyn asked, sounding resigned now.

"I am. I promise it'll be okay."

"I'm coming there next weekend to see you girls."

"We can't wait to see you. It's been too long."

"Yes, it has. So things are better than good, huh? What's up with that?"

"I met someone." Jordan told her about Mason, leaving out the part about the fire and the near-death experience, since Evelyn would worry if she knew those things. She and Nikki had agreed to keep the details from their grandmother, since the repairs would be made before she arrived. "He's really cute and funny, and I like being with him."

"This is wonderful news, sweetheart. Perhaps the best news I've ever heard."

"I'm trying not to get too excited about it."

"Why not?"

"Because. I'm only here temporarily, and he's got a good job and life here. It's a fling. Nothing to get worked up about." Except everything he said and did worked her up in a way that nothing else—and no one else—ever had.

"Do me a favor and don't discount the possibilities in this new relationship."

"It's not a relationship. I don't know what it is, but it's fun. We both know the score. Our lives are very different, not at all compatible."

"Are you compatible in other ways?"

"Gran! What're you asking me?"

"You know what I'm asking. Does he do it for you in bed?"

"Oh my God! I can't even believe you're asking me that."

"Why not? I thought we were both adults here."

"You're my grandmother. Jeez." Jordan's nervous laugh had Evelyn giggling as Jordan felt her face burn with embarrassment.

"Honestly, Jordan, grow up and answer the question. Does he do it for you in bed?"

"I, um."

"It's a yes-or-no question, my love."

"That's an emphatic yes."

Evelyn released her trademark full-throated laugh, which brought a smile to Jordan's face. "Tell me more."

"I will not."

"Oh, come on! I've been widowed for half my life. Throw a girl a bone." She lost it laughing again. "I said bone."

"I can't deal with this conversation."

Evelyn laughed and laughed, which made Jordan laugh, too. "Is he handsome?"

"Very—and he's tall. Six foot six. He's huge, and he's the Gansett Island fire chief."

"I can't wait to meet this tall man who does it for you in bed."

"Gran! If you say that to him—"

Evelyn lost it laughing again. "Relax, honey. I'll be on my best behavior. I can't wait to meet him and Riley and see my girls."

"We're excited to see you, too. Let us know your plans so we can pick you up."

"Will do. I'll see you soon. In the meantime, put all this Brendan nonsense out of your mind and focus all your time and attention on your tall, sexy fire chief who does it for you in bed."

"I never should've told you that."

"No, you shouldn't have, but I'm so glad you did. Love you to the moon and back, my sweet Jordy J."

"Love you, too, even when you're embarrassing the hell out of me."

"My work here is finished. Talk soon and keep me posted."

"I will not keep you posted."

"That's very selfish of you."

"I'm sorry for everything I've put you through, Gran. I should've listened to you and Nik about *him*."

"Sometimes you have to figure things out for yourself, and all the warnings in the world won't register until you see things with your own eyes."

"The video should've been enough. I allowed myself to be sucked back in again after that, and that never should've happened."

"Be gentle with yourself, Jordan. You loved him. You kept hoping he would be better than he was. None of this is your fault. He was lucky to have your love and was too stupid to realize it. That's on him, not you."

"I'm working on coming around to your way of thinking."

"Since I'm always right, come around to my way sooner rather than later, you hear me? And go have some fun in bed with your sexy fireman."

"Lalalala, can't hear you."

They hung up laughing, and as she always did after talking to her grandmother, Jordan felt a thousand times better than she had before. Evelyn had saved her sanity and Nik's when they were growing up. She'd been their touchstone, even going so far as to move to Los

Angeles for several years so she could attend their games, recitals, shows, chorus concerts and every other thing they'd done.

Though they were forced to live with their father during the school year, Evelyn had taken every chance she could get to see them, to take them on vacations, to have them for sleepovers. She'd thrown them birthday parties and made their friends feel welcome in her home, all the while doing everything she could to help their mother combat mental health and substance abuse issues.

It was no wonder that Nikki and Jordan considered Evelyn their personal Wonder Woman. When Nik had been attacked by her college boyfriend, Evelyn had swooped in to bring Nikki to their home on Gansett to recover from the trauma that had been compounded when the young man later died by suicide. Jordan didn't want to think about what might've become of Nik without their grandmother taking care of her through the worst days of her sister's life.

Jordan loved Evelyn Hopper more than she could ever find the words to express. She was determined to make her grandmother proud by dealing with this latest wrinkle with Brendan and moving on with her life.

Nikki came into Jordan's bedroom, carrying a mug of coffee that she handed over to Jordan. "You didn't get in your daily quota."

"Thank you. Did you hear back from Davy?"

"Not yet. Hopefully, he conveyed the message, and we won't hear from any of them again. Were you talking to Gigi?"

"At first. Then Gran, who's off her rocker."

"What'd she do now?"

"She was asking me about compatibility with Mason—in bed."

"Sounds about right. So are you? Compatible with him in bed?"

"Jeez, you're just like your grandmother."

"Thank you. You couldn't pay me a higher compliment." Nik sat on Jordan's bed and curled her legs under her, settling in for some girl talk. "You must've been compatible if you told Gran about him."

"Don't you have to get to work?"

"I'm the boss. They'll wait for me."

Realizing she was cornered, Jordan sat next to her sister, holding back a wince as sore muscles protested the contact.

"Holy crap. Are you *sore?*"

"A little."

"So he's big all over, then?"

"You could say that."

Nikki clapped her hands and laughed. "I love this so much. He's just what you need to get your mojo back."

"My mojo is definitely back. In fact, I'm finding mojo I never knew I had."

"I'm so happy to hear that. He's such a great guy." Nikki practically bounced on the bed as she celebrated Jordan getting laid. "*I love this!*"

"So you said. Twice now."

"You're not excited?"

"I'm trying to keep it real, Nik. He lives here. I live in LA. We're having fun, but that's all it is."

"How can you know that's all it is when you've only known him a few days?"

"Because eventually, I'm going to have to go home and deal with my life."

"Maybe not."

"What're you talking about? Of course I'm going home. I live there."

"Who says you can't live somewhere else?"

"I appreciate what you're saying, and I love how things have worked out for you here with Riley and the Wayfarer and the house. But that's not going to happen for me."

"How do you know that?"

"Because! I do not *live* on Gansett. I *live* in LA. That's where my life is."

"It's where it *was*. Who's to say that couldn't change?"

Jordan put down the coffee, got up from the bed and turned to face her sister. "Nik, honestly, get real."

"Mason is a great guy, the kind of guy who doesn't come along every day. Why couldn't you make something of this thing with him and figure out a whole new life for yourself?"

As she tried to form a logical response to her sister's question, an odd feeling of elation came over her, along with vivid images of what it would be like to live here with Mason, near her sister and Riley, to make new friends who genuinely cared about her and not what she could do for them, like so many of the people she'd associated with in LA. To find work that was meaningful to her, to be far away from the madness that was her former life, to have babies and a family of her own. The flood of emotion that came over her as each new image presented itself in high-definition precision left her feeling gut-punched and breathless.

"J? Are you okay?" Nikki jumped up to come to her. "Is it the asthma?"

Jordan's eyes filled as she shook her head.

"What? What's wrong?"

"Nothing is wrong. For the first time in a very long time, nothing is wrong."

Nikki hugged her tightly. "All I'm asking you to do is to consider it. Nothing has to be decided today or even any time soon. Just consider it. You're the captain of your own ship. You can be and do anything at all. Your slate is blank right now. Draw your own picture of what you want your life to be."

"Is that what you did?"

"It is, and I found every single thing I want and need right here. I found things I didn't even know I needed."

"Just because you found Riley here doesn't mean that's going to happen for me."

"Maybe not, but you just spent the night with a man who isn't *him*, days after you met him. Think about that. You've never been with anyone else, and a couple of days after you met Mason, you're sore after spending the night with him."

"I found out *other* important things were lacking in my marriage besides the stuff I already knew about."

Nikki smiled widely. "Did you now?"

"Oh, *yeah*. It was… I had *no* idea."

"I know what you mean. I felt that way after the first night I spent with Riley."

"Well, you'd only had something awful to compare it to. I was in love with Brendan, and it was nothing like with Mason."

"I feel like I should throw a party or a parade or a fireworks display or something to celebrate this fantastic development."

"No celebrations needed," Jordan said, amused by her sister's euphoria.

"You should celebrate this. It's a big deal to connect with someone the way you have with him."

"I don't want to get ahead of myself, Nik. It's important to me that no one gets hurt here, especially him."

"What does he say about it?"

"That he gets it. My life isn't here. His is. We're just having fun. Everyone else is making more of it than we are."

"Gran and I are excited to see you excited about someone who isn't what's-his-name."

"And I get that. I really do, and I've given you both good reason to be happy to see me with anyone other than him. But please don't jump through gold rings and white picket fences, Nik. That's not what this is about."

"I hear you. I'm only asking that you keep your mind open to all the many things this could be, in addition to fun."

"Okay. I will. Now, can I drive you to work so I can borrow your car? I have a few errands to do today."

"Sure, no problem."

"Let me just grab a quick shower, and then we can go." As she showered and packed a bag to take with her, Jordan tried to erase the array of images that had suddenly appeared before her earlier, each of them featuring Mason at the center of her life.

She was getting caught up in the romantic silliness her grandmother and sister were tossing at her. After everything she'd been through, Jordan didn't have a lot of faith in the power of romance. No, she was a realist and still believed that it was best to keep it real with Mason.

This was about fun and maybe a little bit of a rebound to reset herself after the disaster with Brendan. To make it into anything more than that would be courting all-new disaster, and she'd already had more than enough disaster for one lifetime.

CHAPTER 18

*H*is day had been a mess from the first minute Mason stepped foot into the barn to discover two of his young firefighters had gotten into a fistfight on the overnight shift. Though both were off duty, he called them back and sat them down in his office.

"What happened?" With his hands on his hips, he stood while they sat. When neither of them said a word, he turned up the volume. "Someone had better start talking unless you both want to be suspended indefinitely." He wouldn't and couldn't suspend anyone this time of year, but they didn't know that.

Domenic, one of the first firefighters Mason had hired after he became chief, glanced at Xavier, the newest member of their department. "Someone needs to learn the rules around here."

"That doesn't tell me what happened," Mason said, becoming more annoyed by the second. "Domenic, you've got the floor. Let's hear it."

"We were all out the other night, and he… He came on to the woman I've been dating. When I told him to back off, he got in my face and started something in the bar. I took my girl and got out of there. That would've been the end of it if he hadn't gotten mouthy with me about it last night."

"All I said is she's not into you if she's giving me the look."

Before Domenic could erupt, Mason held up his hand. "Xavier, it's a dick move to come on to another man's woman."

"She's not his woman."

At that, Domenic erupted. "She is, too! We've been seeing each other for months, you asshole."

"Huh," Xavier said. "You'd never know it by the way she's looking at other guys."

Mason grabbed Domenic before he could punch the other man in the face. "Stop it right now before you both find yourself out of a job. I'm not putting up with this crap. Xavier, don't go near Domenic or his girlfriend, do you understand me?"

"Yes, sir," Xavier said with a smirk for Domenic.

"If I hear one more word about this on the job, I'll start suspending people without pay. Am I clear?"

"Yes, sir," Xavier said again.

"Yes, sir," Domenic muttered.

"Xavier, do yourself a favor and keep your mouth shut around here. We're a team, and we don't need new people coming in here and upsetting our team. If you can't do that, you won't last long in this department."

"Apologies, Chief."

"I'm not the one you need to apologize to."

For a second, Xavier appeared to balk at the idea of apologizing to Domenic. Then he seemed to think better of it. "Sorry."

"If I hear another word about any of this, there's going to be trouble, you got me?"

"Yes, sir," both men said.

"Keep your personal shit out of my barn. I mean it. Now get out of here."

They got up and walked out, giving each other a wide berth.

They were no sooner gone than Blaine Taylor came in. "Trouble in the ranks?"

"God save me from twentysomethings. They're insane. One of them hitting on the other's girlfriend, leading to a fistfight at work."

"Good times," Blaine said, chuckling as he took a seat.

"Just what I need this time of year. What's up?"

"This is kind of awkward, but someone mentioned you might be hanging with Jordan Stokes?"

Mason was immediately on guard against whatever Blaine was about to say. "What about it?"

"Her sister called me, put me on notice that the not-yet-ex-husband is out of rehab and asking questions about where he might find her."

That news hit Mason like a ton of bricks to the face. Jordan's abusive ex was looking for her. He stood, feeling an urgent need to find her, to protect her, to... *Shit.* He took a deep breath. She'd told him last night that they were nothing more than fun and games. It wasn't up to him to get between her and her ex. However, he'd do it in a second to keep her safe. He'd do just about anything for her, a realization that sent him reeling.

Blaine flashed a smug grin. "So it's like that already, huh?"

"No, it's not."

"You sure about that?"

"No, I'm not."

Blaine lost it laughing. "You poor bastard. I remember what it was like to be driven insane by the woman I wanted when she was still married to a complete schmuck who didn't deserve her. I waited months for her to be free of him. Thought I'd go mad waiting. But once she was free, that's when things got *really* interesting." Blaine smiled, his entire demeanor softening at the thought of his wife. "Sometimes you just have to be patient to get to the best things."

"That's not what this is. She doesn't even live here."

"Maybe not, but she's here right now, and that's all we've got, my friend. If you show her what life with you on Gansett might be like, perhaps she might be compelled to stick around."

The idea of Jordan sticking around, of staying to be with him, made him weak in the knees even considering such a thing. He no sooner let himself go there than he hauled himself back from the brink of calamity. Her stay on Gansett was *temporary*. Their relationship, such as it was, was *temporary*.

Mason felt sadder than he had in a very long time. "We're not like you and Tiffany. That's not what this is."

"Nothing says you can't make it happen, Mase. If you want it badly enough."

After last night, he wanted her more than he'd ever wanted any woman, even the one he'd nearly married. In all the years since his wedding had been called off, he'd never once been thankful to Kayla. Until now. If she hadn't dumped him, he never would've gotten to spend last night with Jordan Stokes, and that would've been the true tragedy.

Both Mason's and Blaine's portable radios came to life in the same second, with an urgent appeal for help at McCarthy's Marina. A car had driven off the pier into the water. They ran for their vehicles as firefighters and EMTs bolted for the trucks.

Mason arrived first, less than three minutes after the call had come in, to find a frantic scene in the parking area.

Big Mac McCarthy and Luke Harris were both in the water, chest-deep as they frantically tried to open the door to a sedan.

"Windows won't open," Big Mac called to him, sounding grim as they noted the water flooding into the car.

Mason grabbed a window-breaking tool from his truck and jumped in after them. "Watch out. Let me in."

The cab of the car was filling fast with water. Inside, he saw Luke's wife, Sydney, her eyes wide with terror as a cut on her forehead had blood running down her face.

"The baby's in the back," Luke said, sounding as terrified as his wife looked.

Blaine jumped into the water and came up next to Mason. "After we break the window, it's going to fill up fast, so we need to be ready." He banged on the window. "Syd, can you get to the backseat and get Lily unstrapped from her seat?"

She repositioned herself so she could reach the baby, who was crying as the water crept ever closer to the bottom of her seat.

"Mason, *please*." Luke was on the verge of hysteria.

"You got her, Syd?" Mason yelled, speaking as loud as he could so she could hear him through the closed windows.

Syd nodded and raised the baby higher as the water continued to pour into the car.

"Okay, listen up. We're going to break the window and get you out. Stay back against the other side. Ready?"

She gave a thumbs-up.

Mason smashed the tool against the window until it shattered, then used his hands to push on the glass.

"Mason!" Blaine cried. "Your hands."

Mason heard him, but he was like a man possessed as he created an opening big enough for Syd and the baby. "Give me the baby. Hurry."

For a second, Sydney seemed frozen as the water came closer to her chin.

"Syd! The baby!" Mason's body was half in the car and half out as he struggled to keep his head above the rising water.

She handed over the child, and he backed out, handing the child to her father.

"Give her to Blaine, Luke." The water stayed cold on Gansett well into July, and hypothermia was a concern. Mason went back for Sydney, who had moved to the window to follow her daughter out of the car. Mason helped her, but Luke was right there to grab his wife.

She cried hysterically as her husband held her. "I'm so sorry. I don't know what happened."

"It's okay, baby," Luke said as tears ran unchecked down his face. "It's okay."

"Let's get her out of the water, Luke." In addition to the wound on her forehead, Mason noticed Sydney's lips had taken on a bluish tone, and her teeth chattered violently.

Working with Mason's team, Luke half carried Sydney to the ladder and handed her over to Dermot.

"Too close," Big Mac said when he, Blaine and Mason were the only ones left in the water. "Far too close."

"Did you see what happened?" Blaine asked.

"She'd just pulled into the lot to meet Luke for coffee when the car lurched forward and went right off the bulkhead. It's the one spot on the whole pier where a car can fit through. We'll get that taken care of immediately." That the older man was seriously rattled was obvious to Mason. "She musta hit the gas by accident."

"Let's get you out of the water, Mac." When Mason raised his hands to offer assistance to him, he noticed they were shredded and bleeding profusely. "Shit."

JORDAN HEARD about the accident at the marina when she was coming out of the grocery store.

"A car went right off the pier into the water at McCarthy's. A mother and baby were in the car, but the police and fire chiefs got them out."

Mason.

Was he all right? His arm was already injured. He shouldn't be rescuing people! As soon as she was in the car, she put through a call to him that went straight to voicemail. "Hi, it's me. Jordan. I heard you rescued the lady and baby in the car. I'm just hoping you're all right. Call me when you can."

She felt an overwhelming need to see him, to know he was all right, even if it didn't make sense to her. She barely knew him, and yet the need to be with him took precedence over common sense as she drove to the building he called "the barn" to see if his SUV was parked outside. It wasn't. Was he still at McCarthy's? Possibly. She headed toward North Harbor, telling herself she wouldn't bother him at work. She wanted only to see him, even from a distance, to make sure he was okay. After that, she'd leave him alone.

With McCarthy's in view from a distance, she was relieved to see his SUV parked in the lot. Until she realized she didn't see him among the firefighters and police officers still working the scene. As he was taller than most men, he would stand out in a crowd. He wasn't there. As a twinge of anxiety settled in her belly, she parked the car and walked toward the marina, steering clear of the scene where the first responders were still engaged.

At a picnic table outside the restaurant, she approached an older man with steel-gray hair and a towel wrapped around his shoulders. His clothes were wet. "Excuse me."

"Hey, Nikki."

"Um, I'm Jordan, her sister."

He blinked, took a closer look and smiled even though he still looked troubled. "So you are. Apologies. I'm Mac McCarthy Senior, but everyone calls me Big Mac."

Jordan shook his cold hand. "Nice to meet you. My grandmother loves you."

"I love her right back. She's a great lady."

"Yes, she is. Are you all right?" She couldn't help but notice his hands were shaking.

"We had a terrifying accident. My friend Luke's family was in that car."

"I can't imagine how frightening that must've been."

"One of the worst things I've ever seen. The car went right off the bulkhead over there and into the water. Happened so fast. And we couldn't get the door or windows open." He shuddered. "Too close."

"They're all right, though? The people in the car?"

"They will be once they're warmed up. Mason and Blaine were amazing. They saved their lives."

She was filled with an unreasonable feeling of pride. "Are they still here?"

"Blaine took Mason to the clinic. Cut his hands up pretty bad breaking the window."

Oh no. He was hurt. Again. "I, um, do you think it would be okay if I went to check on him? He saved my life the other night." She didn't know what else to say to justify her desire to see him.

"I heard about that, and I think it'd be fine if you checked on him. In fact, would you mind giving me a lift over there so I can check on Syd and baby Lily? I'm a little too shook up to drive."

"Of course. I'd be happy to." Jordan led him to the car, casting a glance at the car in the water as she walked by. What a terrifying thing to be trapped in a car that was filling with water while your baby was strapped in a car seat.

"Nikki must be happy to have you here," he said as she drove them into town to the clinic.

"She is, and I'm thrilled to be with her, too."

"She's a treasure. She's done such a beautiful job running the Wayfarer for us."

"She loves the job."

"That's nice to hear. She's made my nephew so happy."

"And vice versa. She's crazy about him."

"Sometimes things work out for good people."

"It gives the rest of us hope."

"You'll have your turn, honey. You're good people, too."

"How do you know that?" she asked, amused by his certainty.

"You're Evelyn's granddaughter and Nikki's sister. That's all I need to know. And you're far too good for that Zale guy, or whatever his name is."

Jordan laughed at how Big Mac bungled the name of one of the world's most famous musicians.

"He didn't deserve you. Someday you'll find a man who deserves you, who treats you like a queen, who loves and respects you the way *you* deserve to be loved. It'll happen. I promise you that."

His emphatically spoken words touched her deeply. What would it be like to have someone like him for a dad rather than the jerk she'd gotten? "Thank you, Mr. McCarthy. I appreciate that."

"It's the truth, and you should call me Big Mac, like everyone else does."

"I will. Thanks."

Ten minutes later, they walked into the clinic together, and Jordan immediately spotted Mason, standing next to a dark-haired man also in uniform. "I see Mason. It was really nice to meet you, Big Mac."

"You, too, honey. Thanks for the ride, and remember what I told you."

Jordan smiled and, in a moment of impulse, went up on tiptoes to kiss his cheek. "I'll remember." She walked over to Mason, who had blood-soaked towels wrapped around his hands. "Hey." As she noticed his clothes were wet, she squeezed his forearm and tried not to focus on the blood.

"Hey. What're you doing here?"

"I heard you got hurt, so I came to check on you."

As he stared down at her, seeming stunned to see her there, Jordan wondered if she'd played this all wrong. She shouldn't have come.

"That's so nice of you," he said, his face lighting up with a warm smile. He stared at her for a long, intense moment. "Ah, Jordan, this is Blaine Taylor, chief of police."

"Good to meet you, Jordan," Blaine said.

"You, too." Returning her gaze to Mason, she focused on the bloody towels. "Your hands…"

"I'll be fine. The only thing that matters is that Syd and her baby are okay."

"That's not the only thing that matters," Jordan said, looking up at him. "Why haven't they taken you back yet?"

"I told them to focus on getting Syd and the baby warm."

"Since you're in very good hands here—no pun intended—I'm going back to work," Blaine said. "You'll stay with him, Jordan?"

"I will."

"Okay, then. I'm out. I'll check on you later."

"Thanks, Blaine," Mason said.

Jordan led Mason to a chair and sat next to him, taking his right hand into her lap. She steeled herself and unwrapped the blood-soaked towel to reveal his pulpy palm and fingers. "Oh God, Mason. What did you do?"

"It's okay. Doesn't hurt at all."

"It will."

"I'm okay. Really."

Jordan used the unsoiled portion of the towel to wipe away new blood.

"Don't get it on your dress. You look so pretty."

"I don't care about the dress." She dabbed at the wounds on his right hand and then reached for the left one. "How about your elbow?"

"It's fine."

Jordan glanced up to gauge whether he was telling her the truth. When her gaze collided with his, she found him watching her with an unexpected level of intensity. "What?"

"I've never had anyone come looking for me before."

Touched by his sweetness, she said, "Never?"

"Not once ever."

"Well, now you have."

"Now I have."

CHAPTER 19

The most terrifying fifteen minutes of his life. That was how Luke would remember watching the car containing the two people he loved best fly off the bulkhead into the water below. He'd been walking toward the car to greet his girls when the car suddenly disappeared. A surge of nausea had him swallowing hard, trying to contain the pressing feeling that he was going to be sick at any moment. When he thought about what might've been lost...

Sydney continued to sob uncontrollably as Luke sat with her in the hospital bed while Lily slept in her arms after crying herself to sleep. Both of them were under warming blankets, and Luke was lending his own body heat to the cause. "Shhh." He stroked Syd's damp hair. "Everything is okay."

She was crying so hard, she couldn't speak.

He held her while her body seized with sobs. The poor thing had already been through so much after losing her first husband and her two young children to a drunk driver. She didn't deserve another frightening experience.

"It's all over now," Luke said, trying to convey calm even as his own heart still beat so fast, he worried he might need medical attention, too.

"I d-don't know w-what happened," Syd said.

He wiped the tears from her face, which was red and puffy from crying.

"One minute, we were p-parked, and the next..."

"Your foot must've slipped off the brake."

"I was on the phone ordering new furniture for Eastward Look after the fire. It's my fault. I wasn't paying attention."

"The car was parked, sweetheart. You didn't do anything wrong. It was an accident."

"I couldn't figure out what'd happened, and Lily." She swallowed hard, as if she, too, was trying not to be sick.

"You hit your head hard, probably on the steering wheel. It might've knocked you out for a second."

She took a shuddering deep breath. "I was so afraid."

"I know, baby, so was I. When I couldn't get the door open, and the window wouldn't open from inside..." Worst feeling he'd ever had. Thank God Mason and Blaine had gotten there as fast as they did. He owed the two of them everything.

Jenny Martinez came rushing into the cubicle. "Syd." She burst into tears at the sight of her friend. "Thank God you're all right. And Lily." Jenny covered her mouth with a trembling hand. "Thank God." She came to the side of the bed and worked around Lily to hug Syd, the two women sobbing. "I came as soon as I heard." She brushed the hair back from Sydney's face to take a closer look at the bump on her forehead and rested a hand on Lily's back. "Does your head hurt?"

"A little. David said I need a couple of stitches."

"Are you hurt anywhere else? Is Lily?"

"No, we're both fine, thanks to Mason and Blaine."

Jenny rested her hand over Luke's. "What about you?"

"I'll be okay. In a year or two."

"I can't even imagine. What can we do for you? Everyone is asking."

"As long as we have each other," Syd said, "I can't think of anything we need."

Luke couldn't have said it better himself.

196

. . .

MASON STILL COULDN'T BELIEVE Jordan had come to the clinic to find him. While David cleaned and dressed the wounds, Jordan stood by his side, keeping him company through the painful treatment. David applied bandages and showed Jordan how to use skin glue and properly position the bandages when they needed to be changed.

She paid close attention and asked questions to make sure she could take care of him.

He wanted to pinch himself to believe that she was real, that she wanted to care for him and that she'd come to find him at the clinic.

When David discharged him, Jordan walked him to her sister's car with her hand tucked into his right elbow, apparently without a care as to who might see them together and jump to conclusions.

Hell, he was trying not to jump to his own conclusions. In just a few days, she'd become the sun that lit his life with warmth and affection and a kind of true pleasure that he'd rarely experienced—and not just in bed.

"Hang on a sec." She opened the passenger door and put the seat back as far as it would go, a gesture that further endeared her to him.

He was really losing it when it came to her, and he didn't even care that he was probably setting himself up for a painful fall. Every second with her was worth any pain that came later—or so he told himself now. After he was seated, she leaned in to seat-belt him in.

"Hey."

"Hey what?"

"Kiss me."

Jordan smiled and touched her lips to his.

"Thank you."

"I didn't do anything."

"Yes, you did."

Jordan gazed into his eyes for a long moment in which Mason felt the ground beneath him shift and the door to his heart swing wide open to let her in. She came storming in, knocking down the barriers he'd put up to protect himself from being hurt again.

He raised his hand to her face, thankful his fingertips were mostly unscathed so he could touch her. "Jordan."

"Yes, Mason?"

"You're beautiful. Inside and out."

"Thank you." She kissed him again, and he wanted to stay right there all day with her sweet lips attached to his. "Let's get you home."

"I should go to the station."

"No work for three days. Doctor's orders. You need to give your wounds the chance to heal."

Her stern tone made him hard for her. Hell, the sound of her voice made him hard for her. "All right, then. Let's go home."

She drove him to his house, sticking to the speed limit with a precision that amused him.

"You know, if you go five miles over, I can probably get you out of the ticket."

"I haven't driven in ages."

"Now you tell me."

Jordan's husky, sexy laugh made him smile. He could listen to her laugh all day and never get tired of the sound. "You're perfectly safe with me."

She'd told him otherwise last night, but he wasn't thinking about her heartfelt warnings of all the reasons why it wasn't a good idea for him to get overly involved with her. Those warnings were the last thing on his mind after she'd come to find him at the clinic and was driving him home, apparently planning to take care of him, too.

When they arrived at his house, she released his seat belt and came around to let him out of the car.

"I should be opening your door, not the other way around."

"You can stand down on all that business while you're injured." She got the doors for him and then went back to retrieve two bags of groceries. "Thankfully, the cold stuff is still good because I bought a big bottle of cold lemonade."

While he sat at the counter, enjoying the way she moved about his kitchen like she belonged there, she put away groceries. "Are you hungry? I bought some turkey and this loaf of fresh-baked bread. I can make you a sandwich."

"I won't say no to that."

She got out lettuce, tomato and mayo and opened the bread bag. "Cheese?"

"Yes, please."

If Mason had wondered how deeply he had fallen into serious like with her, his suspicions were confirmed when he realized she was adorable even when making a sandwich. Before she finished, he went to answer a knock on the door, determined to get rid of whoever it was so he could be alone with Jordan.

Dermot was outside his door, while another department vehicle idled behind his SUV in the driveway. "Hey, Chief, we brought your truck home for you." As he handed the keys to Mason, Dermot's eyes bugged. "You're that girl on TV!"

She came to the door. "Hi, I'm Jordan."

"Oh my God," Dermot said as he shook her hand with unbridled enthusiasm.

"Enough." Mason's tone and the pointed look he gave his lieutenant compelled the younger man to release Jordan's hand.

"Are you guys… Holy crap! *You and Jordan Stokes?*"

Mason glared at him. "If you breathe one word of that to anyone, I'll remove your tongue with tin snips. You got me?"

Dermot flashed a big dopey grin. "Yes, sir. You got it, sir. Nice to meet you, ma'am. I'm a big fan of your show. Can't wait for it to come back on. You and Gigi are so funny and so hot and—"

"Leave now, Dermot."

"Going now, sir." He saluted as he grinned and tripped over his own feet on his way to the other vehicle, where he would absolutely tell whoever had followed him here that Mason was in there with Jordan Stokes. It would be all over the island before sunset.

"Seems like a nice guy," Jordan said.

"He's a goddamned fool, but a great firefighter and paramedic, so I keep him around." Mason returned to his perch on a stool at the counter.

Jordan handed over a plate with the sandwich as well as pickles and chips on it. As he ate the sandwich, working around the bandages and wincing when the cuts made themselves known, she rolled a slice of cheese and a tomato into a piece of lettuce and took a bite.

"That does not count as a sandwich."

"It does when you don't eat bread."

"How can you live without bread?"

She came around the counter to sit next to him at the bar. "Rather well, actually. I discovered a few years back that I'm gluten intolerant, and since I cut it out of my diet, I've been generally much healthier than I was before."

"I can't imagine life without bread."

"You get used to it."

"So you bought bread just for me, then, huh?"

"I did. I also bought turkey for you since I don't eat that either."

He put his arm around her and leaned in to kiss her cheek. "What did I do to get so lucky?"

"Other than save my life?" she asked with the smile that made her dark eyes shine.

"Other than that."

"You've made me smile and laugh, among other things that haven't happened in a very long time."

He knew what she meant, but wanted to hear her say it.

"What other things?"

She put her lips close to his ear, making him shiver. "Orgasms. Really good ones."

And just that quickly, he was hard as a rock and ready to roll. "Are you still sore?"

"A little."

"You want me to kiss it better?"

"No, I want you to let your hands and elbow heal, which means you have to take it easy."

"I will take it easy. Come with me." He stood and went into the bedroom, tugging the uniform shirt that was stained with blood over

200

his head. Tossing it aside, he fumbled with his belt buckle with fingers that didn't cooperate.

"Stop." Jordan approached him and took over the task, working on his belt until it was unbuckled and then on his pants.

Mason was so hard, he could barely think of anything other than getting her naked as fast as possible. "Clothes off. Hurry." He stood back to watch her strip for him, committing every second of it to memory to ensure that he'd never forget what she looked like as she revealed her body to him. She was so pretty, so sexy, so fucking hot. She was like a dream that had taken over his life in the best possible way.

When she stood before him, completely naked, he could only stare. "What's this plan of yours?"

He hooked his uninjured thumbs into the waistband of his boxers and took them off, watching as her eyes darkened and her lips parted at the sight of his hard cock. Then he got on the bed, situating himself so he was flat on his back. "Come here."

Jordan got on the bed and scooted over so she was kneeling next to him.

"Come over me."

She was so petite that she almost couldn't get her legs wide enough to straddle him.

His cock jumped with excitement as he thought about taking her this way. "Up here." He could tell the second she figured out his plan, because her eyes got big, and she started to say something. The words died on her lips as she moved to straddle his face and grasp the head-board behind him.

"Like this?"

"Just like that, only closer."

"You won't be able to breathe!"

His low chuckle earned him a glare from her. "Yes, I will."

"Mason."

"Shhhh, come closer."

Injured hands or not, he grasped her ass and put her right where he wanted her and then sank his tongue into her.

"Ung, ah, oh, ohhh, *Mason*. Mason!"

Thrilled by the way she lost her mind, he went to town on her, licking and sucking and torturing as she rode him shamelessly, chasing the orgasm. He was determined to make her work for it, to take her right out of the here and now and send her flying. When he got the feeling that she was getting a little tired, he sucked on her clit and drew a keening wail from her as her body seized above him. He stayed with her, making sure she didn't fall or hit her head or feel anything other than the pleasure, and as the orgasm began to wane, he moved her down to press her heat against his erection.

Her eyes flew open as he notched the head inside her tight flesh. "Are you on birth control?"

She had a wild, untamed look to her as she nodded.

"I'm clean. I got tested a month ago, and I haven't been with anyone since."

"I'm clean, too. I got tested in the hospital. After."

Mason knew what she meant and hated that he'd made her think of that ordeal, especially when they were naked and in bed together. "Are we okay to go without the condom?"

"Yes."

The thought of being inside her with nothing between them made him even harder, which, of course, she noticed. "Mason, I can't."

"Yes, you can. Relax."

Her nervous giggle rang through the room. "Easy for you to say."

He reached for her, brought her lips down to meet his. "You got this. You're a stud, remember?"

"No, *you* are."

Smiling, he kissed her again as he rocked against her soft, wet heat. God, she was hot and sexy and sweet and adorable. He couldn't get enough of her.

Dropping one hand from her face, he reached down to where she was stretched to the limit and found the tight knot of her clit.

"Mason," she said, gasping, "your hands. Don't."

"Then you do it."

If he died today, the memory he'd want to take with him into the next life would be the sight of her pleasuring herself as she rode him with unbridled enthusiasm. Her breasts bounced, her lips parted, and her eyes closed as she threw her head back in the second before she came hard, her internal muscles clutching his cock.

Mason put his arms around her and turned them so he was on top and drove into her until he found his own release, which seemed to come from the deepest part of him. His entire body was engaged as he held her and kissed her and absorbed her sweetness.

Ignoring the pain in his elbow and hands, which paled in comparison to the need to keep her close, Mason was on his way to dozing off when her cell rang.

"Ugh, I should get that."

He withdrew from her, let her go, watched her cross the room to where she'd left her purse and noticed when her entire body went rigid. "What?"

"I think it's my ex."

"You don't know for sure?"

She shook her head. "I blocked him. He's been calling from other phones."

That news alarmed Mason. "How often is he calling you?"

"At least once a week."

"Do you want to talk to him?"

"Absolutely not."

Mason appreciated the emphatic way she said that. "Is he out of rehab?"

"Yes."

"Oh, so you already knew that?"

She nodded as she rejoined him in bed. "His manager reached out to me and Nik to ask where I was."

"You guys didn't tell him, did you?"

"God, no. I'd never do that, and neither would she. She hates his guts. But he knows I love it here, so it probably won't take long to figure out where I am if he can't find me in LA."

"I don't like the idea of you being in danger, Jordan."

"I'm not in danger."

"How do you know that? If he comes here, it wouldn't be hard for him to find you."

"He won't come here. He doesn't inconvenience himself. Ever. Coming here would be inconvenient for him."

"I don't like it."

"I'm sorry that it's upsetting to you that I'm still married—"

"That's not what I'm upset about, babe. I'm worried about *you*. He's put you through enough. You don't need to be harassed by him after everything that's already happened."

She propped her chin on his chest, a smile making her lovely face even more so. "It's nice to have someone to worry about me."

"I am worried. He's proven he has no regard for you or what's best for you." He smoothed the hair back from her face.

"And you do?"

"I do. I care. I don't want anything to hurt you." To his dismay, her eyes filled with tears. "Wait, what's this?"

"It's just really nice to be with you."

Could she be any sweeter? "It's really nice to be with you, too."

"We're not supposed to get attached."

He gave a subtle tilt of his hips to remind her of how attached they'd already been.

She laughed, and he went immediately hard for her again as he realized she was going to be a very big problem for him. Perhaps the best problem he'd ever had. Mason put his arm around her. "Talk to me. What're you thinking?"

"I wish he'd go away and leave me alone."

"You're under no obligation to talk to him, especially after what happened the last time you saw him."

"I know."

"What's your lawyer saying?"

"Now that he's out of rehab, she's going to have him served with divorce papers. We've just been waiting for him to get out." She turned those potent eyes on him.

"You'll stay here with me. If he comes to the island, it wouldn't take much for him to find you at Eastward Look. He'd never think to look for you here."

"I really don't think he'll come here. Like I said, he doesn't go out of his way for anything—or anyone."

"He's a fool. Any guy who's lucky enough to have you in his life should bend over backwards for you."

"Is that what you'd do?" she asked with a teasing grin.

"Hell yes, that's what I'd do. If I had you..."

"What?"

Mason stopped himself from sharing his true feelings—that if he had her, he'd never need anything else. If he had her, he'd treat her like gold every day. That if he had her, his life would be perfect. He couldn't say any of that. Not yet. Not when so many things were still so unsettled for her—and thus for him, too. "He's a fool."

She eyed him suspiciously. "That's not what you were going to say."

"It's what I can say right now." He smiled as he drank in every detail of her exquisite face. "So my friends Quinn and Mallory are having a dinner party on Saturday night. You want to come with me?"

"Yes, I do."

"Will you stay with me while your crazy ex is making noise about tracking you down?"

"Yes, I will."

Mason smiled at her easy capitulation. "Are you always this agreeable?"

She returned his smile. "Yes, I am."

"Somehow, I doubt that."

"You'll just have to wait and see."

He couldn't wait to experience every aspect of her, good and bad, not that he expected a lot of bad. Things with her were so good, better than he'd ever had with anyone, and the only thing he could think about was how to keep her right here with him forever.

If that made him a crazy fool, well, then, so be it.

CHAPTER 20

*M*ac returned to the hotel room after having gone to check on Luke, Syd and the baby. He was still rattled after hearing the details of the accident at the marina and blamed himself for the fact that it'd happened in the first place. The curbstone that would've stopped the car from going into the water had cracked over the winter, and he'd removed it, with plans to replace it. He hadn't gotten around to it yet.

As a result, two people they all loved had nearly been lost. He'd felt sick to his stomach ever since he'd heard about the accident, and seeing Luke and Syd, so visibly shaken by it all, had been hard to handle. He couldn't imagine what Luke would ever do without Syd and Lily. Thank God they were all right.

Tomorrow morning, he would ask Shane to get a new curbstone put in at the marina so that couldn't happen again.

Maddie was waiting for him when he came in. She held out a hand to him. "How are they?"

Mac took her hand and sat on the edge of the bed. "Badly shaken, but okay."

"God, what a scary thing to happen."

"It's my fault." Mac hadn't said that to anyone yet.

She raised an eyebrow. "How do you figure?"

He told her about the curbstone that had gotten cracked by a snowplow over the winter and how he'd failed to fix it in a timely manner.

"Mac, come on. Syd hit the gas by accident. That's what caused this."

"The curbstone would've stopped them from going into the water."

"Not if she hit the gas hard enough. The car might've still gone right over it. You can't blame yourself for something that was an accident."

"I should've had it fixed right away."

"Come here."

"I'm here."

"Closer."

"Hang on a second." He removed his clothes, brushed his teeth and crawled into bed next to her. "I'm here. What can I do for you, my love?"

"Not blame yourself for an *accident*, nothing more, nothing less. It was an accident, Mac. Thank God Syd and Lily are all right, but it was an accident. Luke could've done something about that curbstone, or your dad could have. Tell me you know that."

"I do, but I just..."

"You feel responsible for everyone, and that's what is giving you unbearable anxiety. You can't fix everything for the people you love. Despite your many heroic qualities, you aren't actually Superman."

"I'm not? Really? That's devastating."

"You're the most heroic guy I know, always the first to step up for a friend in need. You take care of your own family, your siblings, cousins, parents, employees. But at the end of the day, you're just one guy who can only do so much. The accident at the marina was not your fault. Do you hear me?"

"I hear you."

"Do you really, or are you just saying that to shut me up?"

"I'd never want to shut you up. Yours is my favorite voice in the whole world."

"I love you so, so much, Mac, even when you're trying to be everyone's hero. I just need you to be mine and to let that be enough for you."

"It's more than enough for me."

"Let the rest go. Shit's going to happen. We have to find a way to roll with it that doesn't put us both in the clinic with anxiety issues."

"This getaway that our sisters were good enough to arrange for us was just what we didn't know we needed. I'm still thinking about that massage this morning."

"Me, too, and I agree. This is something we probably need to do more often. We're blessed to have so many people who gladly help us out in a crunch. When we feel ourselves getting too wound up, we need to take a breath and press Pause."

"Do we have so many people who'd help us out with *five* kids?"

"We can farm them out."

Mac laughed. "Our own little stable."

"We had a really tough thing happen to us. Losing Connor changed our wiring. It's made us more afraid than we used to be because we know now that horrible things can happen out of nowhere." She placed her hand on his face, her touch affecting him the way it always did. "We can't be afraid all the time. That's no way to live."

"You're right. I know you are, but it's hard to let go of the fear. I actually talked to my uncle Kevin about it a week or so ago."

"You never said."

"We ran into each other at Rebecca's. Had some coffee. Got to talking. I straight up asked him how people get past being afraid of everything after something bad happens."

"What did he say?"

"It was interesting, but then, talking to Kev always is. He was saying how our hearts expand to accommodate the new people. Our spouse, our kids, our grandchildren. We just keep adding to the love, which makes it so we have more people to be concerned about."

"That actually makes so much sense."

"It does. And he said when something happens to one of them, it's a reminder that something could happen to any of them, and that adds to the anxiety."

"Also a very good point."

"Yeah, for sure."

"Did it help to talk to him?"

"It did. At least I have a good reason for why I feel so on edge all the time lately."

"Your wife is expecting twins after having previously lost a baby. That's a big part of it. Even after we successfully delivered Mac, we still worry about it happening again. I can't wait for you to get the snip, and then we won't have this particular worry again."

He winced at the casual way she threw around the word *snip*. "But we'll have all kinds of other worries, and I have to do better about managing them. I know that. The thought of not being around to raise this gaggle of kids with you is enough to get my attention."

"I couldn't do it without you. I couldn't do anything without you."

"Yes, you could."

"No, I really couldn't. Ever since that first day."

"When you were trying to get rid of me?"

Maddie's smile lit up her gorgeous face. "I wasn't trying to get rid of you, *per se*."

"Liar. You couldn't stand me and wanted me gone."

"I couldn't stand you, but I thought you were hot."

"Is that right? You've never told me that before."

"Yes, I have!"

"Nope. So you think I'm hot, huh?"

She rolled her eyes. "I never should've said that."

"No, you really shouldn't have. Now that I know you're hot for me—"

"That's not what I said!"

"You can't take it back now, so don't even try it." He kissed her so she couldn't object. "Let's have a big party next weekend. I want to see everyone and be with our family and friends and tell them all how hot you are for me."

"I'm not having a party so you can tell everyone I'm hot for you."

"That's fine. They already know."

She playfully smacked his face, which only made him laugh.

"This might be the best day of my whole life."

"A few minutes ago, you were losing it over a curbstone. Look at you now."

"It's all your fault. You do this to me."

"Who's going to plan and provision this big party of yours?"

"Leave it to me. I'll take care of everything."

"Oh, dear God."

OVER THE NEXT FEW DAYS, Jordan dodged multiple calls from Brendan while she cared for Mason and the healing wounds on his hands. Her biggest challenge was keeping him from doing too much. Every time he overdid it, the cuts reopened and set him back to day one.

He was enormously frustrated that he couldn't do much of anything but rest on the sofa and watch movies with Jordan. Nikki had dropped off more clothes for Jordan and groceries so they could hunker down while he recovered.

Despite his annoyance with the situation, Jordan had never been happier as she cooked for them, did their laundry, tended to his wounds and tried to keep him entertained so he wouldn't go mad from what he was missing at work.

On the third day around noon, Jordan took the phone out of his hand when Dermot called for the fourth time since breakfast. "Hi, Dermot, this is Jordan."

"I *love* your show."

Sitting next to her, Mason could hear Dermot's side of the conversation and rolled his eyes.

She smiled at Mason. "Thank you. Could I ask a favor?"

"Of course. What do you need?"

"I need you to not call Mason every five minutes, because he's supposed to be resting and healing. Now, if it's an emergency, that's fine. But if you just want to chat, can you call someone else?"

"Yes, ma'am, I can do that."

"I'd appreciate that."

"Do y'all need anything?"

"Not right now, but I'll let you know if we do."

"You do that. We can be there in a few minutes."

"Yes, you're known for your rapid response time."

Dermot laughed. "Tell Mason to enjoy being stuck at home with his pretty lady."

"I'll do that. Remember—emergencies only."

"Will do."

"Bye, Dermot." Jordan ended the call and handed the phone to Mason, noting the amused expression on his face.

"He's going to talk about the time that Jordan Stokes scolded him for the rest of his life."

"I did not 'scold' him."

"Oh, yes, you did, and it was incredibly hot." He lunged for her, but she darted out of his reach, as she had for three days, since their energetic lovemaking the other day had reopened many of his wounds. Moaning, Mason landed facedown on the sofa. "Come *on*…"

"Not until you're healed."

"Jordan."

"Mason."

"It's mean for you to get me addicted and then cut me off."

He was ridiculously adorable when he was hot and bothered. "I haven't cut you off. I'm taking care of you."

"By ensuring I'm hard twenty-four hours a day and not able to do anything about it?"

"How am I ensuring that?"

"By breathing."

"You're the one who saved my life and got me breathing again!"

"Best thing I ever did, but now I want you to use your second chance at life to put me out of my misery."

"The last time I did that, your hands were a bloody mess afterward."

"That was *days* ago. They're much better now. I've got a much bigger problem than my hands thanks to you."

"It's not my fault."

"It's absolutely your fault, and I need you to do something about it."

That was how she'd ended up straddling him on the sofa and taking care of his very big problem while scoring an epic orgasm for herself at the same time. Nothing like killing two birds with one very satisfying stone.

It wasn't lost on her that she was becoming addicted to everything about him—from the way he made her laugh, to how he hung on every word she said, to the nearly spiritual physical connection that hummed between them every time they were anywhere near each other. She was falling fast and hard for him. Even as she told herself to take it easy, to not dive headfirst into a new relationship when she wasn't even legally separated yet, tamping down her feelings for Mason would be like trying to keep the tide from coming in.

On Saturday night, they attended the dinner party with Mason's friends. Jordan loved Mallory and Quinn, as well as Quinn's brother Jared and his wife, Lizzie. Also in attendance were Alex and Jenny Martinez, Paul and Hope Martinez and David Lawrence and his fiancée, Daisy Babson.

Their hosts had cooked a yummy feast of Mexican food, including the makings for fajitas as well as enchiladas and taco salad.

Mallory seemed to already know that Jordan was a vegetarian and made sure she had plenty of options to choose from.

Jordan noted that, like Mason, Mallory and Quinn avoided the margaritas they'd made for their guests. She wondered if they, too, were alcoholics. "Do you mind if I have one?" she'd whispered to Mason when Quinn made the first batch of frothy margaritas.

"Not at all. Enjoy yourself."

She limited herself to two out of respect for the fact that he didn't drink. The last thing he'd want to deal with was a buzzed or drunk date.

"How're the hands, Mason?" David asked after dinner.

"Much better." He was down to a few Band-Aids on the deeper of the cuts, but the others had healed nicely. "Jordan has done an excellent job of tending to them and making sure I didn't do too much so they could heal."

"We might have a job for you at the clinic," David said with a teasing grin for Jordan.

"I'm the last person you want working there. In the past, I've been known to faint at the sight of blood."

"And yet you held up admirably while I was a bloody mess," Mason said.

"I made myself not faint so I wouldn't be more trouble than I was worth."

The others laughed at that.

"I have to tell you, Jordan," Jenny said. "I love your show."

"Me, too," Hope said. "Jenny and I watch it together. We're addicted."

"That's so nice to hear. Thank you."

"Will you be doing more?" Hope asked.

"I'm not really sure. We're contracted for one more season, but we may not do it. I'm a little skittish about attracting attention to myself in light of everything with what's-his-name."

"I can definitely understand that," Mallory said. "Being famous is probably much more fun in concept than reality."

"For sure," Jordan said. "Not that I don't appreciate how great the fans of the show are. They were amazingly supportive after everything happened with my ex. I've been talking to Gigi about the way forward. I've kind of lost the desire to live my life out loud. She's also my attorney and is trying to get me out of the contract, but we're not sure what's going to happen."

"Well, I hope you get to stick around for a while," Hope said. "It's fun to have a star in our midst."

"I wouldn't go that far," Jordan said, embarrassed to be called a star when she'd really done nothing to deserve that besides be married to a mercurial musician.

"People really connected with you and Gigi on the show," Mallory said. "They appreciated how you kept it real even if you showed the glam side of celebrity. You weren't afraid to talk about your problems. It was refreshing."

Hearing that such an accomplished woman like Mallory enjoyed the show made Jordan feel good about what she and Gigi had created. "We had fun, but it was important to us that it not just be about hair and makeup and clothes, but real life, too."

"You did a great job of that," Mallory said. "We both enjoyed it."

"I didn't picture you for a reality TV fan, bro," Jared said to Quinn.

"Not usually, but Mallory liked the show, so I watched it with her. It was really well done and fun to watch."

"Maybe you could do a Gansett Island version of the show," Paul said.

"That'd be awesome," Hope said. "You could do flip-flops instead of stilettos and talk about the challenges of living on a remote island."

"People would probably be bored senseless by that," Jordan said.

"I don't think so," Jenny said. "You and Gigi could make it hysterical. I have no doubt it would be a huge hit."

"I'm trying to picture Gigi on Gansett."

The others laughed.

"She'd be a riot," Jenny said. "She is so effortlessly funny. Is she always like that?"

"Yes! She's had me laughing since grade school when we sat next to each other. She got me in so much trouble."

"That's the only dynamic you two need to be successful—each other," Alex said. "She's a kook, and you're the one trying to keep her from committing a felony. I actually can't believe she's an attorney."

"I never laughed harder in my life than I did when she told me she was going to law school. And then I realized she was serious. She said she had a feeling she was going to need to understand the law at some point. Turns out, she was right about that. But what's really funny is that she's actually a very good lawyer."

"I can see that," Jenny said. "She's sharp as a tack as well as funny as hell."

"She is. Maybe I need to invite her to Gansett to check the place out. See what she thinks of filming our last season here." The idea of being able to stay, of somehow figuring out a life here, filled her with an unreasonable feeling of elation.

As the others asked about David and Daisy's wedding plans for that fall, Jordan reached for Mason's hand under the table.

He sent her a warm smile.

The idea of being stuck on Gansett Island was looking better to her with every day she spent with him. She'd never been so comfortable with anyone other than her sister and grandmother and a few close friends like Gigi. He made her happy. She'd laughed more with him than she'd laughed in years, and he made her feel safe and adored. Not to mention, their physical connection was positively incendiary.

She nearly laughed at thinking her connection to a firefighter was incendiary.

He would like that. She couldn't wait to be alone with him later so she could tell him about it. And, as soon as she got the chance, she would pitch the idea of moving the show to Gansett to Gigi, who would probably shoot it down.

But it was worth a try. Stranger things had happened.

She tuned back in to the conversation to hear that the activities director at the senior facility Quinn and Mallory ran had decided island life wasn't for her.

"It's such a bummer," Mallory said, "because the residents loved her."

"She was excellent," Alex said.

"Alex and Paul's mother, Marion, is a resident at the facility," Jenny said for Jordan's benefit.

"Ah, I see. What does the activities director do?"

"Organize exercise, crafts, games, music and other forms of entertainment for the residents," Quinn said. "We have a wide variety of capabilities among our clientele. Some are more able to participate than others, but they all enjoy being in the room."

"I can attest to that," Paul said. "Our mom has severe dementia, but she still enjoys making crafts. Sometimes she doesn't recognize us, but she can still create beautiful things."

"It's amazing how the mind works," Alex added. "We're just so happy to be able to see her every day and that she has the opportunity to do things that used to mean so much to her. You guys are life-savers."

"I give my lovely wife all the credit," Jared said, smiling at Lizzie. "It was her idea."

"And your money," Lizzie said.

"Our money."

"*Your* money."

"We appreciate the idea, the money and the incredibly dedicated staff that run the place," Alex said. "It's been such a blessing to our family."

"Your mom gave me the idea," Lizzie said. "I couldn't imagine how hard it would be to have to take a loved one to the mainland to get the care they needed while you were living here."

"It was awful," Alex said. "The day we moved her back here was one of the best days of our lives, and you guys made that possible for us and other families."

As the others discussed Marion's situation, Jordan was stuck on the information about the activities director. When Quinn had described the role, she'd felt a spark of interest that couldn't be denied.

When they were driving back to Mason's, she said as much to him.

"I'm sure they'd talk to you about it."

"Other than a lifelong interest in all things crayon-marker-glue gun-glitter, I'm not sure I'd be qualified. I'm not very musical, and I avoid exercise like the plague."

"You could bring other people in for those things. Julia Lawry is living here now. She's an incredible singer and piano player. I heard her play at Stephanie's Bistro, and she's fantastic. You could get someone from the yoga studio to come in to do classes for the residents. I bet they'd even specialize their program for people who use wheelchairs or have other physical limitations."

"That's true." Her mind raced with the possibilities.

"You should ask them about it."

"I don't know. I probably ought to figure out my situation at home before I do anything here." Jordan wished she could wave a magic wand and make Brendan go away, get free of her contract for the show and deal with her house and belongings in LA. After a few weeks on Gansett, her life in LA felt almost foreign to her, as if it had belonged to someone else rather than her.

"Are you leaning toward wanting to be here instead of there?"

"I might be."

"That's the best news I've heard in maybe ever."

He had such a way of making her feel wanted. After spending most of her life surrounded by men who didn't want her, he was a refreshing and delightful change of pace.

CHAPTER 21

When they arrived home, Mason and Jordan got ready for bed like they'd been living together for years rather than hanging out for a few days. She was so comfortable with him and his tiny, cozy house. He joined her in bed, curling up to her and putting his arm around her.

She ran her hand gently over the curve of his elbow. "It seems better."

"Much. It's bending without agony."

"That's good. Are you sure you still want me underfoot now that you're going back to work?"

"I'm very sure I still want you underfoot, under me, etc."

Jordan laughed at the shameless way he came on to her. "Tonight was fun. I loved your friends."

"They loved you, too."

"I felt like I talked too much about the show and stuff."

"Not at all. They were interested. I love the idea of you doing it from here. How funny would that be?"

"I'm not sure Gansett Island is ready for Gigi."

"It would be awesome. Would you consider proposing it to the network?"

"First, I'd have to propose it to her."

"Would you even do that much?"

"I'd definitely mention it. And I guess it'll depend on what she hears from the network. She's supposed to talk to them on Monday."

"I'd like to cast the first vote for *Jordan and Gigi Live From Gansett Island*. I think it would be a huge hit."

"And you're not at all biased."

"Not one bit biased." Under the T-shirt she'd worn to bed, he cupped her bare breast and tweaked her nipple. "I think it would be spectacular."

"Would you be a guest star?"

His hand froze, and he seemed to stop breathing.

She lost it laughing. "Oh, come on! They'd love you. All tall and handsome and wearing a uniform." She shivered dramatically. "The ladies would go mad over you."

"Um, well, I probably ought to not, um…"

Jordan couldn't stop laughing. "If I do the show here, you'd have to be on it."

"Hmmm, not sure my contract with the town would allow for that."

"Yes, it would."

"How do you know?"

"I have a feeling if I was able to work it out to film from here, you might be happy about that, right?"

"Uh, yeah, safe to say I'd be happy about that."

"Which means you'd do whatever it took to ensure my island show was successful so I would stay here."

"Why do I feel like I'm being shamelessly manipulated?"

"Because you are. I'll only pitch the idea of filming here if you agree to costar. I need to be able to prove to the network that we'd have a viable show here, and featuring the locals would have to be part of it. I pick you as our first costar."

"Um, well, my agent would need to receive a formal offer, and then we'd take it under advisement."

Exasperated, Jordan played her best card. "How about I give you two blow jobs for every day you spend filming?"

"Sold. You've got yourself a deal, my friend. I'd be happy to costar on your show."

Once again, he had her crippled with laughter. That happened a lot with him, and she was finding she rather loved to laugh with and at him. She was finding she rather loved him—a lot. Not that she could say that to him when her situation was so uncertain.

Hopefully, Gigi would soon have progress to report with the divorce and the network. Once those issues were taken care of, Jordan would be allowed to fall the rest of the way in love with Mason. Until then, she had to take care not to let this get so far out of hand that they'd both end up crushed if it didn't work out.

Easier said than done.

MASON WENT BACK to work on Sunday and put in a sixteen-hour shift, dealing with several cases of alcohol poisoning, a moped crash that led to a compound leg fracture, a heart attack on the town beach and a brush fire at the bluffs, near the trail where he liked to ride his bike.

Jordan was asleep when he got home and still sleeping when he left on Monday morning. He left her a note telling her to call him when she got up. After spending most of the last four days with her, he missed her after one day without her.

He attended his usual AA meeting and accepted Mallory and Quinn's invitation to go to breakfast at Rebecca's. After they ordered their usual, Mallory leaned in, coffee mug in hand.

"So, things with Jordan seem really good."

"Subtle, babe," Quinn said. "She promised she wouldn't pump you for info the second she had you in her clutches."

"I'm not pumping him," Mallory said. "I'm merely making an observation."

"If that's what you want to call it," Quinn said.

Mason laughed at their banter. "It's fine. And yes, things are good. For now, anyway."

Mallory pounced, as he fully expected her to. "What does that mean?"

"She's got a lot to deal with before she can figure out her next move."

"She really, *really* likes you, Mason," Mallory said.

"I know she does. And I really, really like her. But she's still married, has a contract to do her show in LA and a house and life there to contend with."

Mallory waved away his concerns with a sweep of her hand. "Those are just details. She's not going anywhere."

"Mallory," Quinn said. "You don't know that, and neither does he."

"What Quinn said. I'm trying not to get too far ahead of myself. There're so many things that have to be dealt with, and not for nothing..."

"What?"

"I don't know if I see her being happy here for the long haul."

"Oh, please. She's totally into you. Everyone could see that the other night."

Hearing that gave Mason the kind of hope he hadn't allowed himself before now. "But would that be enough for her after the shine wears off? You've seen what her life in LA was like. It was all glam all the time. We've got none of that here."

"Has it occurred to you that she might be sick of life in the fast lane, and a slower, quieter life might actually appeal to her?"

"Not really. She's enjoying it right now because of the novelty of it."

"Are you actually calling yourself a *novelty*?"

"I'm trying to keep it real, Mallory. What would a woman like her want with a small-town fire chief long term?"

She stared at him, incredulous. "Mason! I don't even know where to start with that. First of all, after what she went through with the jackass she married, you must look awfully good to her. You're a good guy, dependable, loyal, steady—"

"Boring."

"No! Absolutely not!"

"My life is boring. It's all about work, work, more work, exercise, AA, a few good friends. There's no way I can compete with what she's used to."

Mallory looked to Quinn. "Will you please help me out here?"

"What my beloved is trying to tell you, Mason, is if she loves you, she won't need anything more than you."

"Thank you," Mallory said.

"I'd like to believe that's true, but like I said, I'm trying to be realistic."

"Are you in love with her?" Mallory asked.

"I like her. A lot."

"But are you *in love?*"

"I don't know. Maybe. I could be, if things were different. I'm not looking to be flattened when she resumes her real life." Even though he already knew he would be, no matter what took her away from him.

"You heard her say the other night that the idea of filming here appeals to her. And I couldn't help but notice that she seemed a bit interested in the activities director job at the senior center."

"She did say it sounded like fun."

"The job is hers if she wants it."

"Honestly," Mason said, exasperated and amused at the same time. "You're too much."

"I tell her that every day," Quinn said, smiling at his fiancée.

"What is wrong with offering her a job?"

"I wouldn't want to speak for Mason," Quinn said, "but if I had to guess, he's thinking you're trying to play fairy godmother by offering her a job so she'll stay with him." He glanced at Mason. "How'd I do?"

"Spot-on. You can speak for me any time."

"I know what I saw the other night," Mallory said. "She's crazy about you, and I'll be shocked if she leaves."

"She may not have a choice. She has a contract for one more season of the show, not to mention a husband to contend with."

"She's not going back to him. Tell me you know that."

"I do know that, but she's a long way from free and clear of him."

"Why do I feel like you're setting yourself up to fail with her so you won't be surprised if you do?"

"Mallory." The note of warning in Quinn's tone was loud and clear to Mason, but Mallory pressed on as if he hadn't said anything.

"Hear me out. You don't believe a woman like her, whatever that means, could fall for you and stay with you long term, so you're preparing yourself for it to end when it's still going strong. That's how I see it, anyway."

"I've had a little history with working above my pay grade in past relationships. It never works out well for me."

"Maybe it hasn't in the past, but that doesn't mean it never will."

"You've said your piece, babe. Leave the poor guy alone."

Mason sent Quinn a grateful smile. "I do appreciate the concern."

"I want to say one more thing."

Quinn rolled his eyes. "One more thing, and then I am going to muzzle you if Mason doesn't beat me to it."

"This is important, Mason."

He'd never seen Mallory look more serious.

"I think you love her. I think she loves you, too. If that's the case, *nothing* is more important than doing whatever it takes to make it work, even if that means *you* are the one to relocate."

Her words were like a fist to the face, a wakeup call of the highest order. Here, he'd been consumed with trying to figure out how to keep her on Gansett, when maybe he should've been thinking about how he might go with her if she had to leave. He was ashamed to admit that he'd never given that scenario any serious thought until Mallory forced him to.

"Your point is well taken."

"I know you love your life here, but your life here is going to be a whole lot less ideal post-Jordan."

That, too, was true. He'd been fine before he met her, but now... The thought of not seeing her for one day pained him. How would he get through a lifetime of days without her?

"No job is worth it, Mason," Mallory said softly. "Take it from someone who lost her first love suddenly and tragically and thought

223

she'd never again find what she had with him. It took twenty years for Dr. James here to show up and prove me wrong."

Quinn put his arm around her and kissed her temple. "I was looking for you the whole time."

Moved by them, Mason smiled. "You guys give me hope."

"If you love her, don't let her get away. That's all I wanted to say."

"Thank you."

"You're welcome, and tell her we'd be happy to have her at the center if she wants to be our activities director. No interview required."

"You're just like your father, you know that?"

Mallory stared at him, seeming shocked. "Really?"

Mason nodded. "He can be like a dog with a bone when he gets ahold of something, too." To his great horror, Mallory's eyes filled with tears. "What? I meant that as a compliment."

She waved her hand in front of her face, making an effort to pull herself together.

Alarmed, he looked to Quinn for help. "What did I say?"

"If I had to guess, my sweet girl hasn't often been told that she's just like the father she only recently found out she had."

Mallory used her thumb to point to Quinn and nodded. "That." She used a paper napkin to dab at her tears.

"Well, I mean it in the best possible way."

"I know," she said. "You made my day by comparing me to him. Thank you for that."

"It was the least I could do after all the 'help' you've given me."

The three of them shared a good laugh, and by the time they parted company, Mason was determined to talk to Jordan about their options when he got home from work. And he would leave on time tonight, barring catastrophe. Maybe he would take her out to dinner. Yes, that's what they would do. A real date.

And when the time was right, he'd tell her he wanted them to stay together, even if that meant he had to relocate to be with her.

Did he want to live in LA? No, but he wanted her, and he had to believe he could find a job as a firefighter or EMT with one of the many fire departments in the LA area. It might be nice to return to the ranks and leave the headaches of administration behind. If the fire service didn't work out, he could always bartend like he had in college.

The thought of staying with her, of being with her, of making a real go of this thing with her buoyed his spirits all day. And when Dermot came in to tell him that Jordan was at the barn looking for him, he didn't even try to hide his pleasure from the colleague who would certainly bust his balls about it later.

"Send her in."

Jordan had forced herself not to cry on the way to the barn to see Mason. Under normal circumstances, she'd never disturb him at work, but these circumstances weren't normal, and she couldn't leave without saying goodbye to the man who'd come to mean so much to her.

When Dermot showed her to Mason's office, the first thing she noticed was how happy he was to see her. His handsome face lit up with pleasure that reminded her that he was the first man she'd ever cared about who had given back more than she could ever give him.

But his smile faded quickly when he saw that she was upset. Of course he noticed. He always did. "Thanks, Dermot," he said without taking his gaze off her.

Dermot closed the door, leaving her alone with the man she'd fallen in love with. What a hell of a time to realize that for certain.

"What's wrong?"

"I have to go back to LA. Today."

He didn't even try to hide his disappointment, which was just another reason to love him. He never tried to hide from her, never played games or made her wonder if she had his full attention. "Why?"

"The network is threatening to sue me if I'm not at a meeting tomorrow."

"Oh."

"Yeah. So, Gigi says I need to get my ass back to LA. She's

sending a plane for me because it was too late to book commercial." Why was she babbling to him about logistics? What did any of that matter?"

"You want me to come with you?"

"What? No, you have work and, well, everything. I don't know how long I'll need to be there, and I don't want to mess things up for you any more than I already have."

"You haven't messed up anything for me. This has been so awesome."

"For me, too. I'm so sorry about this."

Mason took a few steps to close the distance between them and drew her into his embrace. He bent his head to breathe in the scent of her hair, wanting to commit every detail of her to memory—as if he wouldn't remember forever every second of the time he'd spent with her.

Only when her shoulders shook did he realize she was crying.

"Aww, sweetheart, don't cry. Go do what you've got to do and come back. I'll be right here."

"I may have to do the full season there. That'd be months."

"I'll wait."

"I can't ask you to do that."

"You're not asking. I'm telling you I'll wait as long as it takes until you're free and clear and can come back or until you ask me to come there."

"You'd do that?"

He pulled back and looked down at her. "I'd do that."

"But this is your busy season."

"So?"

"Mason, you can't—"

He kissed her until she forgot what she was going to say. "I can do whatever I want whenever I want. And if you want me to come to LA, all you have to do is say so, and I'll be on the next plane."

She dropped her forehead to his chest.

He smoothed his hand over her soft, silky hair. "What did Gigi say about the divorce?"

"She can't find him to serve him, but she's got an investigator trying to locate him."

"Is he intentionally dodging the server?"

"Probably."

"What can you do about that?"

She looked up at him. "Take his call. See what it will take."

"I don't want you anywhere near him out there, Jordan. I mean it. He may be sober, but he's still the same guy who hurt you the last time you saw him."

"I know."

"Promise me you won't go see him alone, no matter what."

"I promise."

For the longest time, they stood there looking at each other as if trying to memorize every detail.

"Mason, I want you to know—"

He placed a finger over her lips. "Let's not say anything that makes this harder than it already is. Get your stuff taken care of, and then we'll talk. Okay?"

She nodded. "Thank you for saving my life and then showing me it was worth going through all the shit to get to the good stuff."

"Plenty more good stuff to come."

"I'm going to hold you to that."

"I really hope you do." He hugged her as tightly as he ever had. "Take your inhaler. Just in case."

"I will. Don't get hurt while I'm gone."

"I'll try not to."

"Will you call me?"

"Every day. Just tell me when you're free."

Filled with irrational fear that she might never see him again, she held on for a long time, letting go only when the alarm sounded outside his office and the dispatcher's voice had them pulling apart.

"I've got to go," he said when he released her.

Jordan nodded and forced herself to smile. "See you soon."

"Yes, you will. One way or the other." He kissed her and left the room.

Jordan followed him and watched the apparatus leave the station with a wail of sirens and flashing lights, off to provide assistance to someone in need. He loved this job. She could never ask him to risk it or give it up for her.

That couldn't happen.

CHAPTER 22

*A*s Jordan drove to Eastward Look in Nikki's car, tears rolled down her face as she thought about how long it might be before she saw him again. She went into the house and stopped short at the sight of her sister and grandmother standing in the kitchen.

Jordan ran into Evelyn's outstretched arms, the familiar scent of Shalimar filling her with a tender feeling of homecoming. Petite and still lovely with snow-white hair and nearly flawless skin, Evelyn hadn't changed a bit since Jordan had last seen her.

"What is this about?" Evelyn asked of Jordan's tears.

"I'm so happy to see you!"

"You were in tears when you came through the door," Nikki said. "What's wrong?"

Jordan pulled back from her grandmother while keeping one arm around her. "I have to go back to LA. Today, or the producers are going to file suit. I just came from seeing Mason."

"Oh crap," Nikki said. "How'd you leave it with him?"

"That we'll figure out what's up when I get my shit sorted. If I get my shit sorted."

"If you're crying over him, it's probably safe to say you've already sorted some of your shit," Evelyn said.

Jordan stared at Nikki. "Did she say *shit?*"

"I believe she did."

"Oh, please. You two taught me all the bad words when you were teens. And don't change the subject. This nice young man you're so fond of is going to wait for you to come back. Is that right?"

"Or he said he'd come to me."

"That's awesome," Nikki said. "He's the real deal, J."

Jordan's emotions got the better of her all over again, and new tears slid down her cheeks. "I don't want to lose him."

"Then don't," Evelyn said. "Go do what you've got to do and get back to him. Quickly. If he's your real deal, don't make him suffer."

Jordan hugged her grandmother again. "It's so good to see you. I'm sorry I can't stay."

"I'll be here for a while. Things are far more interesting here than they are in Florida. Now maybe you girls can tell me what happened to the new living room furniture you bought, Nik."

Over her grandmother's shoulder, Jordan grimaced at Nikki. Riley and his brother had worked all week to fix the roof and chimney so there'd be no sign of the fire left by the time Evelyn arrived.

"It's the funniest story," Nik said. "I'll tell you all about it after I help Jordan pack."

As JORDAN DEPARTED from Gansett Island on a sleek private jet three hours later, her heart ached like it never had before, not even after the awful episode that had ended her marriage. Nothing had ever hurt worse than leaving Mason did.

She pulled out her phone and sent him a text. *I just took off, and I already miss you.*

He wrote right back. *Was riding my bike at the bluffs and saw the plane. I wondered if that was you. Come back soon. I already miss you, too.*

Don't fall off your bike.

I only fell off once. Best thing to ever happen. Text me when you land.

I will.

Did I say to come back soon?

You did.

Okay, then.

Jordan couldn't stop crying. She felt like she'd left the most important thing in her life behind on the tiny island that she could now barely see from the window. A panicked feeling went through her, making her wish she could tell the pilot to turn the plane around and take her back.

The only reason she didn't do that was because at some point, she'd have to face what was waiting for her at home in LA. Better to deal with it sooner so she could get back to where she wanted to be.

If someone had told her before she came to Gansett for the Memorial Day weekend opening of the Wayfarer that she'd ever yearn to be back on the island, she might've found that funny. Unlike Nik, who'd always loved the slower pace of Gansett, Jordan had found it mostly boring. Yes, she'd loved being there with her sister, grandmother and her mother when they were kids, but since she became an adult, she hadn't spent much time there.

Why would she? There was nothing to do on the island. She laughed when she thought about that now. How had the most boring place she'd ever been become the most exciting?

Mason, that's how. Being around him was exciting even when they did nothing more than sit on the sofa and watch TV together. He was always touching her, whether it was resting a hand on her leg or putting an arm around her or leaning his head against hers. He was so much bigger than her, but never once had she felt intimidated by his size.

Well, except for…

And just like that, she was crying again as memories of hours in bed with him, on the sofa, in the shower and once on the floor of his living room came rushing back to remind her that nothing and no one had ever made her feel the way he did—all the time, no matter what they were doing.

Married to Brendan, she'd discovered you could feel lonely even if someone else was in the room. She often felt lonely, even when Brendan was sitting right next to her or was in the same bed with her.

He might as well have been on the other side of the world for all the good it did her having him right there.

That was never the case with Mason. Sure, they'd only recently met and were in the rose-colored-glasses stage, as she'd once heard her grandmother refer to the heady early days of a relationship. But she already knew she'd never feel lonely if Mason was there. Even knowing he was only a phone call or text away made her feel better about leaving than she would have if she couldn't have talked to him.

The thought of not being able to talk to him made her feel sick. He was the only one she wanted to talk to about anything lately. Even having Nik close by again paled in comparison to being with Mason.

It was too soon to be thinking of things like babies and forever and happily ever after with him. All she knew for sure was that she wanted more of him and the way he made her feel.

After a rough six hours of emotions and turbulence in the sky, the plane landed at LAX, where Gigi was waiting for her in a lounge where passengers on private planes were met.

"What the hell, girl? Your face is all red and puffy. You look like shit."

As usual, every one of Gigi's blonde hairs was perfectly in place, and her fake eyelashes were so extravagant as to be funny. A Louis Vuitton purse hung from her arm, and her skinny jeans were so skinny that Jordan wondered how she could breathe. Four-inch Louboutin heels had her towering over Jordan when they were roughly the same height when barefoot.

Gigi grabbed Jordan's arm. "Don't make eye contact with anyone, or you'll be all over Twitter grieving your ex or some other garbage."

Her friend was absolutely right about that. With her usual efficiency, Gigi got Jordan's suitcase from the flight crew and hustled her into the white Audi Q7 Gigi had bought when they signed the contract for the second season of their show—after the first season had been a surprise hit.

"What is up with you?" Gigi asked when they were on their way to Bel Air.

"Nothing."

"Try selling that bullshit to someone who hasn't known you since forever. Did scumbag call you?"

"Well, he did, but I didn't take the calls."

"So what's up, then? And don't tell me it's nothing, or I'll just ask Nik. Is this about Mr. Big?" She glanced at Jordan as she weaved through traffic, pissing off every other driver on the road, as usual. "It is, isn't it? Oh my God! Tell me everything."

"I really like him."

"How's the sex?"

"Amazing, stupendous, life-changing."

"Is he big all over?"

Jordan laughed. "He is indeed big all over. *Much* bigger than you-know-who."

"Oh my God, *I love this so fucking much.*"

"It's still very new."

"But life-changing. That's a big term to be throwing around about something new."

"I'm trying not to get too far ahead of myself, especially now that I'm here and he's three thousand miles away." Saying that out loud had new tears flooding her eyes. "Any word from Davy or the scumbag?"

"Nope, the server can't find the scumbag. And I can't get in touch with Davy."

"Ugh. Of course he'd do this right when I want to serve him."

"It's *because* we want to serve him that he's gone under. He doesn't want to be divorced from you."

"Well, that's just too fucking bad. He can hide all he wants. At the end of the day, he's getting divorced."

"I'm so happy you're done with him." She glanced at Jordan. "I dropped him as a client."

"You didn't have to do that."

"Yes, I did have to. He beat up my BFFL. After that, he's dead to me. He should've been dead to me a long time ago."

"Me, too. I'm sorry for all the trouble I've caused for you and everyone else who got caught up in this mess."

"You're not the one who caused the trouble. *He* is the one we all resent."

While Jordan agreed that much of what had taken place was outside her control, she'd stayed with him longer than she should have—and that was on her. While they were stuck in traffic on the 405, Jordan took a second to text Mason to let him know she'd landed.

Glad you're safe.

Well, I'm in LA traffic at the moment, so...

You're not driving, I hope.

No, Gigi picked me up.

Call me later?

I will.

Are you on your way back yet?

Soon.

Yes, please.

Jordan smiled at the way he made her feel wanted even with the entire country standing between them.

"Look at you smiling like a girl who's been getting some of the good stuff."

"Mmm, it's very good stuff."

"Check you out, hitting the rebound. That's my girl."

The comment made Jordan feel immediately defensive of him and what they'd shared. "Mason isn't a rebound."

Gigi's raised eyebrow cleared the top of her oversize sunglasses. "You aren't getting all serious before you're even separated from the douche canoe, are you?"

"Maybe a little."

"You need to slow your roll, sister. Everyone knows the first relationship after a marriage ends is all about the sex and getting back in the saddle. It's not about falling in love."

"*Ever?*"

"Hardly ever. Why? You aren't thinking you're gone over this guy, are you?"

"I like him. A lot. I didn't want to leave him to come here. Not sure if that equates to being gone over him, but there you have it."

"Dude, you can't even do a rebound right."

"I haven't had much experience, don't forget."

"Trust me, I know." Gigi pulled up to the gate at Jordan's home and punched in the code. The gates opened, and Gigi drove in, made sure the gate closed behind them and parked by the kitchen door.

"Home sweet home." After she'd spent a few weeks on Gansett Island, the massive house no longer felt like home. Another thought hit her, rendering her paralyzed with fear. "You don't think he's here, do you?"

Gigi shocked the shit out of Jordan when she opened the glove box, removed a small handgun and slammed the box closed. "I'll check. Stay here."

Gigi let herself into the house with her key. Ten minutes after she went in, Gigi came to the door and waved for Jordan to go in.

She got out of the car, retrieved her suitcase from the backseat and went inside. The place smelled stale, as if it had been closed off. Her cleaning lady had come every other week while she was gone, but it was apparent no one had lived there in a while.

"Where in the hell did you get a gun?"

Gigi tucked the gun into the back of her pants in a maneuver that seemed well practiced.

"Never mind where I got it. If he'd been in here, you would've been damned glad I had it."

Jordan couldn't argue with that.

Gigi went to the fridge and took out an unopened bottle of sparkling water and poured glasses for both of them. "Back to what we were talking about before."

"What were we talking about?"

"Rebounds."

"Oh, right."

"Listen, I know your dad did a number on you and Nik. I get why you steered clear of boys and dating and all the bullshit that goes with it until you met dickwad and lost your mind over him. But you're not going to spend the rest of your life with *the second guy you ever slept with*! That doesn't happen. You're supposed to play the field, date all the guys, have all the sex, and in two to three years, if you find someone who does it for you, then maybe you start having visions of sugarplums."

"What the fuck are sugarplums, anyway?"

"That's not the point! Did you hear anything else I said?"

"I heard you. I think they heard you in Sacramento."

"This is important shit, J. You need time to heal and figure out your life. It's not the time to be falling in love with some random dude on that ridiculous island you and your sister love so much."

"He's not a random dude. His name is Mason, and he saved my life."

"For which we will always be grateful, but you can take gratitude too far. You had a fun time with him. You had some hot sex that you badly needed after limp dick disappointed you for as long as you've known him. That's all it needs to be. You can't fall for every guy you sleep with." She rolled her eyes to high heaven. "Where in the hell did I go wrong with you?"

Jordan was trying not to laugh, which wasn't easy when Gigi was around. Even though the things her friend had said hurt to hear, it didn't change how Jordan felt about Mason. She understood and even agreed with what Gigi was saying, but her friend hadn't spent time with Mason or seen how it was with him.

"Can we talk about the show?"

"Yes," Gigi said emphatically. "Please. Let's talk about the show."

"Would you consider doing it on Gansett Island?"

Gigi's face lost all expression. And then she busted up laughing. She laughed so hard, she nearly hyperventilated. When she finally recovered, she took a deep breath and released it. "I forgot how fucking hysterical you can be."

"I'm not joking."

"You have to be, because that's the most ridiculous thing I've ever heard."

"Hear me out."

"No, J, I'm not going to hear you out. The network wants another season of the show we do *here*. You remember what goes on *here*, right? Nightlife and parties and cool stores and amazing houses and beautiful people. If you go in there tomorrow and tell them you want to move the show—and all the people who work on it—to some remote-ass island in the middle of nowhere Rhode Island, you're almost asking them to sue you."

"The show is you and me being you and me. Who says we can't do that somewhere other than here?"

"I say. That's who. I don't want to live in Bumfuck, Rhode Island. My whole life is *here*."

"You've never even been there. How do you know you wouldn't like it?"

Gigi stared at her as if she was insane or certifiable or from another planet. "Are you listening to yourself right now? Have you *met* me? I can assure you with one hundred percent certainty that I would not like it there."

Jordan's heart sank at Gigi's emphatic dismissal of her plan. It had been the hope she'd clung to on the long flight. "Do you know how to change the code to the gate and the door?"

"No, but Nik does. I'll text her."

With info she got from Nikki, Gigi took care of changing the codes at the gate and on the back door, which made Jordan feel safer about being there alone.

"I'll stay if you want me to," Gigi said. "I'm happy to."

"No need. As long as the codes are changed, I'm fine here."

"I'll meet you in town at noon tomorrow?"

"I'll be there."

Gigi put her hands on Jordan's shoulders and looked directly into Jordan's eyes. "I know your head is all fucked after the last few months, but it's time to get back to normal around here. Come into that meeting with your head on straight. Whether we like it or not, the show has become big business. They're not going to let you out of the contract without a protracted and expensive legal fight that we don't need right now."

"I hear you. I'll see you tomorrow. Thanks for the pickup and everything else you've been doing for me."

Gigi planted a noisy kiss on Jordan's forehead. "Anything for you, kid. See you tomorrow. Call me if you need anything." She lived at the beach but would come running if Jordan needed her. She had no doubt about that. They'd had each other's backs for years, and that would never change.

After Gigi left, Jordan wandered around the big, open, airy house she'd once been so in love with. She looked out at the pool that had been cared for in her absence by the company that came weekly to clean it. Everything was just as she'd left it, but she felt out of place here. And it wasn't because of Brendan. He'd been on the road so much of the time that this had never felt like *their* home. It'd been hers and Nik's before her sister decamped for Gansett.

She sat on the white sectional sofa in the formal living room and tried to remember where it had come from. Most of the stuff in the house had been purchased by a decorator who'd been hired to make the house feel like a home. For the most part, she'd succeeded, but Jordan had no real connection to the house or the furnishings. It was just "stuff." None of it meant anything to her, except for photos she had of her and Nik and their friends and some of her clothes. The rest she could easily live without.

Since there was nothing much to eat in the house, she ordered a taco salad from her favorite Mexican place and went to the gate to meet the delivery person, a young woman on a motorcycle who introduced herself as Amy.

"I love your show."

"Oh, thanks. That's nice to hear."

"I hope you'll be back on soon."

"We're working on it." Jordan handed her a ten-dollar bill. "Thanks for bringing the food."

"You're welcome—and PS, you can do way better than Zane."

"I agree. Thanks again."

Amy took off on the bike, and Jordan went inside to eat while wondering how long she had to wait before she could talk to Mason.

She felt like she'd been picked up by aliens and transported to a world she no longer recognized, which was odd, as she'd never lived anywhere but LA, except for summers on Gansett.

Other than the two times she'd been there in the last year, she hadn't been there since the summer she and Nik were seventeen. After all this time away from there, how could that feel more like home than LA did?

"I'll tell you how," she said out loud as she pushed the food around on her plate. "It's all got to do with a six-and-a-half-foot-tall fire-fighter with a heart of gold." She missed him so much, she ached, and it had been only eight hours since she last saw him.

Gigi was right. She was being silly to let herself get so involved with a man she'd known such a short time, even if the time with him had been the best of her life. Now that she was back in LA, she needed to get her shit taken care of and figure out what was next. She put most of her dinner in the fridge to finish tomorrow and went upstairs to shower.

Forty-five minutes later, she was sitting on her bed staring off into space when her phone rang with a FaceTime call from Mason that wiped out all her resolve where he was concerned. Feeling giddy to hear from him, she took the call. "Hi."

"Hi, beautiful. How're you doing?"

"Better now." That was the unvarnished truth. Hearing his voice and seeing his handsome face made her feel better than she had since she'd left him.

"How are things in Hollywood?"

"Same as always." She paused before she added, "No, wait. That's not true. Everything feels different, like I've been plopped into someone else's life."

"Why do you suppose that is?"

"I think it's because I met you, and I'd much rather be there than here."

"I wish you were here, too. It sucks coming home and knowing you aren't here cooking dinner or sleeping in my bed."

"I liked cooking for you."

"I loved eating what you cooked for me. Are you there by yourself?"

"I am now. Gigi brought me home from the airport."

"Is it safe to be there alone?"

"We changed all the codes. It's fine."

"I'm worried about you running into him and having trouble."

"He's hiding from being served with the divorce papers. I don't think I'll see him."

"I'm still worried about it. I don't want you in any danger."

"I'm okay. I promise. What about you? Any danger on your end today?"

"Nope. We had a fairly quiet day. Wait a sec. I need to knock on wood so I'm not jinxing myself." He knocked on the headboard, and the sight of him in the bed where they'd found so much pleasure together made her yearn to be back there with him. Where she belonged. "When is your meeting?"

"Tomorrow at noon."

"And you'll know more after that?"

"Yes."

"Will you let me know what's up?"

"Of course. I promise I won't leave you hanging."

"If you have to stay out there to film the show, how would you feel about a freeloading roommate?"

"I'd love that, except I wouldn't want you to give up a job you love for me. I'd hate for you to do that."

"It'd be worth it."

"Mason, you can't do that. You just can't."

"Why not?"

"Because we only just met, and you love your job, and you can't go making big decisions that impact your entire life because of me. I won't let you."

"Don't I get any say in what I do with my own life?"

"Of course, but, please don't do anything rash. Promise me?"

"Don't worry. I've still got a job. For now."

Her stomach hurt when she recalled the things that Gigi had said, that she couldn't fall in love with the second guy she'd ever slept with after having married the first one. But maybe… No, Gigi was right. It was insanity to go all in with the first guy she dated or slept with after her marriage ended. She had to rein this in before he did something really stupid, like quit his job to be with her.

"Let's just press Pause and see what happens, okay?"

"Sure, no problem. As long as I can see your gorgeous face every day, I'll be fine. For now."

He kept saying *for now* as if he'd already made up his mind that he was going to give her only so much time to figure things out before he came after her. She couldn't let that happen. Depending on how the meeting went tomorrow, she'd have to figure out what to do about her sexy firefighter before she ended up ruining his life.

CHAPTER 23

$\mathcal{M}$ ason was losing his mind as he tried to carry on like everything was normal when nothing was. Ever since Jordan had left yesterday, he'd felt like he was trying to walk straight up the side of the steepest mountain on earth. He had no energy, no motivation, no interest in anything—except her. He'd listened to the message she left on his phone the day of Syd's accident easily a hundred times the night before, desperate for any connection to her that he could find.

He dragged himself to an AA meeting the next morning because he was self-aware enough to know by now that something like this could threaten his sobriety—if he let it. That couldn't and wouldn't happen.

Seated next to Mallory, he did something he hardly ever did and raised his hand when Nina asked if anyone wanted to share.

She seemed as surprised as all the other regulars were to hear from him.

"I'm Mason, and I'm an alcoholic."

"Hi, Mason," the others said in unison.

"I've been sober for thirteen years."

"Congratulations," one of the tourists said. "That's amazing."

"I have a really good life here on the island. I'm the fire chief. Got a good group of people working for me, have great friends, and I love this place." He rubbed at the chin he'd shaved clean an hour ago. "I met someone. She's…" He leaned on his knees and bent his head.

Mallory's hand landed on his back in a show of support he deeply appreciated.

"She's unlike anyone I've ever known. Sweet and funny and so, so beautiful. I've never connected with anyone the way I did with her. We've only been together for a short time, but I already love her. I really love her. But her life is mostly in LA, and that's where she is now, trying to figure things out. I don't know when or if she's going to come back. All I know is I love her, and she's gone, and for the first time in a really long time, I'm seriously tempted to drink."

Saying the words out loud took some of their power away, or so he hoped. He'd been dying for a drink since he got home last night and found that his house smelled like her, his sheets smelled like her, his towels smelled like her. He saw her everywhere he looked, and the only thought in his head was how much he wanted a drink.

He'd nearly called Mallory and Quinn the night before out of sheer desperation. But he'd powered through and told himself he had to get his shit together. He couldn't go off the deep end over a woman he'd only just met, even if she was the best woman he'd ever known.

"How are you planning to combat the urge to drink, Mason?" Nina asked.

"By keeping myself so busy with work and exercise and friends that I don't have time to drink. It's the nighttime that's going to be hard."

"You're having dinner with us tonight," Mallory said.

"You can come to my place tomorrow night," Nina said.

One by one, every member of the group took a night until they nearly had him in tears. "Thank you," he said gruffly.

"That's what we're here for," Nina said. "To get each other through the hard times and to fight the urge to drink the same way you and your team fight fires. As a group."

Mason nodded. "I appreciate the support."

After the meeting, Mallory and Quinn insisted on buying him breakfast.

Mason went with them because he knew they needed to see he was all right before they went their separate ways.

"You could've called last night," Mallory said when they were seated at Rebecca's.

"I almost did."

"Any time, my friend," Quinn said. "Day or night. Any time."

"Means a lot to have such good friends."

Blaine came into the diner, saw them and came over to say hi.

"Want to join us?" Mallory asked.

"Sure."

Mason pushed over to make room for his friend. Mallory and Quinn would never say anything about what he was dealing with, so Mason took care of catching Blaine up. "Jordan went back to LA, and I'm struggling with the desire to drink. She hasn't even been gone a full day yet, and I'm a mess."

"Oh damn, man. That sucks. What can I do?"

"Have him over for dinner one night this week," Mallory said.

"Done," Blaine replied. "What else?"

"Keep an eye on him at work?" Quinn suggested.

"I can do that, too."

"I feel like a fool for letting something like this rock my boat," Mason said.

"You love her," Mallory said. "We all saw that. Of course you're going to be rocked by her leaving. Is she coming back?"

"I don't know. She's meeting with the suits today about the show. They told her to get back to LA for the meeting, or they were going to sue her for breach."

"So she *had* to go," Mallory said. "It wasn't like she wanted to."

"No, she didn't want to. She was upset about it."

"That's a good thing, Mase," Quinn said. "She didn't want to leave you."

"The thing is, I've been down this road before. I was supposed to get married. A month before the wedding, she said she couldn't go

244

through with it. As bad as that was, and it was pretty damned bad, this thing with Jordan... I think it could be worse, and I've only known her a short time. But everything about the time with her was just... It was fucking perfect. You know?"

"Yeah," Blaine said. "I know what that's like."

"We do, too," Mallory said. "We get it."

"If she has to stay in LA, I'll move out there."

"Don't do anything hasty," Mallory said. "You can't give up your job and your whole life unless you know for sure she feels the same way. As hard as it is, you have to let it play out the way it's meant to."

"I waited a long time to find perfect."

"I know, but now that you have, you need to be patient and give her some room to breathe while she figures things out."

Mallory was right. He knew it, but he didn't like it. "I hear you."

"You need to keep breathing, too." Mallory reached across the table for his hand and gave a gentle squeeze. "If it's meant to be, it will be."

That, too, was true, but God, it was hard to know she was out there somewhere and so far away from him as to be living on a different planet. He would do as Mallory suggested and be patient and stay calm and hope for the best.

For now.

JORDAN THOUGHT she was ready for the meeting with the show's producers and the network that broadcast it, but when she walked into the room full of familiar faces, all she felt was dead inside. When they'd first been approached about doing the show, it had seemed like the most exciting thing that could ever happen.

She'd lived a lifetime and a half since then, and all she wanted was something simpler and more meaningful.

She wanted Mason, even if he was the second guy she'd ever slept with. She wanted him and had no doubt he wanted her just as much. She was about to bet her life on it.

"You good?" Gigi asked when they were seated together on one side of the conference room, across from the execs.

Jordan nodded. She'd worn a black dress with red flowers on it, red heels and was carrying the black Chanel purse she'd bought when Brendan's tour took them to Paris for the first time.

"Jordan, it's so good to see you looking so well." Matilda Spencer, the executive producer and show runner, smiled warmly at her. She was forty-five with red hair and green eyes and was one of the smartest people Jordan had ever met. It was thanks in large part to Matilda's hard work that the show was such a hit.

"Thank you."

"We're very excited to get back to work on the new season."

Now or never, she told herself. *Tell them what you want.* "About that…"

Gigi glanced at her, her expression full of trepidation.

"I'd very much like to do another season," Jordan said.

The relief on the faces across the table was palpable.

"But I want to do it on location."

"Oh my God," Gigi said, her expression incredulous and perhaps a bit angry. "Could I please have a moment with my client?"

"We don't need a moment," Jordan said to her friend. "I heard what you said last night, and I agreed with most of it. But sometimes you do fall in love with the second guy you ever sleep with, and you do get happily ever after with him."

"No, that doesn't actually happen."

"Yes, it can happen."

"Who do you know that's had that happen and had it work out?"

"Gigi, I love you. But I also love Mason, and I want to be with him."

"You barely know him!"

"I already know him better than I ever knew Brendan, and he's *good* to me. I've never had anything like what I have with him, and I'd like to think I'm smart enough after everything I've been through to know a good thing when I find it."

"Um, excuse me," Matilda said as the other suits exchanged confused glances. "I don't mean to interrupt this lovely moment, but could someone please tell me what the hell we're talking about here?"

"Yes, please, Jordan," Gigi said. "Why don't you fill them in?"

Jordan took a deep breath, held it for a second, then released it and met Matilda's intense gaze. "I'm planning to relocate to Gansett Island in Rhode Island, and I'd like to film the new season of the show there."

For a long moment, there was only silence.

Jordan forced herself to hold Matilda's gaze without blinking or otherwise showing the nervous reaction she was having on the inside. This was what she wanted, and she was going to do everything she could to make it happen.

"I'm sorry," Matilda said, "but did you just say you want to film your show, which is about two LA women living their best LA lives, on a remote island in Rhode Island? Or did I hear that wrong?"

"You heard me right."

"I'm afraid I don't understand. What sort of show do you think we could produce on an island in the middle of nowhere?"

"The same kind of show we do here. Me, my friends, my family, my life."

"Your friends including Gigi?"

Jordan glanced at her oldest and dearest friend, hoping she could find a way to support something Jordan wanted desperately, silently pleading with her to at least consider it.

"I don't know," Gigi said, sighing. "I love Jordan with all my heart, but I just don't know if I could do it."

"Think about how fun it could be," Jordan said to Gigi. "With you as a fish out of water on the island." Turning her focus to the executives, she added, "Gansett is the most beautiful place you've ever seen. Rugged coastline, gorgeous beaches, an adorable downtown, bars, restaurants, live music everywhere you go and year-round residents who are such incredible, interesting people. How many reality shows are being shot in LA? Think about how amazing it would be to do something totally different from what everyone else is doing."

"I like the idea," Tom Sturgeon said. He was from the network and had been a big supporter of the show from the beginning. "Jordan is right. LA is done to death. No one is doing what she's suggesting."

Jordan's heart took flight. Was she actually going to pull this off?

"We'd have to relocate the entire crew," Matilda said hesitantly.

"Most of whom will not want to be sent to a remote island for months on end."

"I think we could go with a much smaller crew on Gansett," Jordan said, thinking on the fly and powered by the excitement of actually making this work. "There're fewer locations, and it could be a smaller production overall."

Matilda appeared to give that some thought while Jordan held her breath and tried to keep the hopefulness under control. She was a long way from actually making this happen.

"I'd need to see the place and where we'd be filming," Matilda said. "I can't get my head around it without seeing it."

"That's no problem. I'd be happy to take you there and show you around so you could get a feel for the place and what we could do there. I want to add something that you may not know. When my identical twin sister and I were growing up, we spent our summers on Gansett Island. It's home to both of us. Nikki lives there full time now."

"Would she be willing to be on the show?" Tom asked.

"I don't know. I haven't discussed it with her."

"She wasn't willing to appear when it was in LA," Matilda reminded her.

"Yes, I know, but this might be different. She's engaged to a man who has a big family on the island. They own a marina, hotel and the new event facility that Nikki is managing for them. Perhaps we could feature his connection to the first family of Gansett Island."

"What does the fiancé look like?" Matilda asked.

Jordan couldn't believe she was asking that, and her expression must have said as much.

"Don't look at me like that. You know it matters for this kind of show."

"He's hot, and so is the guy I'm seeing there. He's the chief of the island's fire department."

"And of course he's the reason you want to do this."

"He's part of it, but it's also the fact that I don't want to live here anymore. LA isn't my true home. Gansett is. It's always been my home, and it's where I want to be."

Matilda leaned in, elbows on the table. "I hear what you're saying, and I appreciate what you've been through the last few months. We were all horrified by what happened in Charlotte, and we've tried to give you the proper amount of time to heal and regroup."

Jordan felt like there was a massive "but" coming.

"However..."

Or a "however."

"The show is set in LA. We have a genuine hit on our hands with the current formula. If I've learned one thing in twenty years in this business, it's that you don't mess with something that's working."

Jordan forced herself to remain calm. "I hear you, and I appreciate all the experience you bring to our show. I've always appreciated you, Matilda. You know that. But I have a really good feeling about this idea. It feels fresh and different and exciting in a way that another season here doesn't. The show is about me and my life, right?"

"Yes, of course, but—"

"My life has evolved since we started the show. I'm no longer married to Zane. Or, well, I'm in the process of getting divorced. I'm shaking things up, figuring out what's next, meeting new people. Why shouldn't the show evolve along with me?"

"She makes a good point," Tom said.

If he hadn't been old enough to be her father, she would've kissed him on the lips for his support during this meeting.

"All I'm asking is that you consider the possibility that different won't be bad. It may give the show a whole new shot of adrenaline that'll propel it forward for years to come, rather than one more season of the same old tired formula."

Before Matilda could reply, Jordan's phone rang. She glanced at it on the table and saw Riley's name on the screen and had an immediate and visceral feeling of dread come over her.

"Why is he calling you?" Gigi asked.

Jordan wanted to know the same thing. "I-I'm sorry. I have to take this." She grabbed the phone, stood and walked out of the room as she answered the call. "Riley? What's wrong?"

"Jordan... It's Zane. He's here, and he... He's in the house with Nik and your grandmother, demanding to see you. He... He has a gun, Jordan. The cops are here... It's bad."

The sheer terror she heard in Riley's tone nearly brought Jordan to her knees.

"Can you get here?" Riley asked.

Gigi came out of the conference room to check on her.

"Get me a plane back to the island, Gigi. Right now. Yes, Riley, I'm on my way. I'll be there as soon as I can."

"Please hurry. I don't know. I can't imagine. *Hurry*, Jordan."

"I'm coming. Tell him I'm coming." She ran for the elevator, banging repeatedly on the Down button as she fought off hysteria.

By the time the elevator finally arrived, Jordan was nearly to the point of a full-on meltdown. She tried to call Nikki, but the call went right to voicemail, leading her to wonder if Nik's phone had been turned off. The thought of Nik turning off her phone added to Jordan's panic, because Nikki's phone was never off.

Gigi stepped into the elevator with Jordan, working the phone to arrange for a plane. "No, it's an emergency. We need it right now. We're on the way to LAX. Yes, Gansett Island, so it has to be able to land there."

Thank God Gigi was handling the details, because Jordan could barely breathe as she leaned back against the wall of the elevator car. Tears slid down her cheeks, but she did nothing about them. The thought of Nik and her grandmother being held hostage by that son of a bitch... *What was he thinking?* What did he hope to achieve by threatening the people she loved best?

The thought of losing one or both of them had Jordan shaking uncontrollably as she wept as quietly as she could so Gigi could hear on her call.

"That's fine. Tell him to hurry. We'll be there in thirty minutes."

It would take *hours* to get to Gansett. Would Brendan wait that long for her, or would he do something that could never be undone before she could get there? The thought of life without either her sister or her grandmother or, God forbid, both of them, was unimaginable.

Gigi put her arm around Jordan and hustled her out of the elevator and into Gigi's car. "Try to breathe. We'll get you there."

Jordan's chest tightened as she gasped for air.

Gigi, who had grabbed Jordan's purse from the conference room, rifled through it and found Jordan's rescue inhaler. She held it up to Jordan's mouth. "Breathe. *Jordan!*"

Jordan took hold of the inhaler and forced herself to take a hit that eased her airways even if her chest continued to ache.

Gigi answered a call from Matilda, told her they'd left due to an emergency in Jordan's family, and no, she couldn't say when or if Jordan would be able to finish their meeting. "Look, you heard what she wants to do. Talk it over. We'll get back to you as soon as we're able to."

Jordan couldn't bring herself to care about the show at a time like this. *Mason.* She needed to talk to him. Maybe he knew something she didn't about what was happening at Eastward Look. Though her hands were shaking, she managed to put through the call to his cell, but the call went to his voicemail. The sound of his voice provided immediate comfort. "It's me. I'm sure you've heard what's going on at the house. Call me if you can. I'm on my way."

After ending the call, she tried to keep breathing while Gigi drove them to the airport, darting in and out of traffic with reckless disregard for safety. Who cared about safety when her sister and grandmother were in grave danger?

CHAPTER 24

*N*ikki focused on staying calm while she held her grandmother's hand under the table. The house was surrounded by police and other public safety personnel, not that they could do much about what was happening inside the house.

It was her own fault. She hadn't locked the door, which had allowed him to come strolling into the house, taking them by surprise when he pulled a gun on them. "Tell Jordan I'm here, and I want to see her right now." His eyes had been wild and unfocused, making her realize he was high on something.

"She's not here."

"Yes, she is. Don't fucking lie to me."

"I'm not lying. She flew home to LA yesterday for a meeting with the network about the show."

At about five-foot-nine and thin as a rail, Brendan had close-cropped blond hair and hazel eyes that bugged out of his gaunt face. He looked terrible as he stared at her in disbelief. "That's not true. I was told she's here."

"She was here for three weeks. She's not here now."

"You need to get her here."

"I'll need my phone." She pointed to the kitchen counter, where she'd left her phone earlier.

"Don't call her. Get someone else to do it. Tell them to tell her your life and Evelyn's depend on her getting here. No tricks."

Nikki got up from the table and went to get her phone. She texted Riley. *Zane is here with a gun. He wants us to get Jordan here asap. Call her. Tell her what's going on. I love you. We are fine. He's too much of a coward to kill us. Try not to worry.*

Riley wrote right back. *Jesus, Nik. Are you fucking kidding me? I can't bear that you're in there with him.*

Just get Jordan here. That's what he wants, and tell the cops not to do anything crazy. He doesn't have the stones to hurt us.

Sorry if I don't believe that after what he did to Jordan.

It's okay. I promise. I love you.

Love you so much. I'm dying.

Don't do that. Need you.

"That's enough," Brendan said. "Shut the phone off and go back over there."

"Let my grandmother go."

"No," Evelyn said. "I'm not going anywhere without you."

Nikki returned to her seat, and Evelyn took her hand again, holding on tight. "Don't ask me to leave you in here alone with him."

"Shut up. Both of you." He went to the fridge, opened the door and pulled out a bottle of water that he downed. Then he found a package of deli turkey and began eating that as he paced the kitchen. At least the gun was tucked into the back of his pants. For now, anyway.

Nikki started thinking about how she could overpower him, get the gun and end this thing. She had every confidence that she could do it and would've risked it if her grandmother hadn't been there, too.

Maybe she'd get the chance at some point. If she did, she wouldn't hesitate to act.

RILEY PACED THE YARD, his entire body racked with tension that made him feel like he'd been put through a wood chipper. That Nik was in the house with Jordan's malicious, gun-toting ex was more than he could bear to think about. If anything happened to Nik or Evelyn, Riley would murder that son of a bitch with his own hands.

The yard was full of cops and other first responders he'd summoned. They couldn't do a goddamned thing until the state police's hostage unit arrived. He'd been told they were en route. It wasn't happening fast enough for Riley's liking.

A hand on his shoulder halted him. He spun around to find his dad there. The sight of his father's concerned face nearly reduced Riley to tears. Somehow, he managed to just barely hang on to his composure as Kevin hugged him.

"I came as soon as I heard," Kevin said. "What're they saying?"

"State police are on their way with a hostage negotiation team."

"Good God, what is he thinking showing up here with a gun? Does he think he'll get Jordan to reconcile after a stunt like this?"

"Who knows what he's thinking? All I know is what Nik told me when she texted that he had shown up with a gun."

"I'm so sorry, son. That's horrifying."

"If anything happens to her..." Riley's voice broke along with his heart. He couldn't imagine life without her. Not anymore.

"She's smart and resilient and strong. She's going to get through this and be totally fine. I know it. In fact, I'll bet he ends up sorry that he messed with her."

"I hope you're right."

"I'm always right. You know that."

For once, Riley took comfort in the fact that his father was usually right.

Mason Johns approached them, looking as undone as Riley felt. "What the fuck?"

"No idea," Riley said, conveying what he knew to Mason.

"So he showed up with a gun looking for Jordan?" Mason's usually robust complexion had gone pale.

"Yeah, and now he's got Nik and Evelyn in there and isn't happy to hear that Jordan is in LA."

"She called me. She's on her way. I tried to call her back, but the call wouldn't go through."

Overhead, a state police chopper came swooping in, landing in the field across the street from Eastward Look.

"Here comes the cavalry," Kevin said.

Riley felt like he was going to be sick. If they went in there with guns blazing, would everyone come out alive?

THE FLIGHT to Gansett seemed even more endless than usual as Jordan waited to hear something—anything—about what was going on there. She'd tried to call Mason again from the air, but the call wouldn't go through, so she texted him via the plane's Wi-Fi.

I'm on my way. I hope you get this. What's happening there? I'm losing it.

Hey, sweetheart. It's okay. The state police are talking to him. They're letting him know that he can end this right now before anyone gets hurt and walk out of there.

Please don't let anything happen to Nik and my grandmother. Please, Mason.

Blaine and his entire team are here, and Josh from the state police as well as their hostage negotiation unit. Keep breathing. It's going to be okay.

I'll die if anything happens to them because of me.

It wouldn't be because of you. He's the one doing this. Not you.

I brought him into our lives. It's on me.

I can't wait to hug you.

I need that so bad.

I'm here, and I'll be here for as long as you need me.

Might be a while.

Not going anywhere. Tell me when you're landing. I'll pick you up and get you to them.

I will. Can't wait to see you.

Same, babe. Keep breathing.

Knowing he was there, helping out where he could and waiting for her, made Jordan feel slightly better.

She hit up Davy by text. *Do you know what he's doing? He's got my sister and grandmother held hostage at our home on Gansett. WTF IS HE DOING???*

Davy responded quickly. *OMG, no way.*

YES! He's got a gun. Where did he get a gun!?

I don't know. He went off the grid a couple of days ago, and I haven't been able to find him.

She'd known he was hiding from her and the server but not that his own people had lost track of him, too. *And you didn't think I needed to know that? Seriously!?!*

I'm so sorry. I've been so busy trying to track him down that I never thought to tell you.

He came to my home with a gun. If I'd been there, I might be dead. I thought you said rehab worked.

I thought it had. I'm so sorry, Jordan. I totally should've called you.

Yes, you should have.

Please keep me posted.

She was fuming that he hadn't given her a heads-up that Brendan had fallen out of touch with even his closest circle right when she was trying to serve him with divorce papers. That was not a coincidence.

"What're you hearing?" Gigi asked.

"That he went missing days ago, and Davy never thought to give me a heads-up that he'd gone off the grid for even them."

"Son of a bitch."

"Right? He came to find me with a gun, G. Was he going to kill me for wanting a divorce?"

"I can't even go there. My God. What was he thinking, and why didn't anyone tell you?"

Jordan sucked in a deep breath and blew it out. "How much longer?"

"Two more hours."

"I'll go mad by then."

Nikki and Evelyn remained vigilant as Zane talked on the phone with the state police hostage negotiators.

"I just want to see my wife. That's all I want. I'm not looking to hurt anyone."

Nikki glanced at Evelyn, who raised her eyebrows.

"He's not paying any attention to us," Evelyn whispered. "We need to make a move."

"What kind of move?"

"Did you get rid of the cast-iron frying pan when you renovated?"

"No, because I knew it was your favorite."

"Can you get it?"

Brendan had moved to the foyer, where Nikki could see him looking out the front door at the law enforcement officials positioned all over the front lawn.

"I can get it."

"Get it and come back. We need to bide our time. Move nice and slow so he doesn't notice."

Nikki's heart was in her throat as she kicked off her flip-flops and moved across the kitchen on bare feet. She retrieved the cast-iron frying pan from under the stove without making a sound and was back to her seat at the table within seconds. Adrenaline pumped through her body, making her feel light-headed and supercharged.

"Good job," Evelyn whispered, her gaze fixed on Brendan, who hadn't moved.

"If I come to the door, you'll shoot me," he was saying. "How do I know I can trust you?"

Evelyn leaned forward. "He's going to the front door."

"I'm going for it."

She grabbed Nikki's arm. "Nik, honey, please—if you don't have a clean shot, don't do it. It's all or nothing. You have to knock him out."

"I've been waiting years for this opportunity. Don't worry, I'm not going to miss."

Evelyn bit her lip as if trying not to laugh and gave Nik a thumbs-up.

Taking the heavy cast-iron pan, Nikki got up and tiptoed toward the doorway that led to the foyer. Brendan stood in front of the storm door, talking on the phone and looking out at the police presence in the yard.

Knowing she would never get a better chance, Nikki ignored the pounding of her heart and moved quickly but quietly, coming up behind him, raising the pan with both hands and bringing it down on his head with all her strength. She put everything she had into making sure she took him down.

He collapsed like a felled oak, landing in a pile at her feet.

"Well done, darling," Evelyn said from behind her as she clapped her hands.

Nikki leaned over him, grabbed the gun from the back of his pants and then stepped over him to open the storm door. "Come and get him out of here," she called out to the cops, who rushed the house.

She handed the gun to Josh from the state police, took her grandmother's hand and led her out of the house.

Riley came running up to her, scooped her up and hugged her so hard, she feared he might break her ribs. "Thank God you're okay."

"I'm fine, but he's gonna have one hell of a headache."

"Least of what he deserves. You're like Wonder Woman."

"That's what we call Gran," Nikki said.

"I'm more than happy to turn my cape over to you, darling," Evelyn said. "You should've seen her take him out. It was *awesome*."

"I have no doubt," Riley said. "She's amazing."

Now that she'd taken care of business, Nikki began to shake from the aftershocks. Her sister's ex had shown up looking for her with a gun. Thank God Jordan had been nowhere to be found when that happened.

"He was going to kill her," she whispered to Riley, who continued to hold her like he might never let her go. That'd be fine with her.

"Thanks to you, he'll never get the chance."

MASON WAS ALREADY at the airport when Jordan's plane came into view. A few minutes ago, he'd heard from Blaine about what Nikki had done and couldn't wait to tell Jordan her loved ones were safe. Her ex was on his way to the clinic, where he'd be treated before being arraigned on a wide variety of charges that would keep him far away from her for decades.

The sleek Lear came slicing through the clouds on final approach to Gansett.

Mason got out of the SUV and walked through the terminal to the flight line to meet her as she disembarked. His heart gave a joyful lurch at the sight of her coming down the stairs. When she saw him waiting for her, she broke into a run.

She was wearing a sexy-as-fuck black dress with red flowers on it and red heels that she ran in like she'd been running in heels all her life.

He scooped her up, and the second she was back in his arms, all his agitation settled and everything in his life made sense again. "It's over. Nik knocked him out with your grandmother's cast-iron frying pan. He's in custody."

"Oh my God. That's the best news I've ever heard."

"By all accounts, Nik was a badass warrior."

"That's my sister." Jordan sniffled as tears streamed down her face. "You don't want to mess with her."

"Good to know."

A throat cleared behind Jordan.

Mason put her down, and they turned to face Gigi, who was the picture of LA sophistication right down to the designer handbag looped over her forearm.

To Jordan, she said, "Are you going to introduce me?"

"Sorry." Jordan wiped tears as she smiled at Mason. "Gigi, this is Mason. Mason, meet Gigi."

They shook hands as Gigi tipped her head back so she could look up at Mason. "You are one *tall* motherfucker."

"So I've been told," he said, instantly amused by her.

"Jordan says you're big all over."

"Gigi, oh my God! Shut up!"

"What's going on with the dickhead?"

"Nik knocked him over the head with my grandmother's cast-iron frying pan," Jordan told Gigi.

"Of course she did. I love it. The douche nugget had it coming."

"He sure did," Jordan said.

Mason wanted to kiss Jordan so bad, he could barely resist the urge to do it right then and there. But first she needed to see her sister and grandmother, to see for herself that they were okay. There'd be time for kissing later. Lots of time. He would see to it.

"How's your elbow and your hands?"

"Everything is fine." *Now that you're back*, he wanted to add but didn't since they weren't alone. As they walked to his SUV, he bent his arm to show her his elbow was on the mend. "Hardly even hurts anymore."

He held the passenger door and the one behind it for the ladies, settling Jordan in to ride shotgun. It was all he could do to keep from staring at her or pinching himself to make sure he wasn't dreaming. She'd been gone one day, and he'd nearly gone mad without her. Now that she was back, he would do whatever it took to keep her with him forever.

But first things first.

He drove them to the public safety building where Nikki and Evelyn had been taken to make a statement. "Where are they?" he asked the officer working the reception desk.

The officer's eyes bugged when he recognized Mason's companions. "Conference room."

"Right this way, ladies." Mason led them to the conference room that the police and fire departments shared and knocked on the door before entering.

Jordan ran for her sister and grandmother, the three of them tearful as they engaged in a group hug.

"I'm so sorry," Jordan said. "It's all my fault."

"Don't be silly," Evelyn said. "You didn't send him to the house with a gun, and PS, we're thankful you weren't there, because he didn't come there to talk to you. And PPS, your sister was incredible."

"I heard." Jordan hugged Nikki. "I bet you enjoyed knocking him out."

"Little bit," Nik said as she returned the hug. "PS, it was all Gran's idea. I was just the executor. It's all over now."

"Thanks to you. I love you guys so much, and I'm so thankful you're okay."

"And we're thankful you are," Evelyn said. "We're all okay. That's the only thing that matters."

CHAPTER 25

Mason hadn't left her side since she got off the plane and had even sat with her while she provided background for the officers investigating the incident.

"I have a proposal I'd like to make," Evelyn said.

Her granddaughters gave her their full attention.

"Charge Brendan with a misdemeanor of your choice," Evelyn said to the officers, "and make him reimburse the town and the state for the expenses incurred by his stunt today."

"In exchange for what?" Nikki asked.

"I want several things," Evelyn said. "First, he signs the divorce papers. Second, he makes a public statement on his social media taking responsibility for his own mistakes and making it clear to his lunatic supporters that Jordan was an innocent party in everything that happened. He needs to tell them, in no uncertain terms, to leave her alone. And third," she said, looking to Jordan, "he agrees to never again contact my granddaughter or come anywhere near her or her family."

Josh, the state police officer in charge, looked to Nikki and Jordan. "What do you think?"

"It's up to Nik," Jordan said. "She's the one who was held hostage by him."

"I'd take that deal in a hot second," Nik said, "if it meant we'd seen the last of him."

"In that case, I'm willing to offer him the deal," Josh said. "From what I'm told, he's awake at the clinic and asking to see Jordan."

She felt stricken by the idea of seeing him again, but knew she needed to so she could close the door on that part of her life.

"You don't have to do anything you don't want to do," Mason said to Jordan.

She looked to Josh. "Would you mind if I outlined the offer to him?"

"Be my guest."

To Mason, she said, "Will you come with me?"

"Absolutely."

"I'm making dinner at the house," Evelyn said as they were leaving the conference room. "Everyone is invited. We'll see you there?"

Jordan wanted to be alone with Mason, but they'd have time for that later. She looked up at him.

He nodded.

"We'll be there."

Evelyn crooked her finger at Mason, bringing him down so she could kiss his cheek. "Thank you for taking such good care of my granddaughter."

"It's my pleasure, ma'am," Mason said, his face flushing with embarrassment that Jordan found adorable.

Then again, she found everything about him adorable and endearing and sexy.

While Blaine offered to drive the others home to Eastward Look, Mason took Jordan to the clinic. When they were in his SUV, Jordan reached across the center console for his hand, turning it palm up and examining the healing wounds. "I'm glad you didn't reopen them while I was gone."

"I was careful." He turned his hand to rest it on her leg, under the hem of her dress. "Were you really only gone one night? It felt like a hundred years."

"It did for me, too. You need to know I was going to come back as soon as I could, even if this hadn't happened."

He glanced at her. "That's good to hear. You should know that I was going to come after you if you were gone too long."

"Really?"

"Absolutely. Would that have been okay?"

"Hell yes. As long as you didn't quit the job you love for me."

"I would've done it if I got to be with you." He squeezed her leg, his hand inching upward until she stopped it.

"Hold that thought."

"You're coming home with me later."

"Try and stop me."

The noise that came from him was part growl, part moan as he squeezed her leg. A few minutes later, after parking at the clinic, he looked over at her. "You gotta at least kiss me, or I'll never make it until later."

She had her seat belt off and was halfway across the car in the time it took him to finish the statement. Like it had from the start, the intense connection between them ignited when her lips touched his. They gorged on each other, neither having a care about who might see them making out in his town-issued vehicle in broad daylight. Those concerns were for other people, Jordan thought. Her only concern was getting closer to him.

"Fuck," he muttered when he finally pulled back. "You're going to get me fired."

"That won't be my fault," she said, laughing. "You're the one who started the tongue action."

"Can't help it." He caressed her face as he gazed at her. "So much I need to tell you. Not sure I can wait until later."

"I'd call in sick to dinner, but since it was my ex who held them hostage…"

"I know. We'll eat quickly."

She glanced at the doors to the clinic, noting two police vehicles parked outside. "Let's get this over with." They walked into the clinic together and went to talk to a cop in the lobby.

Mason introduced her to the officer. "Wyatt, this is the suspect's wife."

"*Ex*-wife," Jordan said. She would be soon enough.

"*Ex*-wife," Mason replied with a small grin for her. "He asked to speak to her."

"Come on back." Wyatt led the way to a cubicle, where Brendan was handcuffed to the hospital bed. Had he always been small, or did he just look that way in comparison to Mason?

His eyes went wide at the sight of her. "They said you weren't here."

"I wasn't. I flew back here after I heard you'd taken my family hostage."

"I didn't take them hostage."

"You showed up uninvited at our home with a gun and wouldn't let them leave until you got to see me. That's the definition of taking someone hostage."

"Your sister gave me a skull fracture."

"That's the least of what you deserve." Standing before him, she realized two things. One, she didn't love him anymore, and two, she was no longer afraid of him. "You and I were done long before you pulled this stunt."

"You wouldn't talk to me! I got clean for you, and then you wouldn't even see me!"

"Oh, please, you've never done anything in your life unless it benefited you. Don't waste my time telling me how you got sober for me. Here's the deal. We're over. You may as well sign the papers and be done with it, because after today, you'll never see me again."

"I have things I want to tell you."

"I don't care. There's nothing you have to say that I want to hear. I gave you every chance. I gave you chances you didn't deserve, like after you taped us having sex and posted the video? Remember that?"

"I didn't mean for that to happen! I told you that!"

"I don't believe you. And frankly, I don't care anymore. I've moved on, and my life no longer includes you. As to the shit you pulled today, you're lucky my grandmother and sister are in a forgiving mood. Otherwise, you would've been charged with multiple felonies." She outlined the deal the state police had agreed to and put the papers that Gigi had printed on the table next to his bed. "Do everyone a favor, take the deal, sign the divorce papers, take responsibility for your own shit and tell your fans to leave me the hell alone. Go back to rehab, and don't leave until you're well. Get your life together, and stay the fuck out of mine. That's all I've got to say."

"Jordan!" The cuffs clanked against the metal rail when he tried to get up to give chase. "You have to listen to me!"

"Go fuck yourself, Brendan." Jordan hooked her hand through Mason's arm. "Let's go."

Under his breath, Mason said, "I'm a little turned on after hearing you tell him off."

"Is that right?"

"Oh yeah. Seriously sexy, babe."

Jordan laughed, feeling freer and happier than she had in years. "You know what the best part is?"

"Better than you telling him to go fuck himself?"

"Yep."

"Lay it on me."

"We've got time before dinner to stop at your place. If you can get out of work, that is."

When they got to his car, he opened the door for her, put his hands on her hips and lifted her into the passenger seat. "You want to know the biggest benefit to dating the chief?"

"Other than having him save my life?"

"Even better. I get to set my own hours."

"That's really convenient at times like this."

"Seriously convenient." He kissed her and pulled back before things could get out of hand again. "Hold that thought for ten minutes." His driving on the short ride home reminded Jordan of Gigi darting through traffic earlier in LA. Had that really happened today?

It seemed like a week ago after the longest flight ever to get to her loved ones.

On the way home, Mason called Dermot. "You're in charge for the rest of the day. Don't bother me unless the zombies show up, you got me?"

"Yes, sir. I heard your lady was back—"

Mason ended the call.

"That was rude," Jordan said, laughing.

"He can go fuck himself."

She laughed harder than she had in years, her heart full of love for the second man she'd ever slept with. Jordan didn't care what Gigi said. Sometimes you *could* fall for the second guy you ever slept with. Sometimes he was just so right and so perfect that looking beyond him simply wasn't necessary.

In that moment, she decided that if the network didn't go for her idea for a show on Gansett, she'd buy her way out of the contract, even if that would take most of the money she'd made since the show became popular. She could sell the house in Bel Air and use the proceeds to finance her new life.

And she would apply for that activities director job at the senior center.

The feeling that came with the pieces falling into place was one of peace and contentment and excitement for what was ahead.

"Wait for me," Mason said gruffly when he pulled into his driveway, leaving a cloud of dirt in his wake as he brought the car to a quick stop.

Jordan buzzed with desire and love and so much happiness as she watched him come around the front of the truck like a man on a very important mission. And then he was reaching for her as she reached for him. He picked her up and kicked the door shut and kissed her all the way into the house, even going so far as to press her against the front door until they were in danger of consummating their reunion right there in the open.

Behind her, he fumbled with the door until it flew open and nearly sent them flying.

Jordan shook with laughter as he swore viciously under his breath.

He kicked the door closed and made a beeline directly to his bedroom where they came down on the bed in a wild burst of passion that had teeth colliding with lips.

"Ow," she said, smiling at him.

He shook his head and cracked a big grin. "Let's try this again with some finesse this time, shall we?"

"Yes, we shall."

"How does this sexy dress come off?"

"Over the head."

He reached under the hem and slid the dress up, setting her on fire with his touch as his hands moved over her sensitive skin. By the time the dress cleared her head, she was trembling.

"Mmm, what a sight." His gaze moved over her with barely constrained hunger that only added to her desire. That he wanted her so badly was almost unbearably exciting.

She'd worn a sheer red bra and matching panties that had his full attention.

"I still can't believe that a sweet, sexy goddess like you is in my bed."

"Why can't you believe it?"

"You're way, *way* out of my league."

It pained her to hear him say that. She rested a hand on his face and compelled him to look at her. "No, I'm not. Your league is the best one I've ever been in—kind and sweet and thoughtful and funny and sexy and loyal. I've never had anything like you."

"You've definitely got me. When you left, I thought I'd lose my mind. I was so afraid I'd never see you again."

"That wouldn't have happened. All I could think about was getting back here to you, even after Gigi said…"

"What did Gigi say?"

"Nothing. It's not important."

He kissed her neck and rolled her earlobe between his teeth, sending a jolt of pure need cascading through her that settled into an intense throb between her legs. "Tell me."

"She said no one falls for the second guy they sleep with."

"You never told me I was only the second."

"I told you that."

He shook his head.

"Well, you are."

"What did you say when Gigi said that?" he asked as he kissed her throat and chest.

Jordan squirmed as she tried to get him to focus on the places that burned with need. "I said it can happen."

"Has it happened to you?"

She nodded, thrilling in the relief that overtook his adorable expression.

"Really?"

"Really."

"That's exceptionally good news, because I'm crazy about you, Jordan. So crazy, I had a little sobriety challenge after you left."

"What? You did? What happened?"

"Nothing, but it was a struggle not to give in to old demons when I thought maybe I'd lost you."

"You never lost me. You could never lose me. You not only saved my life, but you showed me something so much better than I ever knew existed. I was always going to come back. I swear."

He found the front clasp of her bra and released it, his eyes going hot with desire as he gazed at her bare breasts.

Jordan's nipples tightened in anticipation, and he didn't disappoint, taking her right nipple into the warmth of his mouth. For what felt like hours, he focused only on her breasts, licking, sucking, tugging, kissing. He made her crazy with everything he did. "Mason."

"Hmm?"

"Hurry."

"I'm in no hurry."

"Ugh."

He laughed and moved down to her belly. Before she caught up to him, he had her panties off and her leg hooked around his neck as he destroyed her with his lips, tongue and fingers.

She came so hard, she saw fireworks behind her closed eyes, which flew open when she felt the hard press of his cock against her sensitive flesh.

"Easy, baby. Nice and easy. Let me love you."

Jordan gave him everything she had, heart and soul, as he made passionate love to her, holding her just right as he filled her to capacity.

"So good," he whispered. "So hot and tight and sexy." He grasped her ass in one big hand and pushed hard into her, triggering a full-body orgasm that made her scream from the pleasure that overtook them both.

He came down on top of her, holding her while their bodies cooled and trembled. "I love you. Maybe it's too soon or too much or whatever, but it's true. I love you."

"I love you, too. And I don't care that you're the second guy I ever slept with. I'm wise enough to know I'll never find anyone better than you."

He hugged her so tight, she could barely breathe, but being breathless had never felt better. "What about the show and everything in LA?"

"I pitched the idea of doing it here."

"What did they say?"

"Our meeting was interrupted when I got the call from Riley about what was happening here." She ran her fingers through his hair as she gazed up at him. "But it doesn't matter what they say. I'm here to stay. If they don't want to do the show here, I'll sell my house in LA and buy out my contract. I have options, and it's time I take control of my life and do exactly what I want. And what I want is you."

Mason leaned his forehead on hers. "Best words I've ever heard."

"I'm worried about the sobriety challenge. What happened?"

"I aired it out in a meeting and worked the program, which is what keeps us sober when things go sideways. I told them about you, that I was in love with you and worried we weren't going to be able to make it work." He rolled to his side, bringing her with him and smoothing

270

the hair back from her face. "I told them it'd taken me a really long time to find perfect, and it was terrifying to think about losing you."

"You're not going to lose me."

"Hearing that makes me happier than I've ever been."

"I want you to know you can always talk to me about the challenge of maintaining your sobriety. I'll always want to hear when you're struggling and do anything I can to help."

"Having you here with me, in my life, in my arms and in my bed is the best incentive I could ever have to stay sober."

"Don't do it for me. You have to do it for yourself first and foremost."

"I know, and I will, but you give me added incentive."

She smiled at him. "I'm happy to be your incentive."

"I'm happy to be your everything."

EPILOGUE

$\mathcal{M}$ ac climbed the stairs to the deck, bringing a plate full of grilled burgers and chicken breasts with him. He delivered the food to the kitchen, where Abby, Stephanie, Owen, Laura and Grace were getting everything else ready. "More coming," he said.

"We're almost ready to put it all out," Laura said.

As he went back out the door to the deck, his cousin Shane and his wife, Katie, were coming in, carrying a huge plate of cookies.

"Oh, I want one now," Mac said. Katie's cookies were to die for.

She held the plate so he could take one for himself and one for Maddie.

"Thanks, Katie."

"You're always my best customer, Mac."

"I'm wondering if I could pay you to make me a couple dozen every week."

"Talk to my business manager." She used her thumb to point to Shane. "I'm sure we can work something out."

"You can't afford my wife's cookies," Shane said.

Mac laughed. "I'll pay any price for regular access."

"I'll take that under advisement."

"You do that."

Mac glanced toward the right side of the deck, where Owen and Julia Lawry had set up to play later on with Mac's brother Evan and Niall Fitzgerald, another local musician.

He went to the left corner of the deck, where he'd arranged Maddie's lounge in the shade. Baby Mac slept in her arms as she gabbed with friends and family, her caramel eyes dancing with happiness the way he liked them best.

He took a quick look to make sure Thomas and Hailey were still running around in the yard with the other kids, being supervised by Blaine and Tiffany. "Excuse me, ladies," he said to the other women, who included Maddie's friend Daisy Babson and some of the others she used to work with at the inn. "I need to have a word with my wife."

"Great party, Mac," Daisy said. "Thanks for having us."

"Thanks for coming."

Mac took a second to hug Sydney, who had her daughter, Lily, in her arms. Lily had her mother's strawberry-blonde hair and hazel eyes. "How're you ladies doing?"

"We're okay," Syd said with a small smile. "It took about three days for my hands to stop shaking."

"Totally understandable."

"We're counting our blessings."

Mac leaned in to kiss her cheek. "As are we, and you two are high on our list."

Sydney blinked back tears. "Thanks, Mac, and thank you for all the food and everything you guys have done for us."

"Anything for you." To Maddie, he said, "Make room for your baby daddy."

She scooted over to give him room to sit on the lounge with her.

He handed over the cookie he'd stolen for her.

Her pretty face lit up with pleasure. "Is that one of Katie's?"

"You know it."

After adjusting baby Mac to find a more comfortable position, she took a big bite of the cookie and moaned.

"Don't do that. It makes me think of appetizers." He loved the sound of her laughter almost as much as the sight of her happy smile. Having their friends and family around always did wonders for whatever was weighing on them. This party, as well as the break their loved ones had arranged for them, had gone a long way toward alleviating their stress.

"I had an idea for appetizers," Maddie said between bites of cookie. "Something we've never done."

Mac's heart nearly stopped at the thought of her thinking such things. Once upon a time, she never would've said that sentence out loud. "There's something we haven't done?"

"Uh-huh."

"What is it?"

After making sure that no one was looking or listening, she pushed her breasts together and touched a finger to her impressive cleavage.

Mac nearly choked on his cookie. "*Seriously?*"

Her face flushed with color as she gave him a shy look that made him immediately hard. "Why not?"

"Stop."

"You don't want to?"

"For fuck's sake. Of course I want to. I want to right this very fucking second, but I can't because you threw this at me when everyone we know is at our house."

She laughed so hard, she shook with it. "Think of it as something to look forward to."

"Sure, as I walk around entertaining our guests while sporting a huge boner."

Her laughter had others looking at them.

"Nothing to see here, folks," Mac said, scowling. "Carry on."

"Is Maddie laughing at you, bro?" Grant asked.

"So what else is new?" Lowering his voice, he said to his wife, "You'll pay for this later. Dr. David didn't say anything about spankings."

"Oh, can we? Please?"

"I'm going to die of boner-related high blood pressure before this party is over."

"Don't do that. I need you too much." She leaned her head on his shoulder. "Thanks for having the party. You were right. It was just what we needed."

"Can I get the part about me being right in writing? I'd like it signed, dated and notarized."

"In your dreams."

Mac didn't need to dream. Not anymore. He had it all, as long as he had her, their kids, their family and friends and the beautiful island they all called home.

MAC MCCARTHY JUNIOR threw one hell of a party, Mason decided as he took in the action from Mac's huge deck and even bigger yard, where half the town seemed to have gathered for the impromptu get-together.

From his vantage point on the deck, Mason spotted Jordan talking to Riley, Nikki, Evelyn, Gigi, Finn, Chloe, Kevin and Chelsea, who was holding her baby daughter, Summer.

Jordan glanced up, caught him looking at her and smiled as she waved him down to join them.

Eager to get back to her, Mason grabbed several bottles of water from the cooler and took them with him when he went down the stairs to the yard.

Two weeks after she'd returned to Gansett, he still couldn't believe Jordan was here to stay and as in love with him as he was with her. He'd been through a lot before he found her, but all the heartbreak had been worth it because it had been leading him to her.

Brendan had signed the divorce papers and had gone live on Instagram a week ago to come clean to his fans, telling them to leave Jordan alone, that she'd been a loving and faithful wife and that she deserved better than what she'd gotten from him. On that, Mason and the man known as Zane were in complete agreement, and Mason planned to make sure she had what she deserved every day for the rest of her life.

Mason handed Jordan a bottle of water. "Anyone else want one?"

"I'll take one," Gigi said. "Thank you."

Mason was fascinated by the exotic creature who was Jordan's longtime best friend. Even dressed "down" in a summer dress and sandals, she was the ultimate fish out of water among the island residents, who were the epitome of casual. After having spent time with Gigi over the last two weeks, he'd concluded that she would come across as glamorous even if she wore a burlap sack.

And while Gigi was stunning, she had nothing on his sweet love, who slipped an arm around him and leaned her head on his chest.

A week ago, Matilda, the show's producer and show runner, had visited the island to try to wrap her head around Jordan's idea of filming the show there. Jordan and Gigi had put a lot of effort into planning for Matilda's visit, going so far as to rough up several scripts for the show that had shown Matilda how it might work there.

As always, the chemistry between the two women had jumped off the screen in the short videos they'd filmed ahead of Matilda's arrival. They were working the fish-out-of-water angle to showcase life on Gansett, and Gigi had agreed to relocate for the summer to film the season before returning to her real life in LA. Under no circumstances, she said, would she be caught dead there in the winter.

Yesterday, Jordan had gotten the call from Matilda with the official green light for filming the next season on Gansett that summer.

With David and Daisy having moved into their new home, Gigi had leased the garage apartment at Jared and Lizzie James's estate for the summer. Next week, she would fly home to LA to pack up what she needed for the summer on Gansett.

Mason and Jordan had celebrated the good news all night long.

"I've learned a valuable lesson over the last few weeks," she'd said to him in the dark of night, which was when they seemed to have their best conversations.

"What's that?"

"I'm in charge of my life, and if I want something—or some*one*—I have to go after it—or *him*—with everything I've got."

"*He* is very glad you came after him." He'd never known the kind of happiness he'd found with her and couldn't wait to see what would come next for them. Whatever it was, he had no doubt it would be fun and funny and sexy and full of love.

"What'd I miss?" Mason asked Jordan.

"We're trying to tell Gigi that she'll have more fun on Gansett Island than she would've had in LA this summer."

"I'm still not convinced," Gigi said disdainfully. "You don't even have clubs here."

"We have the Wayfarer," Nikki said with a goofy grin that made everyone laugh.

Gigi rolled her well-made-up eyes. "*That* is not a *club*."

Mason didn't think they would change Gigi's mind about life on Gansett, but one thing was for certain—Jordan was thrilled to have her best friend hanging out for the next few months. If she was happy, so was he.

Big Mac McCarthy and his wife, Linda, came over to say hello. They both hugged and kissed Evelyn, who introduced them to Gigi.

"It's so lovely to meet you," Linda said to Gigi. "We *love* your show."

"Thank you so much," Gigi said. "Have you heard we're filming the next season here?"

"Get out of here," Linda said, clearly stunned by the news. "That's awesome. I want to be a guest star."

"We can probably make that happen," Jordan said. "We know people."

"Do you watch the show, too?" Mason asked Big Mac.

"I've been known to watch what my wife likes once in a while, and I have to say, the show is fun and funny. Congrats, ladies."

"Thank you so much, Mr. McCarthy," Jordan said.

"You're supposed to call me Big Mac, sweetheart," he said with a wink for her. "Mason, I spoke with Mayor Upton about the situation at the bluffs, and I think we might be heading toward a deal that would include wire fencing that won't block the view."

"That's excellent news. We saved another tourist out there this week."

"Heard about that. It helped me to make the case to the mayor."

"Appreciate your help with that."

"We don't need someone getting killed out there before we make some needed changes."

"Agreed."

When the conversation moved to other topics, Jordan looked up at him. "My hero," she said softly so only he could hear her as she smiled up at him.

Mason liked being her hero. It was the best job he'd ever had.

THANK you for reading *Rescue After Dark*! I hope you enjoyed reading about Mason and Jordan and that all the readers who wanted Mason to get his happy ending are satisfied! Before you can ask, yes, I'm eventually going to do something with Gigi, who was super fun to write, and I do have a fun idea in mind for her.

But before that, I'm going to bring you *Blackout After Dark*, which will feature an island-wide power outage that will give us a chance to catch up with ALL of your favorite past couples and will set the stage for the next few Gansett Island books. I'm super excited to write this next book and to visit with characters we haven't seen in a while. As the cast gets bigger, it's harder to get everyone into every book, and I've been missing some of our old friends. So that's the plan for the next book, which you can preorder now at marieforce.com/black-outafterdark to read in February 2021!

Many thanks to the wonderful team that supports me behind the scenes every day: Julie Cupp, Lisa Cafferty, Holly Sullivan, Tia Kelley, Nikki Haley and Ashley Lopez. Thank you to Dan, Emily and Jake for always supporting my crazy career (and doing Facetime Live chats with me during quarantines), and thanks to my fantastic editorial team of Linda Ingmanson and Joyce Lamb, my beta readers Anne Woodall, Kara Conrad and Tracey Suppo, and to Sarah Hewitt, family nurse practitioner, for her help with the medical elements. And to my Gansett Island beta readers: Gwen, Amy, Melanie, Katy, Betty, Doreen, Laurie, Michelle, Jennifer, Marianne, Andi, Jennifer, Juliane, Tammy, Betty, Kelly, Jaime, Judy and Mona, thank you for being the last eyes on every new Gansett book.

Join the Rescue After Dark Reader Group at facebook.-com/groups/rescueafterdark to discuss Mason and Jordan's story with spoilers allowed and encouraged. Also make sure you're in the Gansett Island Reader Group at facebook.com/groups/McCarthy-Series/ and LIKE the Gansett Island page at facebook.com/GansettIs-land/ to never miss any news about the series.

To all the readers who love this series as much as I do—thank you. I can't believe we're heading toward book 23! That's all thanks to you, my amazing readers. Much more to come from Gansett Island!

Much love,

Marie

Contemporary Romances Available from Marie Force

The Gansett Island Series

Book 1: Maid for Love (*Mac & Maddie*)

Book 2: Fool for Love (*Joe & Janey*)

Book 3: Ready for Love (*Luke & Sydney*)

Book 4: Falling for Love (*Grant & Stephanie*)

Book 5: Hoping for Love (*Evan & Grace*)

Book 6: Season for Love (*Owen & Laura*)

Book 7: Longing for Love (*Blaine & Tiffany*)

Book 8: Waiting for Love (*Adam & Abby*)

Book 9: Time for Love (*David & Daisy*)

Book 10: Meant for Love (*Jenny & Alex*)

Book 10.5: Chance for Love, A Gansett Island Novella (*Jared & Lizzie*)

Book 11: Gansett After Dark (*Owen & Laura*)

Book 12: Kisses After Dark (*Shane & Katie*)

Book 13: Love After Dark (*Paul & Hope*)

Book 14: Celebration After Dark (*Big Mac & Linda*)

Book 15: Desire After Dark (*Slim & Erin*)

Book 16: Light After Dark (*Mallory & Quinn*)

Book 17: Victoria & Shannon (Episode 1)

Book 18: Kevin & Chelsea (Episode 2)

A Gansett Island Christmas Novella

Book 19: Mine After Dark (*Riley & Nikki*)

Book 20: Yours After Dark (*Finn & Chloe*)

Book 21: Trouble After Dark (*Deacon & Julia*)

Sex Machine

Sex God

Georgia on My Mind

True North

The Fall

The Wreck

Love at First Flight

Everyone Loves a Hero

Line of Scrimmage

The Quantum Series

Book 1: Virtuous *(Flynn & Natalie)*

Book 2: Valorous *(Flynn & Natalie)*

Book 3: Victorious *(Flynn & Natalie)*

Book 4: Rapturous *(Addie & Hayden)*

Book 5: Ravenous *(Jasper & Ellie)*

Book 6: Delirious *(Kristian & Aileen)*

Book 7: Outrageous *(Emmett & Leah)*

Book 8: Famous *(Marlowe & Sebastian)*

Romantic Suspense Novels Available from Marie Force

The Fatal Series

One Night With You, *A Fatal Series Prequel Novella*

Book 1: Fatal Affair

Book 2: Fatal Justice

Book 3: Fatal Consequences

Book 3.5: Fatal Destiny, *the Wedding Novella*

Book 4: Fatal Flaw

Book 5: Fatal Deception

Book 6: Fatal Mistake

Historical Romance Available from Marie Force

The Gilded Series

ABOUT THE AUTHOR

Marie Force is the *New York Times* bestselling
author of contemporary romance, romantic
suspense and erotic romance. Her series
include Gansett Island, Fatal, Treading Water,
Butler Vermont and Quantum.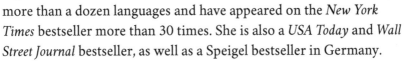

Her books have sold nearly 10 million
copies worldwide, have been translated into
more than a dozen languages and have appeared on the *New York
Times* bestseller more than 30 times. She is also a *USA Today* and *Wall
Street Journal* bestseller, as well as a Speigel bestseller in Germany.

Her goals in life are simple—to finish raising two happy, healthy,
productive young adults, to keep writing books for as long as she
possibly can and to never be on a flight that makes the news.

Join Marie's mailing list on her website at marieforce.com for
news about new books and upcoming appearances in your area.
Follow her on Facebook at www.Facebook.com/MarieForceAuthor
and on Instagram at www.instagram.com/marieforceauthor/.
Contact Marie at marie@marieforce.com.

CPSIA information can be obtained
at www.ICGtesting.com
Printed in the USA
LVHW082109051120
670842LV00007B/225